PRAISE FOR

"If you loved *Bridget Jones's Diary* and *Confessions of a Shopaholic*, you won't be able to put down *Trophy Life*. Smart, humorous, and touching . . . Agnes and her search for meaning is a story that will find a place in your heart."

—*First for Women*

"If you're looking for a light and likable read for your next vacation, *Trophy Life* is a worthwhile pick . . . A charming story about fighting through the challenges and finding yourself on the other side."

—*Nights and Weekends*

"What a breath of fresh air! In *Trophy Life*, Lea Geller gives us a smart, capable, witty, and relatable heroine. Agnes suddenly finds herself in trouble—big trouble—but the path she chooses to find her way back to stability is surprising, entertaining, and ultimately triumphant."

—Loretta Nyhan, bestselling author of *Digging In*

"*Trophy Life* is unputdownable. Lea Geller's writing is fresh, funny, and relatable, and it's impossible not to cheer for Aggie, Geller's plucky heroine, as she wakes up from her so-called dream life and realizes reality offers something even better: a chance to get it right."

—Camille Pagán, bestselling author of *Woman Last Seen in Her Thirties*

"Lea Geller's novel *Trophy Life* is a winner of a book. I sat down to read just the first few pages and looked up a day and a half later—it is that good. This novel examines the ongoing search for true happiness and shows us that sometimes it is found in the most unexpected places, all against the backdrop of an intriguing domestic mystery. It is well written, absorbing, thought-provoking, and satisfying."

—Elizabeth LaBan, bestselling author of *Not Perfect*

"In this absorbing and dazzling debut, Agnes Parsons, a beautiful woman, teacher, and young mother, learns to value the true trophies in life. Author Lea Geller has hit a home run her first time out."

—Marilyn Simon Rothstein, author of *Husbands and Other Sharp Objects*

THE TRUTH AND OTHER HIDDEN THINGS

ALSO BY LEA GELLER

Trophy Life

a novel

LEA GELLER

This is a work of fiction. Names, characters, organizations, places, events, and incidents are either products of the author's imagination or are used fictitiously. Any resemblance to actual persons, living or dead, or actual events is purely coincidental.

Published by Lake Union Publishing, Seattle

www.apub.com

ISBN-13: 9781542026536
ISBN-10: 1542026539

Cover design by Liz Casal

Printed in the United States of America

For Bennett, Efram, Frances, Fiona, and Sidney,
who taught me everything I need to know.

-1-

The day Harry didn't get tenure was also the day I discovered that an IUD is not foolproof. At the time, it was hard to say which news was worse.

I was smacked by the first piece of information while I was moving things around in our apartment. Harry and I moved into this Upper West Side faculty housing near the university when we were expecting our daughter, Alice, and when Sam, our oldest, was three. Back then—well over a decade ago—we were only three people, almost four, and we had clothes, toys, and books, but mostly books. Every six months, I ejected books to make room for an additional pair of sneakers, another gray hoodie, or one more box of indiscriminate white wires.

The grand culling involved tossing about 5 percent of everything we owned, which really meant tossing 5 percent of what the kids and I owned, because Harry was very protective of his things. In Harry's mind, in order for an item to qualify for the purge, it needed to have completely disintegrated, as though soaked in a bath of acid. He would regularly paw through the giveaway bags, making sure I wasn't forcing him to part with that nubby sweater he'd had since college or the pleated rust-colored corduroys he'd bought as a grad student. Coupled with Harry's inability to cull was his careful procurement of what little he did own. Harry had a penchant for locally roasted coffee and small batches of gin—most of it brewed in Brooklyn bathtubs and decanted into darling little bottles that I kept and filled with things but would eventually have to discard in the grand culling.

The kids cooperated, mostly because they rightly suspected that by getting rid of old stuff, they were making room for new stuff. Sam, now almost sixteen, also had biology on his side. He was growing quickly and destructively, tearing through his jeans and shredding gray hoodies. Alice was strategic in her culling, texting me pictures of shoes to replace the ones she had left for me in a pile by the door of her bedroom. Alice is always several steps ahead of me.

Mostly, though, the culling is mine.

Every few months I parted with another vestige of my past life: heels, dress pants, and suits I hadn't worn since I left the office brigade twelve years ago, a few weeks after my thirtieth birthday. Even if I wanted to wear a pantsuit again, the tailoring to bring the turn-of-the-century styles up to date would cost more than a new suit itself. Besides, I wasn't fooling anybody. My pantsuit days were behind me.

The university had offered us several slightly larger apartments over the years, but we knew that if we held out until Harry finally got tenure, we'd win big. That's the way the system worked: it rewarded tenure, but it also rewarded inertia. We were sure it was just a matter of time until more bedrooms, more bathrooms, not to mention more storage, were ours.

In the meantime, we learned to store off-season clothing under our beds, double stack our books, put armchairs in the corners of our rooms, and then shove our belongings in plastic crates behind them. Mostly, we learned to purge regularly.

When my phone rang, I was lying on my stomach, reaching under the coffee table for a missing slipper, trying to stave off the nausea I assumed was due to four cups of coffee with cookie-dough creamer. I was startled and I jumped, hitting my head on the underside of the table. I winced, pulled myself out, and reached for my phone, which was somewhere on the coffee table. I scrambled for it and knocked the coffee over, dousing several days' worth of the *Times* and what looked like Alice's math homework.

It was Harry. I stared at the phone for a second, trying to ignore the uneasy feeling burrowing in my intestine that I'd hoped was just from the creamer. This morning we had been so celebratory. "I'll see you at six at Le Chute," Harry had said, kissing me before he left. He'd booked those reservations three months ago.

I grabbed the phone on the last ring.

"Hey," I said. "How was it?"

"It wasn't," he said quietly.

"What?" I replied, a little too loudly.

"It didn't happen. Arnold pulled me aside and told me I wasn't getting past the committee. He withdrew my name from consideration rather than have me denied."

"What?" I said, even louder than the time before, mopping up the coffee with the newspaper. "I don't understand. How is that possible?"

"I can't . . ." His voice cracked.

"I'm leaving now," I said. "I'll meet you in ten minutes, fifteen max." We were only six blocks away from the university, and the subway had been so unreliable lately that it was faster for me to walk.

"Bells, no. I need to walk . . . to think."

"Harry," I began, standing up and looking around for my coat. My head began to spin, and I fell back onto the couch. No tenure didn't just mean no apartment. No tenure meant no job. Although I needed to be steady for Harry, I felt cold and suddenly weak. "Let me meet you," I said, my own voice trembling slightly.

"I need . . . I need . . . some time," he stammered. "I'll be home later." Before I could say anything else, he'd hung up. I looked around. The apartment felt smaller than it had moments ago, before I knew that I would not have all those bedrooms, before I knew that I'd have to hold on to those plastic crates.

I stared at my phone trying to figure out who to call first. The person most interested in the outcome of the tenure-committee meeting was the person I least wanted to talk to—Vivian Walker, my mother-in-law. The person I wanted to talk to most was Suki, my best friend. I didn't know how to start the conversation, so I wimped out and sent her a text, using our code words for bad news.

Tenure update—THE BREAD DID NOT RISE.

Moments later my phone rang. "Hell's Bells," Suki said, starting the call the same way she had since she learned my nickname on the first day of freshman orientation in college. "How did this happen?"

"I have no idea. He actually didn't want to talk." Suki, who'd grown up with Harry and the Walkers, knew how unusual it was for Harry not to want to discuss something until it was dead and buried. (I'd met Harry at one of the now-legendary parties Suki threw in her post-grad studio apartment. She had a loft bed over a minuscule kitchen, a kitchen in which Suki, the original foodie, prepared trays of food and cocktails long before anyone was talking about food.)

"Where is he going to go? Where will he work? Where will you guys live?" Suki knew that without tenure, Harry had, at most, another year at the university and then had to go back on the job market. The undergraduates would hardly know the difference when their assistant professor suddenly showed up in the course catalog as *adjunct*, but the professor would know, and so would his wife, and even more so in Harry's case, so would his family. And that would only last so long before offers from other lesser schools would have to be entertained, offers that would eventually dry up.

"I don't know, I don't know, and I don't know." I kept moving, piling laundry into a basket and putting it near the front door of the apartment.

"Fair enough," she said.

"I just know that Harry now has to find a job as an English professor. I might as well be looking for a gig as a mermaid. It also means we'll lose this apartment, which I didn't like thirty minutes ago, but to which I am now extremely attached."

"I guess you can finally come to Brooklyn," she said.

"Suki, I write for a free newspaper that probably eight people read, including my mother. Harry is an English professor, or at least he was until thirty minutes ago. Neither of us is qualified for Brooklyn."

"That's not true," she said. "There's no way your mother reads that paper."

As I had explained to Suki many times, to live in Brooklyn you needed to be a writer, an actual well-paid one. Sometimes you can move to Brooklyn and *become* a writer, like Suki, who writes cookbooks about all the things her husband and two daughters like to eat, much of which they seem to procure at the farmers market minutes from their home near Prospect Park, and none of which would make it over the threshold of our tiny apartment. (Kohlrabi frittatas, anyone? Braised chicken and ramps? I didn't think so. I don't even know what a ramp is.) The same thing happened to another college friend, Kate Miller, who had a two-book deal within six months of moving to Park Slope and writes unbearable novels vaguely based on the supposed disintegration of her marriage (six books later and they're still together). While it seems like book deals grow on Brooklyn trees and every third mom is a journalist on book leave, I wasn't willing to risk it. I never bothered applying to Brooklyn.

"Bells," Suki said. "You get paid to write. You're a writer."

"Hardly."

As Suki knew, I wanted to be a writer. I went to college to be a writer, and when that didn't work, I thought about going to more school to be a writer. "To be a writer, Elsbeth," as my mother likes to remind me, "someone has to pay you to write." (My mother is the only person who calls me Elsbeth. To her everlasting disappointment, everyone else calls me Bells.) While I was amassing rejection letters for my short stories, I told her I wanted to apply to grad school and get an MFA. But my mother would hear nothing of it. When my dad disappeared, she went back to law school and became the patron saint of reborn single mothers everywhere. In the gospel according to Hanna Cohn, women who got paid handsomely to write were writers, but short of that, women needed a real career—something they could fall back on when husbands inevitably left. She had no intention of helping me pay for an MFA and would only help pay for law school, so, fearful of student debt and even more fearful of my mother, I went.

After graduating, I took a job in a midsize firm. My mother looked the other way when I had Sam at twenty-six, probably because I went back to work pretty quickly. But when Alice was born, much to my mother's everlasting disappointment (there's obviously a theme here), I left my job. She and I barely spoke in the months after. Having babies early was bad enough, letting them derail my career was another thing entirely.

When Alice was six, I started writing for the *Uptowner*, a free newspaper covering life on the Upper West Side. I was initially assigned to sanitation but then graduated to the entire city services beat, which meant I also covered street cleaning, snowplowing, and if my editor, Andy, was feeling generous, the occasional destructive fallen tree. My mother may have been dismissive, but Harry acted as though I'd won the Pulitzer when I wrote my first article about the politics of alternate-side parking after a snowstorm. He'd framed the first few articles I'd written and continued to mass forward my splashier pieces, even to his midwestern cousins who could not have cared less about the leaky hydrant on Seventy-Second and Columbus.

I had developed a small following of readers who appreciated the humor I infused into the otherwise mundane (Rupturing Sidewalks: The Root of All Evil), and I had gotten a promotion of my own last month when the woman who used to write the City Chatter column moved to Connecticut, where local news presumably took on a different tenor. Even with my ascension from reporter to columnist, and although I was still technically in the business of writing, I was definitely not in the business enough for my mother, or for Brooklyn.

"Bells," Suki promised, "this will all work out."

When I'm nervous, my head sweats. I felt my scalp flush and forced my frizz into a loose ponytail. I leaned over the sink, my chest resting against the Formica counter, and shuddered when I felt a soreness. I looked around the sink at the stacked bowls, crusted with the detritus of cereal and congealed yogurt and granola, and I gagged.

"Bells? Are you OK?"

"I'm just a little queasy this morning," I said, sliding away from the sink.

"If we weren't so old, I'd ask if you were pregnant." She laughed. I would have laughed, too, but instead, with nowhere else to go, I lifted the lid of the Crock-Pot and puked inside.

"Bells?"

"I'll call you later," I slurred, and hung up.

I covered the Crock-Pot, slid down onto the dusty kitchen floor, and leaned back on a cabinet door. The nausea and sore boobs were strangely familiar feelings, even though I hadn't felt them in well over a decade. I could not count back to my period because since I'd been fitted with an IUD, I didn't really get a period. Instead, I counted the days to my birthday. It was May; in three months I would turn forty-three.

When the nausea passed, I got up off the floor and called my doctor, Julia. We'd been on a first-name basis since she delivered Sam after what felt like a marathon labor, during which I apologized for skipping a bikini wax and tried to bribe one of the residents into sneaking me a cupcake. I could run out and grab a pregnancy test from the drugstore, but something told me this could be more complicated than peeing on a stick. When the nurse sent me to Julia's voice mail, I began to ramble.

"Julia, it's Bells Walker. I'm super nauseated. I puked, and my boobs really hurt. I'm not sure what it means. I mean, I think I know what it means, but I don't get a period, so I don't really know. Anyway, please call me when you can. Thank you." I had circled the table so many times while leaving the message that I was once again dizzy. I walked into my bedroom and lay down on the bed, sliding in between loads of unfolded laundry.

Within minutes, Julia called me back.

"You should come in today," she said.

"Like right now?"

"That's what today usually means." Julia laughed. "We need to make sure that if you *are* pregnant, it's not ectopic. Then we would need to take out the IUD, which can be risky. Either way, you need to come in."

"Ectopic?" I asked. "What are the odds that I'm actually pregnant?"

"Let's talk when you come in."

"Maybe this is just perimenopause," I pressed, suddenly begging for a word I never thought I'd be happy to hear.

"Bells, you need to come in."

"Got it." I relented, looking over at the black boatneck dress I'd set out for dinner, a dress I would not be wearing to dine at Le Chute. I canceled the reservation, texted the kids in case the appointment ran late, and after changing into pants with a button, was out the door.

I stared at myself in the elevator mirror under the world's least flattering fluorescent lighting, pretending not to see the gray at my hairline. I made a mental note to order more hair color and closed my eyes until I was safely in the lobby.

An hour later I'd taken a pregnancy test and was lying on an exam table, swaddled in a paper gown. I stared at a poster of the female reproductive system and tried not to think about the status of my insides. I doubted that my tubes were as vibrant and springy as the ones on the poster.

Julia walked into the room and smiled at me sympathetically. "It's good to see you, Bells," she said, washing her hands. "Let's prep you for the ultrasound."

I pinched my knees together, shivering in the gown. "I did some research on my way over," I began. "It's kind of amazing what you learn when you google 'failed IUD.'"

There was a light knock on the door.

"Hold that thought," Julia said, scooting her rolling stool to the door. She stuck her head out of the room, conferred with her nurse, and popped back in again.

"Your test came back positive, but let's have a look and see what's going on," she said, pulling up my gown and thankfully not looking at my face, which felt like it had been slapped with a meat cleaver.

I could feel sweat pooling in my armpits and beneath my lower back.

Julia began the scan and looked at the screen. "You're definitely pregnant," she said, mincing no words. "And it's not ectopic."

"OK . . ."

"That's a good thing, Bells," she said, looking over at me. "But because of its placement, I need to take this IUD out."

"OK . . ." Really, I was anything but OK.

"I just have to warn you that there is a real risk you could miscarry." She was still looking at me.

I nodded my assent. And then, seeing that Julia needed more, I whispered, "Yes."

"I'll be using this ultrasound to guide me as I retrieve the IUD, but I need you to lie perfectly still," she ordered, prying open my knees with her gloved hand.

She pointed the ultrasound screen in my direction. "Want to take a look?"

"No, I'm good," I said, keeping my eyes on the ceiling, wishing there were a screen up there like my kids had at the dentist. I'd much rather have watched *Dora the Explorer* on an infinite loop than peek inside the current workings of my uterus.

"A real risk?" I asked, eyes fixed above.

"Yup. But so far, so good," she said. "Just keep still."

I wanted all of this to work out, and at the same time, a small piece of me wished that I could go back a few hours in time to when everything was less complicated. I gripped the sides of the exam table. When Julia was done, she pulled down my gown.

"Bells, it looks fine," she said, smiling at me.

"Wow," I breathed, still gripping the sides of the table. "What are the odds?"

"Actually, about one in a thousand."

"Damn," I said, exhaling. "I have all the luck today."

"You certainly do." She took off her gloves and washed her hands at the sink.

"How far along am I?" I asked, looking at her.

"About nine weeks." She pulled a paper wheel out of a drawer and did the math. "Which puts your due date roughly at the end of December, maybe a little later. You'll do some testing over the next few weeks to make sure everything is alright with the baby."

"I can't believe this is happening," I said.

"Why don't you go home, discuss this with Harry, and we can talk over the next few days."

"I'm old," I said to her.

"I have other pregnant clients your age, and some even older than you. Besides, we prefer to say 'advanced maternal age,'" she said, grinning at me.

"Excuse me?"

"I just don't want you to freak out when you hear that. It's how we refer to pregnant women over thirty-five."

"OK, I'm freaking out right now."

"Hey, this is an improvement." She laughed. "A few years ago we called it a geriatric pregnancy."

"Now I want to cry."

"Don't cry. Go home. Talk to Harry, and I'll call you tomorrow to discuss all your options."

Harry. I bolted upright and jumped off the bed, tearing the paper gown. I rummaged in my bag for my phone: four missed calls.

I quickly texted him, my hands shaking:

Something came up. All good. Be home in 30.

"Bells." I had forgotten Julia was still in the room. "You'll be fine." She smiled at me, and I almost believed her.

~

When I ran into the house forty minutes later, I was greeted by a mountain of empty cereal boxes. In addition to my two children, I saw several of Sam's bandmates crowded around our kitchen table, shoveling food into their mouths. The ground was moving under this family, and still, my most pressing task was feeding my bass-playing teenager and all of his friends.

"Hey, guys," I said, holding up an empty cereal box and shooting Sam a look. He looked down. Sam went to bed one night a few weeks ago and woke up the next day six feet tall. He and Harry were now the same height. He had Harry's thick sandy-brown hair, but it was often hard to see because he wore a gray hoodie, hood up, every single day of his teenage life.

"We're out of cereal," he said, dribbling Chex. I'd just bought cereal. "And there's a weird smell coming from the Crock-Pot."

"Hey, Mrs. Walker," said his friend Asher, a saxophonist, swinging on the doors of the cupboard, scouring for the next snack.

I got a wave from another friend, Levi, the drummer, who lifted an empty snack bowl and poured crumbs into his mouth. I saw popcorn on the floor.

Alice ran up to me. "Where were you? What happened with Dad?" She ran her hand through her own frizzy hair and moved closer to me. If Sam had won the hair lottery, Alice, the recipient of the Cohn curls, had definitely lost it. I was about to answer when she blurted, "Why is he in bed? Is he sick? Did something happen?"

"Dad's in bed?" I asked, taking a step back.

"What happened with the tenure committee?" Sam called, putting down the box of cereal.

"Hold tight, guys," I said. I stumbled into the bedroom and found Harry curled up in bed, his back to the door. As much as I wanted to roll up into my own ball and disappear, I slid off my shoes, climbed in, and spooned him. "I'm so, so sorry," I said, my lips on the back of his neck.

"The worst part was the look on Arnold's face," Harry said, speaking into his pillow. "He actually looked sorry for me."

"Arnold always looks like that."

"I just don't know how I didn't see it coming," he said, flipping over and turning to face me. "And I have no idea what I'm supposed to do now."

"We'll figure it out," I said, putting my arms around him. "You'll find another job."

"I'm a literature professor," he groaned. "There are no other jobs."

He was right. There were no other jobs, or at least there weren't many. But I knew that *my* job was to keep calm and carry Harry when he freaked out. I leaned over and kissed him.

"I'm serious, Bells. I have to go back on the market now, and if there is another job somewhere, that somewhere is not Manhattan. We'll lose this apartment; we'll have to move."

I started to remind him that everything was going to be alright, but he cut me off.

"Where were you today?" Harry asked.

I briefly contemplated lying, but in addition to being a head sweater, I am also a bad liar.

"At the doctor."

Harry stiffened. "What's wrong?" He sat up, and I looked into his hazel eyes, which were darker than usual. His brow was a furrowed mess.

I took a sharp breath. "I'm fine," I said. "I'm just . . . pregnant." *Please don't freak out. Please don't freak out. Please don't freak out and leave me.*

"What?!" Harry bolted off the bed. "But you have . . ."

"Yeah, the thing about an incredibly low failure rate is that someone still has to be in the 0.8 percent of people who get pregnant with an IUD."

"Wow," Harry breathed.

"Yup," I agreed, standing up and facing him.

"And here I was thinking you had to have sex to get pregnant."

"Nice, Harry." Here I was comforting him, and he was about to launch into one of his favorite topics. After alternate-side parking and the voice of the *other* in nineteenth-century American literature, what Harry loved to talk about most was how much more sex everyone else was having. Because he had a fine attention to detail, Harry even named names, running through lists of all the people we knew. I'd listen to him rattle off all our friends, knowing full well that these women were not putting out anywhere near as much as Harry thought they were—hell, nothing could match the orgy he had in his mind. I was pretty sure the couples who talk about all the sex they are having are not having any at all, but I never told this to Harry. I didn't want to burst his orgy bubble.

"Fine," he said. "I may not be good enough for tenure, but I can impregnate a woman with a near-foolproof birth control device, even with sporadic sex."

"You are a rock star," I said, sitting back on the edge of the bed. I took some breaths to steady myself.

"So this means we're going to have a baby? How will that work? Where will the baby sleep? What if we really have nowhere to live?" He ran his fingers through his hair, and I watched his face change from amusement to terror. He started pacing, circling the room, increasing his speed with each lap. I watched his perfectly square broad shoulders tense up. Those shoulders were the first thing I'd noticed about him. You couldn't miss those shoulders.

"Harry," I said, getting up again and trying to block him. He kept swerving to avoid me. I reached for him.

"Jeez, Bells. Aren't you too . . . old?"

"Actually, I prefer the term *advanced maternal age*," I said.

"Huh?"

"I'm only four years older than you," I said, hearing my mother's voice in my head. *Just remember: You'll be middle-aged first. You'll be gray first. Think about it. You'll be everything first.*

"Yeah, but I'm not the one at risk. I'm not the one carrying the baby."

I was about to respond when he crumbled in front of me. "Oh my god, a baby. A baby's coming, and I went and lost my job." He sank into the armchair next to our bed and grabbed both sides of his perfect hair. Moments later he looked at me as though he'd just remembered something. "Bells, where are we going to live?" And because—enormous man-child that he was—his suffering was always greater than mine, I comforted him and not the other way around. I was kneeling in front of the armchair when we heard a crash from the kitchen. I swear I could hear the crumbs scatter under the kitchen table.

"Harry, you know that we may still have a choice here." I stared at him and put my hands on his beautiful face. *Never marry a man prettier than you,* I heard my mother say. I shut up her voice and focused on Harry and his face.

He looked up at me. We'd never really discussed this before; we had never needed to. "Do we have a choice? Do we really?" he asked.

"No," I whispered, verbalizing what I knew all along.

"I didn't think so, either. Besides, you know I do love the babies," he said. It was true. Harry Walker was a sucker for an infant and would gladly have fathered a hundred newborns if I'd agreed to it. Harry loved children when they were a physical extension of him, when he could wear them. I had albums full of Harry toting the kids around the city in a BabyBjörn. He even devised a way to wear both children at once—he put Alice on his chest and Sam in a backpack.

"I promise. This will all work out," I said. At the time, I even believed it.

~

The next morning, while I loaded the dishwasher and wiped down the counters, I called my sister-in-law Molly. Molly was married to Harry's younger brother, Alex. Harry is a middle child, the second of three boys. With no sisters of my own, I forged an alliance with the two other women who'd married Walker boys.

"What happened?" Molly asked immediately. Molly is a pediatrician and, along with the rest of the Walkers, lives in Upper Westchester, a hornet's nest of overachievement. I briefly wondered if Harry was the first boy from Chappaqua to be denied tenure.

"He didn't get it. He didn't even get to the vote."

"God," she said in a tone that made me wonder if she'd ask whether the decision was benign or malignant.

"And Vivian texted me. He's dodging her calls."

I was about to ask Molly for advice when I saw a call coming in. Vivian. "Crap, she's incoming," I said.

"That was quick. Good luck." She laughed, hanging up and leaving me alone with my mother-in-law.

"Bells?" I swear I could hear her playing with her pearls.

"Hello, Vivian."

"What kind of news do you have for me?" she demanded.

"Not the good kind," I said, and then bathed in the long pause. I knew she was still alive because I could hear her breathing.

"Vivian?" I asked.

"I was already planning on coming in tomorrow to celebrate. I'll take a late-morning train and be with you for lunch," she said, recovering quickly and hanging up.

I once saw a bumper sticker that read **PARENTING IS ABOUT SHOWING UP**. If that were really true, then Vivian Walker would be parent of the century. Her solution to every problem was showing up and making things worse. When I miscarried after Sam, she showed up and stared at me until I got out of bed. She then told me multiple times that I should count myself lucky, because while children are a blessing, having children too close together was impractical.

And now, Vivian would be showing up here.

-2-

I bolted out of bed the next morning after what felt like only a few hours of sleep. I needed to clear my head and clean the apartment before lunch with Vivian. When I'm nervous, I also bake. I waited for the first round of nausea to pass, then pulled out my grandmother's speckled pink melamine bowls. The sight of them immediately calmed me down. I whipped up two batches of carrot ginger muffins and a pear crumble, congratulating myself on resisting licking a single bowl. I fed the kids and cleaned the kitchen again. Harry went for a run, Sam left for school, and I walked Alice, who went to school ten blocks away. Alice spent those ten blocks yelling.

"I can't believe you made me wear this sweater," she said, tugging at the bottom of it. "It shrunk."

"I didn't make you wear anything. I just told you we had to leave or we'd be late." For Alice, leaving the house involved multiple trips back inside for all the things she'd forgotten, which meant ushering her out of the house a full ten minutes early.

"Maybe if you weren't baking all morning, you could have helped me," she muttered and looked down at her legs. "And oh my god, I'm wearing gray tights with a black skirt!"

"I'm sorry," I said, because I was, for all of it (maybe not the baking). We hadn't told the kids about the tenure rejection yet. Neither of us felt ready for the barrage of "what next" and "what if," so we punted and told them the decision had been postponed a week or so.

"It's fine," she said, stopping at a corner and assessing me. Then, as if seeing me for the first time that morning, she asked, "Why are you wearing that coat?"

"Huh?"

"It's not that cold, and you're wearing a big coat," she said.

Alice, I am in a big coat because even though I am only nine weeks pregnant, after a light breakfast I already look about four months pregnant, and I don't think this pregnancy is news you can handle.

"I'm cold," I said, wrapping the coat around myself.

"Whatever," she replied. "It just looks weird."

At the door to the school, Alice looked around—presumably to see if anyone had noticed her odd, out-of-season mother—forced a large smile, and ran inside. I walked back to the apartment, and fifteen minutes later, I dashed back out with her homework, promising myself that I needed to stop being the kind of mother who lets herself get berated by a sixth grader only to run back to school with her homework.

I got texts from both Molly and my other sister-in-law, Jess, both wishing me some form of Good luck with Vivian. All I could do was text back a series of exclamation points, because while I didn't know what to expect from her visit, I also knew exactly what to expect.

When I finally got home, Harry was still in his running clothes, waiting for me at our circular kitchen table. I made a pot of his pour-over coffee, boiling the water, setting up the paper filters, even grinding the beans the way he liked them. He drank his coffee black. I didn't want him to know about the cookie-dough creamer, and we were out of milk, so I drank mine black, too.

"I have a meeting with Glynis at eleven thirty," he said, hunched over the steaming mug. Glynis Moore was the English-department chair. She dressed like a Druid and spoke with a soft Scottish accent.

"Apparently we are discussing my options." He pronounced the last word like it was in a foreign language.

"What do you think she'll say?" I put my mug down and clasped it for warmth. I hated black coffee. If I could just have a little creamer . . .

"I have a hunch she'll tell me I'm done here," he said, sitting back in his chair and looking away.

Generally, I was not one for Harry's hunches. In the winter, Harry thinks he has the flu about once a month. In the summer, it is dehydration or sunstroke. One year, the man was convinced he had Zika. Still, I knew Harry well enough to know that there must have been something he'd said to Glynis, some correction he'd made to one of her departmental pronouncements, some question he'd asked that had his colleagues squirming in their seats.

Before I could reply, I was interrupted by a text from Vivian.

I'll be there in 15.

"Shit," I said, jumping out of my seat. "It's your mother. She'll be here in fifteen minutes."

"What? Why so early?" Harry was now the color of my secret creamer.

I knew exactly why. I'd had a nagging feeling that Harry's meeting with Glynis would run conveniently late, causing him to miss Vivian's visit entirely. That feeling was also tugging at Vivian.

I got up and walked to the fridge. I must have made a sudden movement because I felt a large wave of nausea wash over me. I leaned on the fridge door and breathed. For a few minutes, I'd forgotten I was pregnant.

"Harry," I said in between gulps of air, "are we telling her about this baby?"

"No," he said, walking over and putting his hands on my stomach. "We need to tell the kids first. Although she'll be so devastated by the tenure news that we could tell her we're picking up and moving to Bangladesh and she wouldn't care." He put his arms around me. I pulled away to burp.

"Sexy," he said.

"You know what's really sexy?" I asked. "Cleaning for your mother."

I looked around. The apartment was nowhere near Vivian clean. The living room was stuffed with garbage bags full of things we were tossing to make way for other things we didn't even know about yet, with the exception of Alice, who had texted me pictures of wedge booties and a phone case because she got rid of a sweater and a pair of tights. I grabbed the garbage bags and stashed them out on the fire escape, careful not to knock over my terra-cotta pots of basil and thyme.

Harry helped by loading the dishwasher, although I knew full well I'd be reloading it later in the day because Harry believed you should be able to put things in however you want, and the machine ought to figure out how to clean them. I removed the clean but as-yet-unfolded laundry from the couch and threw it onto our bed. For good measure, I tossed the comforter over it. I didn't have time to shower, so I rummaged through my closet for something to hide a midsection, which looked a lot less pregnant yesterday. I found a loose khaki shirtdress and stood on the edge of the bath to see the full length of myself in the mirror. I looked like I was wearing a paper bag. I ran into the bedroom to change, then changed again.

Vivian Walker was a sucker for pink. She breezed in wearing a pale-raspberry bouclé suit with a scarf tied round her neck, her hair in a shellacked bob. My own hair immediately felt unruly. She gave me a brief hug, then held me at arm's length to assess my situation. I tried to strike the least pregnant pose possible. Vivian took stock of outfit number three—a long black sweater, gray skirt, gray tights, and black suede boots that were not as old as they looked. Luckily, her eyes lingered on the boots.

"This city gets dirtier every time I'm here," she said as her eyes moved up and landed on my face. Vivian took our not living in Westchester as a personal affront. When she finished assessing me, she walked into the living room, raising an eyebrow to survey the scene.

"Where's Harry?" she asked, smiling. "Has he done a runner?"

"Of course not. He's in the shower." I laughed nervously, wondering if Harry was halfway down the fire escape.

"It's just as well," she said, brushing off a couch cushion and taking a seat. "I wanted to talk to you alone." She motioned for me to sit next to her, and I obeyed.

"Well," she asked before I was even seated, "what are you going to do?"

"I'm not really sure," I said, bracing myself with a throw pillow. "I want to give Harry some space."

"Wrong, Bells," she said. "You know full well that it is a wife's job to—"

"Grease the wheels of her husband's career," I chimed in, watching her nod knowingly. I should have known better. I should always know better.

Vivian's whole life had been about Harry's father, Steven—his job, his hobbies. Until Steven died suddenly three years ago, for almost forty years Vivian had learned to love the things he loved and never seemed to resent them. Steven was a surgeon who loved to read and play the stock market, and because he loomed so large, there was an unspoken agreement that each son would take one-third of him and run with it. Harry's younger brother, Alex, became a doctor, and his older brother, Mark, ran a hedge fund. I don't know who was in the room when it was decided that Harry would become an English professor, but there you have it.

"I don't need to tell you that Harry's job is your job," she reminded me. "Academics need extra care, and we both know that Harry needs even more than most." Vivian believed that all wives should shepherd their husbands' careers, but academics, especially academics like her son, were a special breed. "For a group of people so socially challenged, their jobs require an inordinate amount of socializing, and you know reading a room is not Harry's forte." I practically had this lecture memorized. I often wondered if Vivian thought that she needed to teach me what she considered the basics of being a good wife because she assumed that my own mother must have been a bad one.

"You're right," I said through a forced smile.

"Who will you call?" she asked.

"Colleagues, contacts, whoever I can find," I said. I was obviously making no calls of any sort. "His job is my job."

"Until it's not," she said, crossing her ankles, bearing an expression I couldn't read. She gave her head a small shake, then proceeded to grill me about the kids. I was dodging questions about Sam's plans for college when Harry walked in. (I was pretty sure we might have to resuscitate Vivian if she heard the words *B-minus average*.) It didn't matter. When Harry glided into the room, she leaped off the couch.

"My clever boy," she said, wrapping her arms around him. "My beautiful, clever boy."

~

Unlike Vivian, my mother never showed up. Showing up was inefficient and would take time away from her work. Hanna Cohn made little time for hobbies, for interests, for exercise, and for me. She never tried to hide it. She lorded her singular drive over me as a reminder of how consumed I was by my husband and children.

"I see" was what she said when, later that day, I called her with the tenure news. "I suppose Vivian has already paid you a visit."

"She has," I said as I cleaned Alice's room, trying to organize the mess of clothes in front of her closet. I picked up a pile of what I thought were sweaters, and a boot fell out on the hardwood floor.

"What's that sound?" my mother asked.

"Oh," I said, looking for the matching boot, "I'm cleaning Alice's room." The words were not yet out of my mouth before I regretted them.

"Elsbeth," she said, "this is why these people can do nothing for themselves."

"These people?" I grabbed Alice's oldest teddy bear and lay down on her bed in defeat. "Can we please talk about something other than what an enabling mother I am?" I asked.

"No. I have a client meeting in ten, so we can't. But Elsbeth, remember, you can change course at any time."

"I know," I said.

"Do you? Do you know that you can pick yourself up and be the breadwinner? You have an excellent degree you don't use. It's waiting for you, Elsbeth."

"Thanks, Mom," I said, hanging up and rolling over onto my stomach. My boobs hurt so much that I quickly rolled back onto my side. One thing was very clear—my mother was not going to react well to my pregnancy news. I could imagine her coming over in the middle of the night with a satchel of surgical tools and a bottle of whiskey, ready to stage her own medical intervention. I groaned. Maybe I could have this baby and keep it a secret from her. Even though we lived in the same city, I barely saw her. I closed my eyes and pictured myself presenting my mother with an eighteen-year-old child she knew nothing about.

As for that baby . . . all of me ached. Even my ears were tired. I sank farther into the bed and groaned. I looked down at my almost forty-three-year-old body, wondering how it would bear the brunt of this pregnancy. I knew that women older than I was had babies, but this body didn't seem to have the juice for it. I put my hands on my sore boobs, so bedraggled and neglected, and wondered what they had left to give.

When I was younger, I thought about being in my forties the way I thought about all the years that lay ahead of me. At twenty-five, I was going to have a blossoming writing career and a husband. In my thirties, I would have children punctuated by book tours. (At no point in any of my imaginings did I factor in gray hair.) Forty, though, was the magical future age when my magical future self would have all the things she wanted—a family, an enormous apartment with enough storage that I didn't have to store out-of-season clothes under my bed, and long lines at my book signings all over the world.

Somewhere in the back of my mind, I remembered a Greek myth about a god who swallowed his children, but I knew in reality that it was actually the other way around. Your children swallowed you. Was I ready to go through life in the fog of infancy, preoccupied with feedings and naps? Harry was shockingly present for the baby years, so much so that other parents would hand him colicky newborns to calm when they were at the very ends of their parenting ropes. But was he really ready for a return to middle-of-the-night pacing, a restless baby in his arms, and that constant feeling of exhaustion?

I tried not to take stock of my life too often, but I couldn't help wondering if I was headed in the wrong direction. Lying in bed that night next to my snoring, rejected husband, worrying about his job, his ego, our home, and whether my body was ready for another ride on the pregnancy carousel, I knew one thing for sure: I was moving further and further away from the fortysomething woman I thought I'd be.

-3-

"Dutchess College," Harry announced one week later, throwing himself down next to me on the bed. I was exhausted and lying down. It was three o'clock in the afternoon.

"What?"

"Dutchess. It's a few hours north, in northern Dutchess County, hence the name."

"Sounds like a finishing school for royals," I said, staring up at the popcorn ceiling.

"It may very well be, but even royals need to read the classics."

"All of them? Even Faulkner?"

He smirked.

"I know it's a step down, but it's a good school, Bells. Dutchess has a strong liberal arts program and a lot of money."

"Do they have a Manhattan campus?" I asked, only half joking.

"No. But they do have an opening in their English department, and they really want me." He dropped his head to the side and looked at me, letting me take in his symmetrical face. He'd had his meeting with Glynis, and he'd been right—she had told him to look elsewhere. Elsewhere turned out to be several hours north of urban civilization.

I couldn't think of anything to say, but Harry kept talking. "You'd get a house."

"I'd be OK with a bigger apartment," I said, scooting back on the bed and propping myself up with pillows.

Harry reached out and put his hand on my knee. "Bells, I know this wasn't part of the plan, but I need to consider it. *We* need to consider it. Besides," he said, moving his hand to my bloated stomach, "think of all the extra space this baby will need. With a big house, you may never need to cull again."

"But my life is here, Harry. My job is here. I know the City Chatter column may be small potatoes, but it's *my* small potatoes." *And I waited so long for it.*

"I've put feelers out everywhere, really I have. There's nothing." He moved closer to me. "You'll be the most famous columnist in Dutchess County," he promised. "A million papers will be vying for you. Just picture yourself in your home office . . . with windows."

I closed my eyes and waved goodbye to the column I'd been planning on the fight between local skaters and Upper West Side safety moms over a proposed skate park. Farewell, clever skater boys (and girls) title. Farewell, byline—Elsbeth Cohn, columnist.

"What would I even write about up there? A bumper apple crop? The biggest pig at the county fair?"

"Don't joke," he said. "I will be reading and forwarding all your apple and pig articles."

I could hear the kids out in the living room. "I guess Sam can't decide if he loves or hates us, so a move won't change much," I murmured, shuffling toward Harry and resting my head on his chest. "But can I have another week until we tell them?" The night before, I'd been in Alice's room under the guise of helping prepare her for a social studies vocab quiz.

"What do you think of these?" she'd asked, showing me a picture of heeled black booties covered in tiny metal studs, presumably to match the pleather jacket she'd saved up for, which was also covered in studs.

"You know the rule," I said. "No heels, and please focus. What is federalism?" It was hours after her ADD medication had worn off, and getting through a third of the vocabulary words would be a victory.

"They're not heels, they're wedges," she said, ignoring my question and rolling her eyes. It was hard for me to remember what Alice was like before she learned to roll her eyes. I was about to repeat the vocabulary word when I got a text from Sam, who was in the next room.

Can I sleep out tonight? Study group at Evan's.

Evan was the guitarist in Sam's band. "Study group at Evan's" was code for "Evan's parents are out of the country," and any study plans involved ordering pizza and playing video games until the early morning hours. Fool me twice, Sam Walker.

No sleepovers on a school night, and why are you texting from your room?

My phone rang. It was Sam.

"Front desk," I answered. "Bells speaking."

"Whatever," he said, and hung up.

I recounted the story to Harry. "Yeah, we should definitely wait," he agreed, sitting up. "What's for dinner?"

"I made lasagna," I said.

"And a soup?" he asked.

"Of course," I said. "And a soup."

~

The next day I met Suki at a Starbucks a few blocks from the apartment. As a Brooklyn food writer, Suki could not frequent Starbucks in Brooklyn, or to be safe, even Lower Manhattan. She ordered a drink with whipped cream and two hundred shots of caramel, then sat down at the table.

She took a long sip and unzipped her coat. "If I drink another cup of locally roasted pour-over, I'll die," she said, throwing her coat over the back of her chair. "What's going on? How's Harry?"

"Harry is fine. He wants to take a job upstate in the middle of nowhere. In other news, I'm pregnant."

Suki slammed her caramel drink down on the table and coughed up about 150 calories. "YOU'RE PREGNANT?!"

"I am."

"Hell's Bells! What happened to your IUD?"

"It failed." How long was I going to keep repeating this story? Couldn't I just change my Facebook status or tweet it out?

"I guess that explains the tent dress. When are you due? How far along are you? How do you feel?" she asked, pausing to take another gulp.

"Late December. About ten weeks. Like hell." I drank some seltzer.

"Damn. You really know how to shake things up." She stopped for a second and then looked stunned, as if something had just hit her.

"Hanna," she said. "Does she know?"

"No. I am considering not telling her. Besides, if Harry takes this job, we'll move over an hour away, and I may never see her again."

"How far upstate?"

"Dutchess County," I said, feeling another wave of nausea that I was sure had nothing to do with being pregnant.

"Well, the Hudson Valley is all the rage. It's practically the new Brooklyn," Suki said, polishing off her drink.

"Don't say that," I said. "I don't want to get rejected."

"Hardly." She smiled. "I can picture you sitting in a big country kitchen, writing the next great American novel." Of course she thought about the kitchen. "You could write about a woman who gets pregnant in middle age." I winced, and she pressed on. "Could be pretty funny. Teenagers and babies in the same house."

"I'm not sure I have a novel in me anymore. Besides, I can't think of anything less interesting than writing about myself, and nobody really wants to read about an older mom. Everyone loves a nubile pregnant woman."

"I don't know about that," she said, making an enormous slurping sound.

"I don't want to go, Suki," I said. "I had planned to grow old in the city—I was ready for the gray hair and NPR tote bag. I had it all mapped out."

"Um, Bells," she began, "you already have the tote, and about that hair . . ."

"What's your point?"

"You are already a gray-haired NPR lady. Maybe it's time for something else."

I looked at her.

"I don't like it, either," she admitted, scraping the bottom of her creamy drink with her straw. "Who knows? Maybe you will even have a gaggle of mom friends this time."

"I thought you said posses were overrated."

"Kind of." She laughed. "I just got left off an invite list for the Earth Day block potluck, and it wasn't by accident."

"They're all probably intimidated by your thyme–sea salt cookies," I said, thinking that I could probably polish off a tray of those cookies right about now.

"It's just good to have people," she said, sounding suddenly serious. "Even if you don't like them all the time."

We looked at each other for a few long moments, and then our hour was up.

As we left Starbucks, Suki hugged me. "Tell her," she said. "Just rip off the Hanna Band-Aid."

I took her advice and called my mother as I walked home, past storefronts and apartment buildings whose sequence I had practically memorized (Starbucks, dry cleaners, new drugstore, building, building, Dunkin' Donuts, vegan desserts that used to be a watch store, Starbucks) but would soon likely forget. My mother did not pick up. My mother never picked up during the day. I didn't trust myself to call back, so I only half ripped off the Band-Aid: I left a message.

"Hey, Mom. It's me. Just checking in. I'm pregnant. OK, bye!"

I ended the call and threw the phone into my giant bag, as if it were radioactive or as if Hanna Cohn would materialize if I kept it in my hand.

She called me that evening as I was folding laundry on the couch.

"Elsbeth, you can't be serious."

"About what?"

"Don't play dumb. You are almost forty-three. You have two children and a husband who might as well be a third child. Do you really think another baby would fit into this?"

I started to answer, but she wasn't done yet. "You know you have a choice in this matter," she informed me.

"Thank you, Mother," I said, lifting couch cushions in search of missing socks.

"You're forty-three," she clipped.

"Esme Katz-Wong had a baby last year at forty-five."

"Esme Katz-Wong didn't get married until she was forty, and she'll be in a wheelchair when that baby graduates from college. Don't be a fool, Elsbeth."

"Mother, I am having this baby," I said, raising the found socks in victory. Once the words were out of my mouth, I knew for sure that they were true. I felt myself smiling for the first time in days. "I am having this baby, and now I am going to fold some laundry."

"You will never go back to law," she warned.

"I was never going back anyway."

~

Even though we were all living in a few increasingly crowded rooms and I was throwing up into any receptacle I could find, the kids had no idea I was pregnant. Adolescents are special that way. I could have grown a third arm, and Sam would still come home and ask me what was for dinner while Alice pawed through my purse for gum, prattling on about her day. Still, Harry had accepted the job at Dutchess, and I was growing by the minute, like one of those spongy toys that balloons in bathwater. We had to tell them.

A week after I'd told Suki and my mother, Harry and I sat the kids down on the couch. I had just gotten the results from a big batch of testing, and so far everything looked good. Well, everything looked good for the baby. We were about to rock the kids' worlds in one fell swoop.

"We have news," Harry announced, sitting on the ottoman, his hands clasped in his lap.

"I knew it," Sam interrupted. "You guys are getting divorced!"

"What?" I felt dizzy, and I perched on the coffee table.

"Evan's parents are getting divorced."

"OK . . ."

"And I knew you'd be next," he said, his voice shaking. "You guys are always fighting."

Alice chimed in. "What are you even talking about? They never fight."

"Whatever, Alice. Why do you always take her side?"

"Just because I'm not a jerk doesn't mean I'm taking sides," she charged.

This was not how I envisioned this conversation going. "Guys!" I yelled, leaping up from the table. "We are not getting divorced!"

"Then why make us sit here?" Sam huffed, visibly shaken. "I have to practice, and this sucks." He got up to leave, tossing a throw pillow at Alice.

"Because," Harry said, standing up and squaring off with Sam, "I didn't get tenure, and we are moving."

In a rare moment of collusion, the kids turned their heads to look at each other, almost to make sure the other was still there, that they hadn't vaporized with the bad news.

Sam spoke first.

"Is this a fucking joke?" he demanded.

"Sam, language," Harry said. "And no, this is very much not a joke. I didn't get tenure." He looked down. I put my hand on his back.

"Where are we going?" Alice asked.

"Dutchess County," I said. "It's an hour or so north of here. There's a university that wants Dad."

"Does the middle school do plays?"

"Yes, I checked." I had not checked. "And Kayla Lewis won't be there to get every good part."

Alice beamed at the thought of upstate stardom.

"You guys have got to be kidding!" Sam yelled, moving away from us.

"There's more," I said. I had the feeling he was about to bolt, and we needed to get all the news out while we had the nerve.

"We're pregnant," Harry announced, looking at me. "Your mother is having a baby."

"WHAT THE ABSOLUTE FUCK?"

Harry opened his mouth to reprimand Sam, but I jumped in (the kid had definitely earned a curse or two). "Sam, I promise. This will all work out." I reached for him, but he backed away.

"I'm outta here," he said, heading for the door, his voice breaking.

"A baby?" Alice asked, reminding us she was still here. "Is it a boy or a girl?"

"We don't know yet," I said. The door slammed.

"When is it coming?"

"Around the end of the year."

"Am I gonna have to share a room?"

"Probably not."

"I have to tell Sophie and Tanya," she said, pulling out her phone, her purple nails flying over the screen. Without looking at us, she walked away and into her bedroom.

She ran back out twenty minutes later.

"I just finished telling everyone I know, and then I realized that I just told the entire sixth grade that you guys have sex."

"Actually," Harry began, but I shot him a look.

~

An hour later, I had tracked Sam's phone and was up on the roof, begging him to come down. Wherever we lived next, I really hoped it wouldn't have roof access.

"Come inside and we can talk about this," I pleaded. The buildings around us were lit up, and the air was cold and clammy. Was summer really only weeks away?

Sam was leaning against a post, his hands in the pockets of his hoodie, the hood pulled over his head. He had been crying. "You're moving me in the middle of high school? What about the band?"

"It's not my first choice, but yes, and we'll find another great band, even if it's out of school. Every school band wants a bass player." I took a step closer to him.

"I finally made all-city and you want me to leave? Why can't you wait a couple of years?"

"We could wait, but tenure probably won't happen then, either, and Dad has an offer, a good offer."

Sam exploded. "A good offer! You guys always tell me how selfish I am, but he couldn't hold out until I get through high school. Nobody moves in high school. It's social suicide."

"I'm sorry, Sam. I really am. Dad is in a tough spot. These jobs are hard to get."

"Liar," he spat. Competing sirens from the street below threatened to drown us out.

"What?"

"You're not sorry!" he yelled. "You're always talking about a bigger apartment, and now you're getting a whole house." Standing there on the roof against the backdrop of enormous buildings, Sam looked so small.

"We're losing this apartment, Sam. It came with Dad's job." I took a step forward and reached for him, but he brushed me away.

"Well, you always say how much harder we are as teenagers and how you wish we were babies again." He stood up straighter and adjusted his hood. "You got what you wanted."

"Do you really want to have this discussion? Do you really want me to regale you with tales of failed birth control?"

"No . . ."

"And I never wanted to leave the city," I said, looking around us at the buildings lit up with the lives of people inside them. "I love it here, Sam. I never thought we'd have to go." The words, thick and heavy, stuck in my throat.

"Whatever," he said, storming away from me and heading to the stairs. "I'm not going, and you can't make me."

"I'm so sorry," I said, calling out after him.

"You suck," he said from the stairwell.

"I know I do," I said.

-4-

Three months later, in the middle of a steamy August, Harry turned thirty-nine, and one week later, I turned forty-three. Andy took me out for lunch after I filed my final *Uptowner* article—on the death of a beloved busker at the Seventy-Ninth Street station.

"I can't believe you filed your last piece," Andy said, pulling his reading glasses out of his cargo vest to examine the menu.

"Never mind the piece. I can't believe I'm giving up the column," I said, sipping my lemonade. "Especially when you went and gave it to Lyla Levy."

"Lyla's not that bad. She's just not very funny."

"You always were a master of understatement."

Andy smiled. He wasn't the one leaving, giving everything up.

I spent a few weeks saying goodbyes, but other than Suki, I couldn't count many people I'd miss. Over the past ten years, most of our friends had moved out of the city, many for greener suburban pastures in Westchester and New Jersey, and some to pastures farther west. I'd never managed to fully connect with the other academic moms. Our family's copious free time made us suspect in the university crowd: we had no riding lessons, chess tournaments, or enrichment math tutors. Sure, Sam played in a band and occasionally in a few trios, and yes, he was even all-city, but that was pretty much it. Despite Harry's constant and unsubtle suggestions, Sam resisted anything academic once his school day had ended—which meant no chess team, no math league. He was a smart kid for whom school was a challenge, and there seemed to be fewer and fewer kids like him around.

Alice's ADD left her emotionally and physically wrung out at the end of the day. Other than rehearsal, after school she couldn't do much more than become one with the couch and binge-watch arguably inappropriate television, or spend hours sketching outfits I'd be terrified to let her wear and shoes with eight-inch high heels. As I'd learned when she applied to middle school (yes, that's a thing), neither her school play performances nor her volumes of sketch pads qualified as an extracurricular activity. Even outside the university crowd, compared to the overprogrammed, overenriched kids in our neighborhood, my kids stuck out like two slacker thumbs. I wasn't sure how it turned out this way. I know that Harry would have preferred it otherwise ("Sam, I see they're accepting applications for the student newspaper"), but I'm more of a bunny mom than a tiger mom. Maybe I lacked the energy, or the drive, or maybe I just want my kids to like me more than I liked my own mother. Even though Suki wanted me to have "people," most of the moms on 110th Street avoided us because they worried that slacking off might be contagious.

Suki showed up one morning laden with tote bags. She rushed past me and set them down on the living room floor.

"What's this?"

"Your Dutchess County survival kit. All the things you'll miss the most."

"Food things?" I asked, catching a fishy whiff from one of the bags.

"Naturally," she said, beginning to unpack. "I brought you a dozen bagels and a dozen bialys. I also hit Zabar's and Barney Greengrass and bought you some lox, sable, and whitefish."

"I'm driving with a car full of smoked fish?"

"If it was good enough for my grandparents who drove a trunkful of it up to the Catskills each summer, it's good enough for you."

"Fair enough."

"I also brought you a little dim sum and some cannoli, and I thought about hitting the Union Square farm stand," Suki said as I stared longingly at the containers of food. "But I think you'll be up to your ears in those."

"Funny."

We looked at each other.

"We could eat all of this now," I said, pawing through a bag.

"We could."

And with that, we both sat on the floor and tore into some cannoli.

~

The only person left for me to see was my mother, but she'd stopped talking to me. It wasn't an official estrangement, but she returned none of my calls and made sure to come over and say goodbye to the kids when she knew I'd be at the doctor. She had taken each of the decisions of my adult life as a personal blow, but this baby had sent her over the edge. At least she and Vivian were finally on the same side. Between our move to a lesser university and my "late-in-life" pregnancy, Vivian was worried about the optics—her form of currency. At least Vivian had made several trips down with Ernst, her own personal handyman, and watched while he disassembled furniture and removed shelving.

I spent the week of my birthday taping boxes, then untaping them to recover whatever it was I had accidentally packed. The city was steaming. I sweat through three outfits a day, and my hair, unruly at the best of times, was out of control. I dumped serums and oils onto it, but nothing worked—it entered the room a good ten minutes before I did.

At almost six months pregnant, I was swaddled in a giant maxi dress, squatting in front of boxes, a giant roll of tape in hand. The maxi dress wasn't ideal for packing, or squatting, but I refused to wear pregnancy shorts. I wasn't much of a shorts wearer even when not pregnant, but in early June, I tried on a pair in a maternity store and made the epic mistake of looking at my backside in the mirror. When I saw what looked like a giant horse's ass shoved into a pair of denim cutoffs, I nearly fainted with shame. I also noticed a thick, dark vein on the surface of my skin that looked like a rubber hose working its way down my leg. It's the kind of thing you miss when you get dressed in pitch darkness. I called Julia.

"It's a varicose vein. If it's not painful yet, it may be soon."

"Wonderful," I said, staring into the empty carton of what had been mint chip ice cream, commanding more to materialize.

"Keep an eye out for more," she added. "And get yourself some support hose."

"Support hose? I thought you said I wasn't really a geriatric mom?"

"This has nothing to do with your age," Julia promised me. "This happens to women of all ages, and it's totally manageable."

"What am I going to do without you?" I asked, my head now on the kitchen table. "Why do I have to have this baby with a random country doctor?"

"You'll be just fine. Margaret Ross is a good doctor affiliated with a good hospital, and this time you won't have to share a room." That was certainly good news. When I delivered Sam, I had to share a room with a woman whose husband called her Mother even though this was their first baby. With Alice, I shared a room with a woman giving birth to her fourth child. The room was pretty crummy, and our food arrived cold, but she thought she was at the Ritz. They practically had to throw her out of the hospital.

So, with the help of tan-colored support hose, which made me look and feel like my grandma Pearl at the end of her life (all I really needed was a set of curlers and tea-rose-pink lipstick), I managed to pack the last of our boxes. Alice tried to pack her own things but had an impossible time starting a box and was frequently distracted by her phone, or by anything happening in the apartment that did not involve packing. At most, she packed in six-minute increments. Sam told me he wasn't coming so he didn't need to pack, which meant I was responsible for packing the eighty-five gray hoodies and clumps of tangled white wires.

~

The night before we left, I colored my hair. When I first started covering grays, I sat in a colorist's chair for over an hour once every few months. But as my appointments grew closer together, I let Suki talk me into coloring it myself. Suki's daughters were still doing the after-schools my kids had long since abandoned, and she could not fathom losing one hour every six to eight weeks. Following her directions, I went online, described my hair color and texture, and uploaded a picture of myself. I took about forty pictures until I found one that didn't make me look like I was in need of an undertaker or a hundred thousand dollars' worth of surgery. Every six weeks a packet of hair color arrived at my door, and I even let Suki talk me into texting her all the things I had accomplished while self-coloring. Suki would write things like:

> Proofread poem, helped with math homework, made dinner for the week, tested two recipes, ironed ballet recital outfit, colored hair.

I would reply:

> Folded laundry (it was more of a bundle than a fold), paid Spanish tutor, studied vocab with a distracted middle schooler, cleaned up dinner, baked a coffee cake, served second dinner, colored hair.

Luckily, Molly, my pediatrician sister-in-law, had preempted any concerns I had about coloring my hair while pregnant. Unprompted, she'd texted me:

> If you can wait it out, hold off until end of first trimester to color your hair. After then, have at it. No need to go gray for a baby ;)

That night, I slapped on some color, rubbed it all over my head, and sent Suki my final hair-coloring text from the city:

> Packed the last of the boxes, took a break, packed some more boxes, cried about leaving, gestated, cried some more, colored hair.

-5-

We were leaving Manhattan, the city that neither sleeps nor stops, and moving to a town called Pigkill. I kept this detail away from the kids, airily tossing around the words *Dutchess County*. Dutchess County had a pastoral, almost regal sound to it. Pigkill sounded like something you did behind a shed, when no one was looking.

We rolled into Pigkill on the hottest day of August and were greeted by an enormous sign that read **Welcome to Pigkill, the Pearl of Dutchess County.**

Harry turned around and beamed at the kids. "This is it, kids. Welcome to Pigkill."

"What's Pigkill?" Alice asked. For the journey, she'd donned a tank top and a skirt covered in pink feathers.

"It's the name of the town we'll be living in. It's our new home," I explained, the last word sticking deep in my throat.

"How can I tag myself in Pigkill?!" she moaned.

"It sounds like something from one of *your* books," Sam said to Harry, who raised an eyebrow in delight.

"Sam," he said, "*Lord of the Flies* isn't one of *my* books. I didn't write it. William Golding—"

"Whatever," Sam muttered. "This still sucks."

I couldn't blame them. I was trying my best to be positive for Harry, but I could barely bring myself to say the name. The night before, I'd wondered: *Maybe I was mispronouncing it! Maybe it was from the original Dutch. Maybe we should all be saying Peegkill?*

"I need to pee again," I said, putting my hand on Harry's shoulder. He sped up slightly, and a rattling came from the back of the car.

"Sam," Harry yelled over Sam's enormous headphones and presumably awful music. "You know what to do!"

Sam banged on the inside of the car, and the rattling stopped. In preparation for the move and the looming new addition to our family, we sold our old sedan and inherited a minivan. The previous owners were university acquaintances who'd moved to Germany on a Fulbright and who were planning on trading up when they returned. Even though Dutchess College was paying for our move, and even though every third person told me how much less it cost to live upstate (cue Harry: "The Hudson Valley is not upstate!"), money was still tight, and I was happy to take someone else's rejected car. Harry thought he was being cute when he named the minivan Fulbright.

The name was the only distinguishing thing about the car.

"Pee," said Alice when we took our first ride. "This car smells like pee. I'm not getting in."

"No worries!" chirped Harry, whipping out a can of Lysol from his orange canvas messenger bag. (The bag looked new. Hadn't we agreed to hold off on new purchases?) He sprayed a thick mist everywhere, and the car soon smelled like pee and pine.

It wasn't just the smell. If we drove over sixty-five miles an hour, we heard a loud rattling from the back right corner, which was only silenced when Sam slammed his fist down on the inside plastic panel above the wheel. When the air-conditioning crapped out somewhere in Westchester County (after we'd stopped at Vivian's for lunch, and she'd sent us on our way with Ludmilla the housekeeper's famous sandwiches in waxed paper), Harry stopped at a gas station, purchased a spray bottle, and shot ice water at anyone who claimed to be dying of heatstroke. (Naturally, he believed he was legitimately suffering from heatstroke and sunstroke and that he'd narrowly avoided Lyme disease by stepping over a small patch of grass at a service station.)

"I'm excited to see the house," Harry announced, brimming with optimism. Among other perks, professors at Dutchess received faculty housing in the form of actual houses. We were going to be living in a home built in the late 1800s.

"What are we going to do with all the space?" Harry asked, desperate for enthusiasm.

"Maybe you guys can keep having babies and fill it up super quick," Alice sneered, for which she received a rare high five from her brother.

The kids may not have been excited, but I was. Even though I hadn't seen a single picture of the house, I'd fallen in love with the words *washer/dryer* and *driveway*. I would never have to worry about the old guy in 4H pawing through my underwear or fight for a parking spot again, and I would never, ever have to listen to Harry drone on about alternate-side parking and the inefficiency of city street cleaning. I'd also been promised a vegetable garden (no more pots on the fire escape!), a home office, and something called a baker's kitchen. If I closed my eyes and tilted my head a certain way, I could almost envision myself—writing articles for a local paper from my sunny home office with a Bundt cake in the oven and parsley growing in wooden boxes just outside my window.

"Farmers market!" yelled Harry, pulling me out of my reverie.

Harry had been waiting his entire adult life for local honey, unpasteurized dairy products from tiny farms, and barn-brewed liquor. As soon as we saw signs for the Sunday market, he did a little dance in his seat.

"We have arrived!" he announced. "And we will celebrate by eating locally!"

The kids groaned, but Harry persisted. He followed signs to downtown and parked the car on the corner, next to something billing itself as an artisanal micro-batch ice cream store. I wanted to climb out of the car, but my legs had melted into the leather and were welded to my seat. Eventually I peeled myself off and tumbled out.

The market was three streets long, maybe four, and full of stalls. I looked around. Suki wasn't wrong about the Hudson Valley. Although I saw trees, trees, and then more trees, I didn't see an actual farmer—just a couple of man buns, some tattoos, and a sea of yoga pants.

Harry was already forging ahead. He was wearing a long-sleeved shirt and long pants with rubber bands around his wrists and ankles, which he read online would keep ticks away and spare him from Lyme disease. The kids made sure to walk a few feet behind him at all times. I grabbed my enormous purse and followed.

"Look how happy these people are!" he announced, waving his sleeved arms proudly, as if he himself had created this scene of marketgoers. "No angst. I do not see angst!"

I looked past the farm stalls and saw a playground. I squinted and saw moms, young moms, very young moms. Very young moms and their healthy babies, which despite all my test results, I still was not convinced I'd be having. These fresh-faced moms, who still produced their own natural collagen, were moving fast—pushing swings, following kids down slides. I put my hand under my stomach and looked for a bathroom.

"Bells! Bells!" I heard Harry call as I emerged from a diner whose bathroom I'd used. I followed his voice and arrived at the ice cream store.

"Lavender and goat milk!" He beamed, wearing an enormous sun hat he must have bought at one of the stands. It even had a massive flap for the back of his neck. Sometimes it struck me how someone so naturally attractive could do so much to make himself look like an enormous insect. He stuck out his cone, and I took a lick. It tasted like bubble bath and goat. I gagged.

"Where are the kids?" I sputtered.

"Exploring," he said. "I think this is going to be good, Bells. Just smell the air. Want your own cone?"

"I want to see the house, Harry," I said, looking around and immediately spotting Alice's pink feathers.

"Our house?" he asked.

"Yes, Harry. I want to see our house."

"Onward, then!" he bellowed. The kids made their way back as Harry quickly bought two jars of honey, a bottle of cold brew, and some soap made from goat milk. I briefly wondered if it was from the same goat whose milk I just licked in ice cream form. We piled back into Fulbright and prepared to drive on. "I think you're all going to love it," Harry said as the kids buckled in. "You'll have bigger bedrooms and more living space than we could ever have in the city, but . . ."

"Here it comes," laughed Sam.

"I think we all need to have an open mind," Harry said, handing me his market stash.

"What?" Alice, Sam, and I said in unison.

"It's an old house, that's all I'm saying."

I should have gotten that ice cream.

-6-

The first thing I noticed were the two white columns in front. Maybe it was the motion sickness, but I could have sworn that one column was taller than the other. We had driven past rows of houses that Harry explained were mostly colonial. "Both Dutch and American," he'd explained, his arm extended out his open window. Some had just been painted, their black trims bright and crisp; others were in states of peeling, overgrown disrepair. The odd Victorian was thrown in the mix, complete with spires and brightly colored exteriors. Every street had one boarded-up house and another one being drastically remodeled. It was hard to tell whether the neighborhood was coming or going.

We arrived at a long, narrow, steep driveway with a brick portico, which must have been built when cars were much narrower, because Harry and Fulbright came to a stop halfway up the driveway when it was clear we might get stuck. Harry put on the parking brake, and we all climbed out.

I walked up a small flight of brick stairs, and rounding the front of the large colonial ("American!"), I saw the uneven columns. The front door in between them was a deep red, and the house itself was gray, with black shutters. My head was cocked to one side when Harry came up behind me and put his arms around my waist, or the area where my waist once lived.

"What do you think?"

"It certainly is grand," I said.

"And old," Alice added, coming up alongside us.

"Don't knock old and grand," Harry said, taking my hand. Was he referring to me?

"It's great, isn't it?" he prodded.

"Harry. This is our house. You don't need to sell it to me." I was feeling more hot and tired than old and grand. My back hurt, my legs ached from sitting, and I was experiencing the all-too-familiar feeling of needing to lie down and take a walk at the exact same time.

"Let's go inside," I said as warmly as I could.

We swung open the red front door and were greeted by a giant foyer. To the right and left were large rooms, both of which were lined with windows and window benches. I picked a direction and walked to the right, noting that the floor creaked with each step.

"Where are you going?" Harry asked, following me.

"The kitchen. I'm looking for the kitchen."

I could hear the kids behind me, taking it all in. Before I could get to the kitchen, I walked into a third large room and immediately saw a potbelly stove. I took a picture and texted it to Suki and my sisters-in-law, all of whom quickly texted me back some version of OMG.

"Look at this!" Harry yelled, jumping in between me and the stove, holding out his arms proudly, as if he had birthed it himself.

"What are all these rooms for?" I asked him. "And why is there a stove in the middle of one of them?"

"They look like living rooms," he answered.

"Three living rooms?" I asked. "How much living are we planning on doing?"

"One can be a dining room, one a living room, and maybe the third a sitting room," he said.

"A sitting room?" Given that sitting in the car had nearly finished us all off, I had a hard time envisioning all of us sitting in one room for long periods of time. The kids seemed to agree, because they had quickly grown bored with the copious living space and were already climbing a carpeted staircase in search of their bedrooms. I looked at the carpet. It was deep red, almost burgundy, and it would have to go.

I followed the maze of large rooms, but other than the potbelly stove, I saw nothing that resembled an appliance.

"Where is the kitchen, Harry?" I asked, turning to him. "I don't see a kitchen."

Harry looked like he'd just accidentally eaten someone else's birthday cake. "Here is where we need to open our minds," he mumbled.

"Harry, please tell me there's a kitchen."

Harry took my hand, presumably the only part of me that was not swollen, and led me through the entire sunlit ground floor. When we found no kitchen, we had no choice but to walk out a pair of French doors at the back of the house. Harry pulled me along until we stood in the large rectangular yard under an enormous tree.

"The kitchen is out here in the yard?" I asked, swatting away a bug.

Harry pointed to a stand-alone building.

"That's a garage, Harry. Please tell me the kitchen isn't in the garage."

"It used to be the garage," Harry said, pulling me closer to it. "I guess this is what the housing coordinator meant by stand-alone kitchen."

I pushed back. "Harry, how could you not tell me our kitchen is not attached to the rest of the house? What are we going to do when it rains? Oh my god, what will we do when it snows? Because I think it snows upstate . . ."

"I have a plan, and this is not upstate."

"Whatever," I spat. "I might as well have a look." I marched ahead of him and opened a side door to the garage kitchen.

It was, in fact, a beautiful space. I faced a wall of windows that looked out onto the vegetable garden. The kitchen cabinets were a creamy white, as were the countertops. There was a fridge the size of our Manhattan bedroom and two shiny double ovens, and in the middle of the kitchen stood a large island with a marble slab. There was plenty of storage and room for our table and chairs. I got my baker's kitchen. I just got it in the middle of the yard, separated from the rest of the house by a patch of grass and empty vegetable boxes.

"Tell me," I said to Harry, "does your plan to get here in the winter involve umbrellas?"

"And boots," he admitted.

I was about to respond when Alice came running in.

"Mom, Dad. Sam is on the roof!"

"What?"

"He got mad, and he climbed onto the roof," Alice cried, looking around. "Are we in the kitchen?"

"Yes, but don't worry. Your father has a plan." Without looking at Harry, I walked out through the yard and back to the house. Once inside, I trudged upstairs. The old not-pregnant me wanted to run up the stairs, but I leaned heavily on the banister that, like everything in this house, creaked under my weight.

Alice ran ahead and planted herself in a large room with a walk-in closet and a bay window. "This is mine," she announced.

"Actually, this looks like the master bedroom," Harry said. "Let's take a walk." Alice and I followed Harry down the hallway past two more bedrooms, each with a small attached bathroom. We ended up at another flight of stairs, which looked like it went up to the attic. I took a deep breath as we kept climbing.

The attic was a large room with a sloping dormer ceiling, a floor of thick, painted wooden planks, and its own bathroom. I walked to an open window and saw Sam perched outside, level with the treetops.

"I guess you found the roof," I said.

"Can I sleep up here? Can this be my room?" he asked, his eyes full of tears.

For a moment, I saw the face of the small boy he once was, the boy who lit up and raised his chubby arms when I walked into his room to take him out of his crib, the boy who clung to my jeans on the first day of school, the boy who wrote his first songs for me. I wanted to climb out onto the roof and wrap my arms around that boy and reassure him that this would all be fine, but I wasn't sure how he'd react; it had been months since he'd let me hug him. I also didn't want to tumble to my death. Instead, I reached out and put my hand on his arm.

"Yes," I said. "This room is yours."

Sam nodded and swallowed.

"I love you, and this will all work out," I said, our moment coming to an abrupt end the minute I made promises I couldn't keep. Sam turned his face away from me, giving me the side of his hoodie instead.

Harry and I let Alice choose one of the two remaining rooms on the second floor, and we decided the other would be for the baby. She immediately whipped out her phone to give Sophie and Tanya a guided tour of her "own personal bathroom." I had almost made it to the bottom of all the stairs when I noticed a tall gray-bearded man standing in the hall in front of the fireplace. He was examining the mantel.

"Can I help you?" I asked. He turned to me. He looked like an old hipster Abe Lincoln.

"I'm Richard," he said. "I'm the handyman. I come with the house."

"Why's that?" I asked.

"You'll see," he said, leaving a piece of paper on the mantel.

I felt a little dizzy and leaned hard, the banister shifting audibly under my hand.

"I'll fix that," he said as he walked to the door. As he let himself out, he added, "And the plumbing."

"What about the plumbing?"

"You'll see."

-7-

One week in and the house had practically swallowed me alive. Although I was growing larger by the day, I felt myself shrinking inside cavernous rooms, rooms that I'd spent the past decade fantasizing about. The house was screaming for furniture, window coverings, and rugs, and instead there were only piles of boxes. Every time I went online to buy something, I got overwhelmed and ended up reading stories about women who gave birth at sixty. (Vivian had sent some pieces of furniture she had in storage, but they were from her shabby-chic phase, which meant that even though the furniture probably cost as much as our house, it looked as though she'd bought it at a garage sale, then left it out in the rain for six months.) I tried to make a dent in the unpacking, but it seemed that whatever I unpacked was never the thing I was looking for.

Anything I couldn't order online could be procured by Harry, who was always up for some shopping. Granted, I sent him out knowing he'd return with the first overpriced, unnecessary object he saw. When I sent him to the drugstore for medicine to treat a pregnancy condition I cannot even bring myself to name (hint: it almost rhymes with asteroids), he blew into the house an hour later. "The drugstore—it's an old-fashioned apothecary!" He beamed, clutching several brown paper bags, regaling me with their contents, most of which came in amber bottles.

For a moment, I worried about where we'd store all these bottles, but then I remembered—we had bathrooms aplenty in this new house.

As for those bathrooms, I'd left increasingly hostile messages for Richard. He wasn't lying about the plumbing. Whenever Sam showered, water dripped directly down into Alice's closet, and whenever Alice showered, water dripped down onto the potbelly stove. Two toilets weren't flushing at all, one seemed to be flushing continuously, and there was a sewage-inspired smell coming from the basement that nobody was willing to investigate. When I was able to get in touch with Richard, he listened to my list of complaints.

"Sounds like you need some plumbing parts," he said. What it sounded like to me was that I needed a house built in this century. "I'll be there when they arrive."

"When will that be?"

"When they arrive."

"Richard," I said, putting on my sweetest voice, a voice that bordered on creepy when I heard it coming out of my mouth, "what am I supposed to do in the meantime?"

"Buckets."

"Buckets? That's the best you can do?"

"Mrs. Walker," he said, putting on what I suspected was his sweetest voice, "there are some things one cannot rush. Plumbing parts are among those things."

"But . . ."

"You'll find a stack of buckets in the closet at the foot of the basement stairs. I'll be there when the parts come in."

I quickly learned there was no rushing Richard or the plumbing parts, and not needing any more of his country wisdom, I thanked him and promised him a coffee cake if he showed up by the end of the month. Then, holding my nose, I ambled down the stairs in search of the buckets. I found Harry in the kitchen when I came back up.

"Listen, Bells," he said, taking his toast from the toaster, "I found this fantastic new coffee shop near the college that makes a mean bulletproof coffee, even decaf. Why don't you come in with me, walk around campus, and I'll drive you back when I'm done with my meeting?"

"I'd love to," I lied. (As much as I loved butter, I did not want it stirred into my coffee.) "I have things to do here today. Rain check?"

"Bells, I'm not going to force you to meet me, but you really need to leave the house."

"That's easy for you to say," I said, pulling up a chair next to him at the kitchen table. "You're not the one responsible for all the unpacking."

"Fair enough," he said, disputing none of that statement. "But I think you still need to take a break. Why don't you head into the *Gazette* and show them your clips?"

"I was kind of hoping to have the baby, lose the weight, and then make an appearance," I admitted, licking my finger and picking up crumbs from my plate. (I'd made a batch of blueberry muffins when the baby awoke me with a kick at 4:00 a.m. I had obviously unpacked the kitchen immediately.)

"What?"

I couldn't look at Harry, so I focused on my plate, methodically picking up every last crumb. "The minute I leave this house, everyone will know that the hot new professor is married to an old pregnant lady."

"What? That's nuts."

"Great. So now I'm old, fat, *and* crazy."

Harry got out of his seat and knelt down in front of me, taking my hands in his.

"Bells Walker, you are not old, fat, or crazy. You are beautiful and glowing, and you need to leave this house."

If Harry knew what I would soon do, he probably would have told me to stay home. Forever.

~

A week later, Alice emerged in her first-day-of-school outfit, one she'd spent days working on and that made her look like a drummer from an '80s girl band. That morning, she searched frantically for the one pair of shoes she could not live without, while Sam prowled from room to room tearing open boxes looking for *that* gray hoodie.

Harry gave them both a pep talk, mostly taking the form of "Think of Pigkill as a fresh start," which we all knew was his way of encouraging Sam to discover his inner A student and for Alice to believe him when he said that the Hudson Valley could be the cure for her ADD.

"You know it doesn't work that way," I muttered in between sips of decaf.

"We don't know that," he said, screwing on the cap of his glass water bottle and strapping on yet another new messenger bag. "For all we know, she could leave that all behind in the city."

I knew this was code for "She doesn't need medication for her ADD," but rather than go down this road in front of Alice, I turned and focused on the kids.

"Guys, we have to go," I said, swallowing a final bite of a middle-of-the-night babka. "Even I am making a fresh start today." All heads turned my way. "That's right," I announced, getting up and putting my plate and mug in the dishwasher. "I'm going in to the *Hudson Valley Gazette* to see if they want or need another writer."

Harry beamed from behind his own mug. "They will both want and need you. I'm sure of it."

"So am I," said Alice. "They're gonna love you . . . but no offense, you need to change your outfit." She eyed my green wraparound sleeveless dress and gold Birkenstocks.

"You will not shame me or my outfit today," I proclaimed. "And especially because this was outfit number six. Let's go." We all marched from the garage kitchen into the house.

"I'm not ready!" Alice shrieked, leaping from zero to crazy in five seconds. She leaned over a box and threw all the wrong shoes over her shoulder. "Where did you put my silver sneakers?" Even though she'd been like this for over a year now, it still threw me in a tailspin every time she went from my biggest fan to a complete lunatic.

"In a week or two, we will know where everything is. Until then, let's go."

"This sucks," Sam said from the driveway.

"You know I can hear you," I called to him. (What Harry liked to call my "bat-like hearing" was the bane of my children's existence.)

Sam just shrugged. I headed for the door. Alice and her phone followed. I paused before I unlocked the car, then stared at the two of them. Alice look frazzled, as was her norm in the morning and at all moments of transition, but she also looked terrified, her eyes wide and frantic. Sam looked fearful but angry, his expression screaming, *I can't believe you did this to me, I still can't believe this is happening.*

"You've got this," I said to them, and when neither replied, I went on. "I know neither of you wanted this, but you both can do this." Alice nodded with her entire body, then fumbled her way into the car as I unlocked the doors. Sam just stared at me. "I have your back," I said. He looked away.

Right before we left, Harry ran over to Fulbright, leaned in the driver's window, and put his hands on my shoulders. "Next time I see you, you'll be a star reporter for the *Hudson Valley Gazette*!"

"I think you may be putting your cart a few blocks before your horse, Harry. They don't even know I'm coming."

"Nonsense," he said. "They'll love you. Make sure you show them the clippings from the snow-day series. Besides, you are hardly a horse."

I couldn't decide whether to kiss him or kick him, so I opened the car door and did both.

As instructed, I dropped the kids a block from school, making sure to squeeze Alice's hand as she climbed out, and made my first foray out of Pigkill since the day we arrived a week ago. I drove two towns over to Beacon to the headquarters of the *Hudson Valley Gazette*. From what I could see, even though it was just as leafy, Beacon was several times larger than Pigkill and a hundred times more fabulous. For starters, there were fewer boarded-up stores and homes and many more streets that looked like they'd been plucked from the hipster corners of Brooklyn. I drove past rows of boutiques with pale wood and Danish lighting and past even more coffee shops than we had on the Upper West Side. It wasn't just the stores and cafés; the Pigkill farmers market crowd had nothing on these people. I saw at least five women whom I may or may not have recognized from television (or maybe they just had that very tall, very thin, very large head look). I passed men wearing perfectly worn jeans, fitted lumberjack shirts, and just the right amount of stubble. Everyone was walking at least one good-sized dog.

I climbed a flight of stairs, opened a glass door with **Hudson Valley Gazette** etched on the front, and was greeted by walls of exposed brick and the smell of coffee. The newsroom was small but fitted with cubicles and a glassed-in room at the back. I didn't see a front desk or a receptionist.

"Hello?" I called out.

"Can I help you?" asked a small twentysomething man, wearing the enormous glasses I'd been forced to wear in middle school. He and his ironic eyewear peered over a cubicle wall.

"I'm Bells Walker. I'm here to talk to the editor," I began.

"Does Gary know you're coming?" he asked. Gary Wallace was the editor of the *Gazette* and, according to my internet research, had been for almost three decades.

"No."

The man and his glasses headed to the back of the newsroom. He stuck his head in the back room and emerged moments later with an older man.

"Let me guess," the older man said, walking toward me. "You just moved here from the city and you want a job . . ." Gary Wallace was probably in his midfifties and had a smattering of gray hair circling his otherwise bald head. He was trim and wore jeans, a faded T-shirt, and a worn blazer I was almost certain his partner had been trying to throw out for years.

"I have clippings," I said, not sure how to answer him.

"I'm sure you do," he replied. "Listen, if I had a dollar for every New York City writer who got priced out of Brooklyn, moved up here, and asked me for a job, I wouldn't have to work anymore." He spun around and called out to the newsroom. "Everyone in here who came up from Brooklyn, stand up." Two men (including the little man and his big glasses) and three women rose from behind cubicles. They were all noticeably younger than I was. "If you moved from another borough of New York City, stand up," he continued. Two more men stood. "Anyone else?" A slightly older man reluctantly got out of his seat, holding a cup of coffee. They all had the rested look of people who were neither pregnant nor living with teenagers. The air around me suddenly felt thick and soupy. All of me felt frizzy.

"I can work from home," I sputtered. "You wouldn't have to give me office space."

"They all say that. And by home they usually mean from some coffee shop with Wi-Fi where they will take many breaks to check their email and walk other people's dogs."

"Oh."

Gary smiled. "Listen, I'm sure you're a good journalist, and these are probably terrific clips." I heard a snicker coming from the direction of Large Glasses. "The Hudson Valley may be exploding, but it's also exploding with writers. I don't think there's anyone left in Brooklyn."

"I can write about anything," I said, pretending I hadn't heard the Brooklyn remark. "I can write about food, parenting . . . I was actually about to start writing a column for the paper when I moved."

Despite himself, Gary looked at my stomach. "In that case, maybe start a blog," he said. I heard more snickering.

"A blog?"

"Yeah, they still seem to do really well. Some local mommy blogger with six kids just got a book deal." He turned to the cubicles behind him and called out, "What was her name?"

"Hudson Mom of Six," someone called out.

"Can you at least hold on to my clippings?" I asked, pretending I hadn't heard him.

He smiled and nodded at me sympathetically. I handed him the manila folder and saw myself out.

Hot, hungry, and desperate for some air, I ran down the stairs and out of the building, not exhaling until I was outside. I walked to Fulbright as quickly as I could, filling my lungs while fielding a barrage of texts from Alice.

How did it go? Did they hire you?

No. Why aren't you in class?

Why couldn't I hold off on judging her?

In the bathroom. Don't worry—I'm trying to pay attention.

We texted until she returned to whichever class she'd been avoiding, and I stumbled into the car. *I don't think there's anyone left in Brooklyn.* I let my head rest on the steering wheel until I'd composed myself, then drove to the diner in Pigkill, which I noticed had a **KOMBUCHA ON TAP** sign out front. I walked in and slumped down at the bar.

"Oh, look, we're the same," said a very young waitress with shoulder-length dark-brown hair, her hands on her tiny pregnant belly.

"So we are."

"I'll be right with you," she said, carrying a burger out to a group of women at a booth. She came back and took a sip from a drink she had stashed behind the bar.

"I'll have a decaf, please," I said. The waitress nodded and lifted her glass. "You should really try the egg creams. They're kind of my specialty."

The last time I had an egg cream was when my grandfather was alive. I smiled at the thought. "Sure," I said. "Chocolate."

"Obviously." She smiled and returned moments later with a tall glass. I watched as she beat together milk and chocolate syrup with one hand while adding seltzer with the other. She kept beating until the milk frothed, then handed me the glass. I took a gulp. It was milky and sweet with a kick of salty, seltzery fizz.

"Wow, this is excellent. Even better than I remember."

The waitress took a sip of her own egg cream and put it back behind the bar when the booth of women beckoned her over. One of them handed her a dish that she took back to the kitchen.

I took out my phone and looked up Hudson Mom of Six.

Sure enough, there she was, with her six "little blessings," all of whom were living their "best lives, the Hudson Valley way." The blessings all wore coordinated outfits in neutral shades and were set against a gauzy blush backdrop of peaceful domesticity. Hudson Mom of Six seemed to take lots of pictures of the blessings' feet, lined up at the water's edge or on a bath mat, and her blogs were short but treacly sweet. Mostly, though, she seemed to do a lot of shilling for things like graham crackers and food storage containers.

I looked up. The waitress was still shuffling back and forth with whatever dishes those women had ordered.

I went back to the blog and read a back-to-school post in which the Hudson Mom detailed her children's locker decorations and bento box lunches. I'd happily sent Alice to school with a locker mirror, but

I'd be damned if I was going to shape a mound of rice into a panda's head and decorate it with seaweed.

As I read a post about making art with your kids by filling LatexFun! balloons with paint, attaching the balloons to a canvas, and then popping them with a skewer, I slurped the last of my egg cream and marinated in my rejection. Somehow, this Mom of Six and her paint balloons had landed a book deal while I'd just been rebuffed by a small-town paper even after I'd basically offered to write for free.

"I bet you're having a better day than me," the waitress said, coming back.

"I'm not sure about that."

"Did someone just leave you a quarter for a tip after you'd taken back her meatless burger three times?" I looked and saw that the booth was empty.

No, but I'm going to fade into the scenery up here while some woman nabbed a book deal by combining cheesy craft projects and product placement. "You win." I smiled.

"Anything else?" she asked.

"No, thanks," I said, leaving her money for the egg cream and a tip to cover me and the booth of women. I got up to leave, and my phone buzzed with a call from Suki.

"How did it go?"

"The bread didn't rise. In fact, the bread fell flat."

"Oh no! What happened?"

"There are more writers than stories up here," I said, climbing into Fulbright. "Apparently, writers are the pigeons of the Hudson Valley, especially writers who move up from the city clutching a folder of clippings."

"Pigeons. That's funny," she said. "You should write that down."

"I'd be happy to write it down, just tell me where to write it. As of now, my witticisms have an audience of one."

"I promise something will turn up. Besides, you're missing nothing here. I sat on the subway for an extra hour last night. Think of all the time you're saving not waiting for trains."

I wasn't so sure about that. I closed my eyes and pictured myself jostling along on the subway in the comfortable anonymity of my old life. It may not have been perfect, but I knew where everything was; I knew where *I* was.

The one thing I knew for sure about Dutchess County was that the life I envisioned here was quickly receding from view.

- 8 -

"I guess that gives us a reason to fix up the office," Harry said later that night when I told him about my *Gazette* rejection. He stripped out of sweaty clothes and headed to the bathroom, while I lay in bed in the same position I'd been in for about six hours, unable to tear myself away from the dewy life of the Hudson Mom of Six. I'd gotten up to stretch, pee, and change my sweaty T-shirt, but the magnetic force of my pillows and laptop kept pulling me back. I was toggling between reading about the secret blessings of the picky eater and a draft article Harry had sent me to proofread. Proofreading was something we'd been doing for each other since he was in grad school and I was in law school. Back then, we had signature colors—I edited in green, he in red, and we'd leave notes for each other in the margins. *Change to active voice . . . also, you smell great.* Now we edited on laptops, but we still left each other notes, or at least I did now that I was giving Harry nothing to edit. If I had been a cheerier version of myself, I'd have written something witty in the comments, like, *So hard to concentrate while you walk around naked,* but this bedridden version of me had nothing.

"Why the office?" I called out.

Harry walked back in from the bathroom as he let the shower run hot. "Your novel." He grinned.

The night I met him, in Suki's tiny loft, Harry asked me what I did. I told him I was just another good girl who went to law school even though what I really wanted to do was write. He looked at me like I was the most exotic creature he'd ever met, even though I was in a loft full of good girls who went to law school but who really wanted to write. Harry was looking at me the same way now. Nobody else ever looked at me like that. "You can go back to creative writing, use the office to write your book," he said, leaning over me and kissing my forehead.

I flashed him the most grateful smile I could muster. Neither Harry nor I had any idea how creative I was about to get.

While he showered, I tried to read his article (Melville, blah, blah, nativism, blah, blah), but found myself zoning out and dipping back into a *Hudson Mom of Six* blog post. If this woman could build a career for herself taking a milk carton, covering it with graham crackers and Pillsbury icing, and calling it a gingerbread house, as well as spewing out fictionalized dreck (there are absolutely zero blessings of a picky eater, and I would know this as the mother of a boy who only ate five foods until he was fifteen, one of which was cheese sticks), then why couldn't I write something?

"What are you thinking?" Harry asked me, fresh from his shower.

"Huh?"

"Looks like you're chewing a hole in your lower lip."

I turned the laptop around and showed Harry the Hudson Mom. "This woman just got a book deal. What does she have that I don't?"

"I don't know," he said. "How about several more kids and a penchant for unimaginative crafting?"

"That's funny," I said. "I should write that down." I also jotted down some notes—*pigeons as the writers of the Hudson Valley*, which was funnier when I said it than it was on the page.

"Seems a little silly if you ask me," Harry said.

"What, unimaginative crafting?"

"No, a blog. You can do better than family pictures and cookie recipes. You're a journalist," he said, scrolling up and pointing to a picture of six children finger knitting under a Christmas tree. "And I'm serious about the office," he added, getting up and looking for his slippers. "Richard said he can blow insulation into the room."

I was pretty sure that Harry had no idea what that meant. Either way, the thought of another Richard project was not at all comforting, especially because neither he nor his plumbing parts had yet to make an appearance. I'd texted him earlier in the week to ask for an update and received the following reply:

Adopt the pace of nature. Her secret is patience—Emerson

To which I replied:

Emerson didn't have to move buckets around while pregnant—Bells Walker

I closed the laptop, got out of bed, and walked over to the proposed office space, peering through the glass-paned door. Maybe Harry was right. It wasn't just the Hudson Mom who'd gotten me thinking. I'd also read Lyla Levy's first two City Chatter columns, both of them whiny, trite diatribes about the death of the family-owned store and unending subway delays (less cliché, more chatter, Lyla), and both of which, silly or not, made my fingers itch to write something of my own.

~

My itchy fingers took me to a PTA meeting.

Even though I was on time, the meeting was already underway when I arrived, so I sat in the back of the classroom and watched a slideshow of the first few days of school. Wearing what I'd hoped was a somewhat flattering black sundress and slides, I shifted uncomfortably in the hard plastic chair, hoping to see a picture of Sam, but I only saw pictures of what looked like the same small group of students over and over again, all of whom looked happy to be reunited after the world's longest summer vacation. When the show was over, the lights went on, and a blonde, athletic-looking woman who seemed about my age stood up and faced the room. Her lower half was clad in workout gear, but atop her sneakers and leggings was a fitted T-shirt and cotton blazer. She reminded me of a faun, if fauns were one-half spin instructor, one-half business casual.

"Hello, everyone, and thanks for coming. I'm Cynthia Plank. I run the PTA." Cynthia paused so we could all take that in, basking in her own importance. "I see a couple of new faces, which is so great. We pride ourselves on community here in Pigkill, and I know you'll find this is a wonderful place to raise kids." She paused and looked around, again allowing us all to appreciate her. "Why don't we go around and introduce ourselves?"

As Cynthia Plank went around the room, we heard from old and new moms, including Avery, a mom who just moved up from Westchester, whose twins were freshmen and already known to the crowd as star lacrosse players. Each mother was happier than the next to be here, as though she'd won some location lottery and ended up in Pigkill. As Cynthia drew closer to me and the witty introduction I should have been rehearsing in my head, I began to sweat in my seat. I was practically drenched by the time she got to me. If I hadn't been in public, I would have fanned my armpits with the handout I'd picked up on my way in.

"I'm Bells Walker," I said, ignoring the feeling that a spotlight had landed on my midsection. "My son, Sam, is a junior. I have a seventh grader at the middle school—Alice. We're new." *I am too old to be pregnant and find it difficult to leave my home for long periods of time. My hair is not usually this large. Also, I like to bake in the middle of the night.*

"Welcome to Pigkill and to the high school PTA." Cynthia beamed, seeming to grow an inch taller in her sneakers, and a lot blonder. "Make sure you check out the sign-up sheets at the back of the class." I was grateful when she moved on to someone else in the room and the spotlight shifted. After everyone had spoken, we were directed to a table where we could sign up for committees. I saw the words **BAKE SALE** on the top of a spreadsheet and began to fill out my information.

"Be careful," said a British accent. "The bake sale is Cynthia's pet project."

I turned. The accent belonged to a striking woman with a dark bob and eyebrows that looked like bats about to take flight. She was wearing a vintage-looking baby-doll dress and booties. I tried not to stare, but I'm pretty sure she had a tiny nose ring.

"Also, be careful where you put your name. Cynthia takes these forms super seriously." She paused. "She used to work in finance." (This was pretty common in the city, too; it was always the finance moms who liked to shame the rest of us with their overwrought spreadsheets.)

"Got it," I said, making sure not to put my cell phone number under the email tab.

"Anna Mills," she said, extending her hand. "My son, Thomas, is a junior as well. He's already taken six practice ACT tests, but who's counting?!"

"And Cynthia?" I asked, intentionally ignoring her comment about a standardized test that Sam had yet to see. "Does she also have a junior?" I may have been miles from the city, but I was getting a quick picture of the moms of the Pigkill PTA. I'd have bet that Cynthia's and Anna's children had packed after-school schedules and starring roles in the opening video.

"Yes, a girl—Hayley. It's a huge grade. We're all 9/11 refugees," said the third voice, a woman several inches shorter than the rest of us with thick, straight red hair, very white teeth, and an out- of-place suntan.

"Huh?"

"We moved from the city after 9/11," she explained as Anna nodded. "We all came up around the same time, and because this is Pigkill, we bonded pretty quickly."

I thought about 2001, the year Sam was born, and what it was like to be pregnant, give birth, and become a mother when it felt like the world was falling apart. So many of our friends left the city that year and in the years right after. Nobody in the room bothered to ask me why I'd moved up; maybe they all knew. I did have to field questions, though—just not the kind I wanted to answer.

"When are you due?" Anna asked, her eyes fixed on my stomach.

"Sometime around the new year," I said, my eyes on the door.

"Do you know what you're having?"

A baby. "No, we like to be surprised." *And this year's understatement of the year award goes to . . .*

"It's so exciting," Cynthia chirped over my shoulder. "I'm sure your older kids are *thrilled*."

"Sure," I said. "What teenager doesn't want a pregnant mom?" A few mothers laughed, and Cynthia looked uncomfortable.

I wanted to go home, and looking back, I probably *should* have gone home, but I was already out, and I knew that if I went home, I'd stay there. For a week. Instead, I resisted the magnetic pull of the house, got into Fulbright, and headed downtown.

~

I drove to the main square and parked along the water. From what I could see, downtown Pigkill really was about four blocks long. I sat in the car for about twenty minutes, answering texts from Alice, who was currently holed up in the school bathroom.

WHAT DO I DO?

She sent a picture of a tiny red dot on her forehead.

When you get home I'll help you cover it. Don't worry.

OMG It's huge. I can't.

Yes, you can. Now please put your phone away and go back to class.

I also hate my hair.

Her texts did remind me to check my own skin and hair in the car mirror. I pulled down the mirror and did a survey. I saw the beginnings of a tiny stray hair in the center of my chin and made a mental note to attack it with a pair of tweezers later.

I climbed out of the car, then walked past the goat-milk ice cream store, the diner, and a store that claimed to sell both vinyl records and vintage soda. I arrived on the corner at a bookstore cleverly called The Dutchess Reads.

I swung open the door and was immediately awash in a sea of hipsters. Even my brief foray into Beacon had not fully prepared me for the parade of man buns, tattoos, and piercings, all on very thin people. (I was officially at the stage of my pregnancy where just about everyone looked very thin.) The store itself was dark, despite hanging filament bulbs and two large skylights. I could smell coffee and spotted a barista, a pastry counter, and some tables in the far-right corner. I ambled through the crowd, almost knocking a porkpie hat off a twentysomething's head. I ordered my coffee, bought a muffin, and found a seat behind a freestanding bookshelf. I heard the whispers almost instantly.

"I don't get it," said a voice from the other side of the bookshelf, a voice I recognized as belonging to Cynthia Plank. (I turned my head slightly and confirmed that she was sitting a few tables away and couldn't see me unless she craned her neck.) "How much kombucha can these people drink?" she asked.

"Remember what this place was like before they arrived," said a British accent belonging to Anna with the eyebrows.

I looked around the room, then pulled out my phone to text Suki.

This place might as well be Brooklyn. Think farm-to-table food, kombucha, and hipsters in ironic hats.

Oh no!

Oh yes!

I glanced at the people sitting next to me.

Someone is actually wearing those high-waisted acid-washed pants we wore in high school, and there are two guys looking at a vinyl record.

LOL.

I heard a third voice. I couldn't turn my head without being too obvious, but I assumed it belonged to the mom who told me about being a 9/11 refugee. I never got her name. "All that stuff we hated, and they can't get enough of it."

I texted Suki.

What's next? Roller skates and five-foot-deep TVs with aluminum-foil antennae??

I keep telling you—YOU SHOULD WRITE THIS DOWN!

"Peggy," said Cynthia, "as long as they keep coming up here from the city, our home prices go up. They may be annoying, but all that kombucha just let you refinance." They all laughed. I quietly laughed with them and made a mental note of the third woman's name. Maybe Suki was right about posses; maybe these women would be mine. If that was going to happen, I at least had to remember their names.

"Enough about them," Anna said. "I want to talk about *her*, the new one at the meeting."

"Which new one?" Peggy asked. "That fabulous lacrosse mom? I hear both her kids are already DI recruits."

"No, the very pregnant one. How old do you think she is?" *Very?*

"Old enough to have a junior in high school," Cynthia whispered. The voices laughed.

I felt my entire head start to sweat. I instinctively slid down in my seat and patted down the top of my hair.

"What kind of name is Bells?" Peggy giggled. Somewhere, Hanna Cohn was smiling with approval. She may not have liked the nickname, but Hanna Cohn would have marched over to the table and introduced herself, made piercing eye contact, and left with the scalps of the town gossips in her soft leather briefcase. She was miles away, though, most likely in a suit, and I was alone, dressed in what I thought was a hip, shapeless dress, but what I now realized was a glorified muumuu. I was no Hanna Cohn. I slunk deeper into my seat to drink my decaf latte and finish my muffin while scanning the room for the least visible way out.

"Can you imagine having to be pregnant now?" Cynthia whispered. "Would you ever go back there?"

"Never," the voices agreed.

"Since I turned forty, if I even look at a baked good, I turn into an actual muffin top," Cynthia added. "I'd never be able to lose all that baby weight."

"Maybe we should buy her some high-waisted jeans as a baby gift," Anna laughed. "They're incredibly forgiving."

"Not *that* forgiving."

I choked down the last of my own muffin and fled.

~

Once home, I raced upstairs, those women's voices chattering in my head. I didn't think there was any room up there, what with Hanna and Vivian competing in the disapproval space race, but it seemed I had all the room in the world for disapproval.

I still heard their voices—*Would you ever go back there?*—as I grabbed my laptop and found the doc I'd started in bed. But now I didn't just have their voices in my head, I had Suki's as well: *You should write this down*. With my eyes closed, I tried to remember everything I'd overheard, everything I'd seen, and most important, everything I thought. I opened my eyes and began to write.

Later that evening, I really did try to make conversation and take an active if slightly inauthentic interest in everyone's day, but I could not stop myself from running blog titles through my head (*City Mouse*? Too obvious . . .). I tried to listen as Alice regaled me with the minutiae of middle school squads and posses. Because it seemed that middle school girls only socialized in groups of three, she had found membership in a new trio of girls. If Sophie-Tanya could be replaced by Abigail-Courtney, order would be restored in the whirl of her universe.

I even attempted to make conversation with Sam, who spent most of his time upstairs practicing for his upcoming school band audition.

I lured him into the kitchen with some oatmeal cookies (with chocolate chips, because who really wants raisins?), which I traded him for any small nugget of news I could get about his life outside this house.

Just as Sam was telling me about his English teacher, who ended each week with a slam poetry challenge, Harry walked in. "I got called a cidiot today," he said, holding a piece of paper.

"What's that?" Sam asked.

"An idiot who has moved up from the city." Harry turned to look at me. "You know the light that went on in Fulbright?"

I nodded.

"We waited too long to change the oil. It's lucky for us the thing is still running."

"What the hell is wrong with people up here?" I asked.

"Bells . . . ?"

"I mean, they've never met someone who hasn't changed his own oil? They've never seen a pregnant fortysomething? There has not been a single IUD failure in all of Dutchess County . . . ?"

"Um, Mom," Sam interjected, in the gentlest voice I'd ever heard come out of his mouth, "I don't think—"

"Never mind," I snapped. "This just makes it much easier for me." I ran out of the room, leaving them baffled in my wake.

Once in the main house, I pulled out my phone and called Andy.

"Hey, Bells, it's good to hear from you. How's life up in the country?"

"About that, Andy. I have an idea." I heard myself breathing heavily.

"OK . . ."

"I want to write about life in Dutchess County."

"For a city paper?"

"That's the thing. So many hipsters are coming up from the city that it's starting to look like Brooklyn up here. I think there could be real interest, especially if I can make it funny."

"I'm not sure, Bells. You sure you don't want to try and find a local gig?"

"Andy." I inhaled. "I got rejected by the *Gazette*."

"Oh."

"Just let me try this, please," I begged.

"Fine." He paused. "A trial. But I can't promise anything. Send me something, and I'll see what I can do."

"One more thing. I want to write under a pseudonym. I'm new here, and I want to stay anonymous for as long as I can." As for my anonymity, I thought for a second about how I was going to tell Harry about this but decided it was probably going nowhere. Telling Harry could wait.

"Do you have one in mind?"

I thought back to the coffee shop where I'd overheard Cynthia and her friends, with its hanging filament bulbs and customers in porkpie hats. "How about the County Dutchess? Get it? Misspelled royalty?"

"I get it, and it's good. Send me something by this weekend, and we can run it on Monday. Remember—no promises."

"Thank you!" I squealed, holding the phone out and almost kissing it. I felt victorious for a moment and had to remind myself that I'd just convinced the editor of a free city paper to let me write—on a trial basis.

I looked around to see if anyone had heard me, and when I was in the clear, I sat down, opened up my laptop, and continued to write.

~

The Great Kombucha Migration

Sitting in a Hudson Valley coffee shop, which until three years ago was an auto parts store, it's not hard to notice the change. Writers have been flocking here forever, fleeing overpriced city living, but the latest Valley invasion is more of the young, tattooed, kombucha-drinking variety. (I was just in a café with three kinds of the fermented beverage—ginger, berry, and something called *sencha*.) But it's not just the drinks. The entire decor of the Hudson Valley has undergone a rapid makeover. Trucker caps and fluorescent lighting have made way for porkpie hats and filament bulbs, and instead of one tattoo parlor in town, there are now four and counting. Farm stands don't just sell corn and strawberries; they now sell goat-milk ice cream and something called microgreens. (I'm all for eating miniature salads, or better yet, no salad at all, but I don't think that's what it is.) Everywhere I look, there are new, younger Valley dwellers bobbing and weaving through our towns, complete with ironic eyewear, farm-to-table eating, and yes, overpriced beverages sipped through disintegrating paper straws.

It's official: the millennial invasion is near complete.

Someone needs to warn these millennials, though. Someone needs to tell them that Dutchess County may look like a farm-to-table utopia built with reclaimed wood and mason jars, but it's just another place full of the kind of people who smile and act friendly and then talk about you when they think you're out of earshot—the kind of people who talk about community, but whose main goal seems to be exclusion. This may make Dutchess sound like a lot of other places, but it's worse because people like to pretend that it's better here than everywhere else.

I know this much is true: something is rotten in Dutchess County. I'm sorry, millennials, I hate to break this to you, but if this is a utopia, it's a fermented one.

I also know this: with each new wave of immigrants, the last wave grows increasingly irritated. Nobody dislikes a recent city transplant more than someone who fled the city a few years earlier. The true locals call them *cidiots* up here, and I, too, was once one. They remember a time when the Hudson Valley was a days-long horse-and-buggy ride away from the city and you could eat iceberg lettuce in peace. With tension growing between all parties, this place is set to explode like home-brewed kombucha on draft.

In this column, I'll address the changes to this once-sleepy county. I'll also let you know what's going on in Dutchess, and even better, what's *really* going on behind the scenes.

More soon,

The County Dutchess

PS: Porkpie hats look good on NOBODY.

~

After Harry fell asleep, I lay in bed listening to the house groan, and I proofread the piece obsessively. As a city kid, I had only lived in apartments, but Harry grew up in a great big mock European house surrounded by Tudors. (He liked to joke that there were so many Tudors in Westchester that Henry VIII must have had a secret wife from Scarsdale.) He said the nighttime noises were just the sounds of the house settling, but to me the house sounded anything but settled. I climbed out of bed and crept down the stairs, trying to step on the middle of each stair, which I'd learned was the quietest way to tread. I walked from room to room looking for the perfect place to sit, but the only room with any furniture was the potbelly room, which had our tiny city couch on one side of the stove and a large gray tufted couch we'd recently had delivered on the other side. Harry had come home with a pile of firewood for the stove and had shown me how to use it after he himself had googled "How to use a potbelly stove." I opened the door of the stove, put in two logs and some kindling, and lit the fire. I curled up in the corner of the tufted couch and opened up my laptop. I read the piece one more time, sent it to Andy, and with the potbelly stove in full force, I finally fell asleep to the sounds of the house.

-9-

I'd be lying if I said that I didn't expect to wake up to the sound of my phone buzzing off the hook with congratulatory texts and emails, but instead, I awoke to Alice standing over me.

"That guy is at the door," she said, still in her pajamas. "And why are you down here?"

"Which guy?"

"He says his name is Richard."

I bolted off the couch and ran to the foyer. When I realized I was not wearing enough to greet a man who had not seen me give birth, I ran up to my room and threw on a robe.

"Richard!" I sang, a little too enthusiastically. "You're here! You're really here!"

If he looked embarrassed, I didn't notice.

"Hit some really bad traffic," he said, sitting down on the couch, making me wonder what Emerson had to say about being wary of handymen who sit down on your couch. "I used to live here in Pigkill, but I got priced out and now I drive in."

"Yes, that sounds rough," I said, still standing, hoping to speed things along.

"Took me an hour to drive thirty miles," he huffed.

I nodded sympathetically, although hopefully not too sympathetically.

"Take Beacon, for example. Used to be normal, and now it's full of ice cream for vegan people."

Eventually he stood up and strapped on his tool belt. "Where to first, Mrs. Walker?"

I thought you'd never ask. "Follow me," I said, leading him on a tour of dripping taps, running toilets, and leaky showers. I capped it all off by opening the door to the basement and asking him to take a whiff. He snapped his suspenders and got to work, or so I hoped.

I knew people were about to start looking for breakfast, so I grabbed my phone and headed to the garage kitchen. There was a fall chill in the air, and I was glad for my robe as I made my way through the garden. I made some coffee and checked my messages. There was one from Andy.

Love the column! It will go live later this morning.

Great! I'll probably need a new handle on Twitter—I've checked and @TheCountyDutchess is available.

Remember, Bells . . . just a trial.

Andy's hesitance aside, I felt a little more regal as I swanned around the kitchen mixing oatmeal, pouring coffee, and cutting up fruit.

"What do you have on today?" Harry asked me, which was code for "Are you leaving the house?"

I opened my mouth to tell Harry about the Dutchess, but there was a very good chance I'd just written my first and only column. "I have to unpack," I said, wondering if the Dutchess would ever unpack a box herself.

"Um, Mom. No offense, but you've been unpacking for weeks, and it still looks the same," Alice said, smiling and mixing blueberries into her oatmeal.

"These things take time," I said. "Besides, I'm unpacking for two."

"I forgot to tell you," Harry said, intentionally avoiding my eyes. "My mother said she's sending Ernst up to do a day of unpacking for you."

I was about to launch into a you-really-must-stop-letting-your-mother-do-this tirade when Quick Richard (as Sam had recently dubbed him) appeared and asked if we knew where the snake was, at which point Alice jumped three feet in the air and spilled her water.

"Snake?"

Richard explained that a snake was a plumbing device used to dislodge extreme plumbing clogs.

"Extreme?" Harry asked, setting his toast down and helping me mop up the spilled water.

"Have you been down into the basement?" Richard asked.

Rather than hear the details, I offered Quick Richard a zucchini muffin and a cup of coffee, then threw on a hoodie to drive the kids to school. The Dutchess could wait.

~

Apparently she'd have to wait until I watched Harry model new bike shorts in the bedroom. He already owned a bike, but it had recently acquired some accessories, and Harry had acquired spandex. The kids were at school, and I realized this was the first morning we'd spent alone in the house since we'd moved in—Quick Richard's presence in the basement aside. In the city, we had breakfast together most mornings, doing the crossword with two pencils and one of our phones in stop-watch mode, but that was before Harry did things like bike to school with the head of the English department.

Unlike me, Harry Walker was truly blooming where he'd been planted. He roamed the county in search of produce and anything that came in an amber bottle. ("Did you know that there's a Wappinger *and* a Wappinger Falls?!") In addition to his newfound love of esoteric leafy greens, meals in jars (he came home with a blue glass jar he said would be perfect for overnight oats), and locally brewed beverages, any fears or doubts about taking a job at a second-tier school were assuaged by his status as a glossy big fish in a small upstate pond. Barely on the radar in the city, Harry was now being invited to department-chair meetings and dinners with donors. In addition to biking in with the department head, he was even asked to join golf games with trustees. Harry does not golf.

I was assessing the spandex situation when my phone buzzed with a text from Andy.

Check the comments!

I shielded my phone from Harry and opened the link to my column. "Are you still reading that god-awful blog?"

"Blogs are the modern form of social commentary," I shot back. "You don't think Edith Wharton would have blogged?"

Harry made a face and walked out of the room. It didn't matter. I had a growing fan base of my own.

> Love the Dutchess!
>
> Kombucha on tap! Love it.
>
> Porkpie hats! More Dutchess, please.
>
> We love Sundays up in the Hudson Valley. But agree, way too many hipsters. (Come for the foliage, stay for the sencha . . . ?)
>
> Who are you? Why the handle?

I shot a text to Andy.

Does this mean I can write more?

Let's try a few more columns and go from there.

It's a deal!!!!!!!

Normally I'm not a fan of a parade of exclamation points, but they suddenly seemed appropriate. I felt the frisson of publication and, even dare I say it, the risk of anonymity, and I smiled to myself.

If I'd had an assurance from Andy that the Dutchess had a future, this would have been the perfect time to tell Harry. But given how "silly" he found *Hudson Mom of Six*, I didn't feel right telling him that even though Andy and I were referring to it as a column, I'd basically started a probationary, gossipy blog about a fictional woman who dished on life in the county. I certainly couldn't tell him until I was so enormously successful that he'd have no choice but to toss his sanctimony aside and be proud of me. (I understand how those two points seem completely inconsistent, but that's how writers think, even fledgling writers—either nobody will read this or the whole world will read this, and next thing you know, I'm in every celebrity book club.)

"Bells," he said, lacing up his shoes, "I really think you should get out today, even for a walk."

"Who am I getting out for?" I asked, placing my phone facedown on the nightstand.

"What do you mean?" he asked.

"Do you want me to leave the house because you think it will be good for me, or because it will be good for you?"

Harry sat down on the end of the bed and began to rub my incredibly swollen feet with his magic hands. "I really want it to work for us up here, and I think for us all to be happy, you probably need some friends. At the very least, you need to get out of the house once a day, other than to drive the kids to school."

"And your job?" I asked.

"What about it?"

"Do I need to socialize for my own sake, or because I'm married to a professor?"

Harry paused for moment. Then, fully resplendent in biking gear, he stretched out next to me on the bed, his head level with my stomach. I ran a hand through his wavy hair.

He propped himself up on an elbow and widened his eyes, now green and playful. "If I play it right this year, I'm basically guaranteed tenure. But that's on me—it's *my* job to go to cocktail parties and bike to school with the department chair. You just need to settle in." He began to massage my feet again, his hands working their way up my tight calves. (The best wedding present we'd gotten was from Suki, who enrolled us in a six-week massage class. Harry's specialty was calves and feet. My specialty was forgetting just about everything I'd learned in class.) I'd have socialized with all of Dutchess County at that point if he'd agree to keep massaging until my due date. But Harry had a point—he didn't just need to talk to all the right people this year, he also needed to play it safe.

"Got it," I said, putting the issue to bed in my mind. Harry lifted my shirt and spoke directly to my belly, his lips cool on my skin.

"Please don't eat all the cookies," he said, which was a joke dating back to when Sam was inside my stomach. Harry once walked into the kitchen, looking for a snack. When he asked about the chocolate chip cookies I'd baked in the middle of the night, I told him the baby ate them all.

"Fine." I relented, leaning forward. "I'll go into town and meet some of the locals."

Harry's jaw dropped, and I hauled myself out of bed.

~

Suki sent me a link to a Hudson Valley calendar, following up with a phone call to explain.

"Life up there is divided into two categories," she began. "Fairs and fests."

"I see," I said, not at all seeing the difference between the two.

"The season begins in the fall, continues through the winter and spring, and hits fever pitch in the summer, culminating in the Renaissance fair and the mother of all large gatherings, the county fair."

"This is all very overwhelming."

"Any gathering over five people is overwhelming for you," she said knowingly. "These are more fun than you think, and often, there's pie."

I looked at the calendar. Within the next few months, I had my choice between the Cheese Fest, the Apple Fair, the Antique and Waffle Fair, a Pumpkin Fest, a Honey Fest, and something called the Sheep and Wool Fair. In search of a story, I decided to head one town over to the Apple Fair.

I would soon learn a few things about the Valley's fairs and fests. Just like the Mexican corn stands and huge woolen sweater stalls at all the farmers markets on the Upper West Side, regardless of the main attraction, up here there would always be an artisanal taco truck, vegan and gluten-free baked goods, and someone selling cheeses made from animals other than cows.

Mostly, though, at this fair, there were apples, and lots of them. I walked past a chalkboard emblazoned with the words **Pie Contest! Double Crust Pies Only—No Crumbles, Crisps, or Bettys**. In front of the sign was a large table brimming with pie samples on small plates, with a large glass bowl in the center. In front of each pie was a stack of tickets. My job was to sample each pie and place the ticket of the best pie in the glass bowl. I was now officially a lover of the Apple Fair.

I picked up a plate and took my first bite of pie. I felt my stomach expanding as I worked my way through the samples, each one buttery and flaky. (This may have been the wrong day to test out a new pair of support hose.) I was taking a bite of the fourth entry when I heard someone call my name. I turned and saw Cynthia and Peggy walking over from the apple-butter stand, drinking cider out of compostable cups.

Cynthia and Peggy looked around nervously and stopped a few feet from me. "We can't come too near the counter," Peggy announced. "We have pies in the contest."

"Really?"

"Yes," Cynthia said. "It's pretty much the only fair we can do this year." She looked over at Peggy. "For obvious reasons."

"Obvious?"

"Junior year," Peggy explained. "In addition to all the usual essays to edit and tests to study for, not to mention all the AP classes"—they both nodded—"this year we also have college."

I nodded, too, wishing I had some cider to wash down the mountain of pie lodged in my esophagus.

"And we can't compete with the big bucks in the city or Westchester," Cynthia said.

"Yeah, we can't build a wing for Harvard or pay for someone to take the SAT for our kids," Peggy retorted.

"Or pretend our kids are field hockey stars," Cynthia added.

They both stared at me nervously.

"We really have to up our game," Peggy said, breaking the sad silence.

Then they began speaking simultaneously, listing everything that lay before them this year. I tried to tune them out, but I heard the words *tutoring*, *test prep*, *enrichment*, more *enrichment*, and *volunteer hours*. As they spoke, they began to blend into one person, one very loud and tightly wound person. I noticed they were both wearing necklaces with small discs bearing the first initials of their children. Upon further inspection, I noticed they were also practically wearing the same outfit. They both had on yoga pants, jeweled flip-flops, and long jackets that could also have doubled as dresses. Cynthia just looked a little more fabulous. Her baby discs had little birthstones.

"Hello, girls!" chirped a woman with long streaked hair, a camouflage hoodie dress, and cropped skinny jeans. I recognized her immediately.

"I'm Meegan," she announced, pivoting to me and sticking out her bangled arm. "Rhymes with vegan. You might know me as Hudson Mom of Six."

I managed to affect a look of having absolutely no idea who she was while knowing I'd been hate-reading her blog almost daily since I discovered it.

"Because I have six kids," she added.

"That's a lot of kids," I said, playing it as cool as possible.

"They're a blessing," she said, suddenly very solemn.

"Meegan has a blog, and she just signed a big deal, so pretty soon she'll have a book," explained Cynthia. "She's something of a Dutchess County celebrity." Despite all the pie, I felt myself shrinking. What was it about this woman that was book worthy, and if her blessings and crafting were enough for a book deal, would there be one for me one day?

Fortunately, Meegan had a crowd to work. "Great meeting you," she said as she wandered off to share her light with someone else at the fair.

"That woman never misses an opportunity to tell you how many children she has," Peggy remarked.

"It's hard to miss with a handle like that." I laughed. (*Look at me,* I thought, *out making small talk. Who's agoraphobic now, Harry?*)

"We're having a grade mixer for parents," Cynthia said, changing the subject. "Bring your husband."

My husband? Did they say this to everyone, or had they already heard about Harry and his hotness? (Suki always told me to count my lucky stars that Harry often insisted on dressing like an aging explorer. I thought about his flappy sun hat and Lyme disease prevention bands and smiled.)

At some point, Anna came swooping in, wearing a tie-dye variation on the yoga pants and flip-flop theme.

"I just got off the phone with the school board," she announced. "They agreed to let us meet in the school."

"We're forming a support group for parents," Peggy said, turning back to me, a look of concern on her face. "To help us manage our college anxiety." Someone walked past with a tray of samples of CBD-infused sodas. Peggy grabbed three and chugged them in one shot. "It's really good for inflammation and stress," she said, swallowing.

The Dutchess was just what I needed. She gave me somewhere to put all I'd been thinking for as long as I'd been a parent. I may have been far north of the striving moms of the Upper West Side, but not much had changed. I was the mother of two average students. A million tutors and enrichment hours might have helped, but only marginally. Mostly, they would have stressed out two kids who, for different reasons, preferred the middle of the academic road. Maybe it was because my fancy degrees hadn't served me all that well, or maybe it was because a fancy college ultimately failed Harry, but I wasn't about to get sucked into the college frenzy. Luckily, Harry was the just-right amount of self-involved to keep the kids shielded from his own higher-learning insanity.

I didn't want to tell these women that my stress took the form of lying awake worrying about reentering the world of the breast pump, not to mention the damage that breastfeeding would do to breasts that were no longer in their thirties, so I excused myself and stepped away to text Suki.

> Took your advice. Went to Apple Fair. Pie is good but local moms are awful.

Give it time, she replied moments later. Proud of you for getting out. xxxx

I noticed a stand promising something called apple pigs next to a stall selling wool crafts. I walked over and bought Alice a teal cross-body bag with three small daisies on the front—she'd just made plans to go to Abigail's house after school, and I, in my unending ability to buy the *one* thing she would never wear, thought she'd like it. When Harry saw the bag later that night, after Alice looked up from her phone and rejected it as ugly, he smiled with approval. I was perched on the window seat, secretly working on another blog post. Harry sat next to me rubbing my feet.

Sam walked in as I was jotting down notes about the Apple Fair.

"I'm not going, so you can ignore the email."

I looked up from my laptop. "Huh?"

"You're gonna get an email about a college-application workshop. It's gonna be full of stressed-out kids and their parents." He looked at me, making actual eye contact. "Mom, I really don't want to go."

"You don't want to go to college?" Harry asked, dropping my foot.

"I do, but I'm not exactly the target audience for an application pep rally," he said, still looking right at me. I nodded at him. *I've got you, Sam.*

"Then who is the target?" Harry asked.

"The smart kids."

"Sam, you are smart," I jumped in.

"It's for kids who think it's a good thing to be working on college applications a year before they apply," Sam said. "The same kids who are doing fake community service and paying a ton of money for private college counselors."

"Do you really want to give these kids a leg up on college just because they make you feel bad about yourself?" Harry asked.

"They aren't the only ones who make me feel bad about myself," Sam mumbled, turning to walk away.

"If you think the kids are bad," I said, "you should meet their mothers."

~

The 9/11 Refugees of the Hudson Valley

Don't get me wrong. I love day-trippers. I was one once. (The Duke and I would drive up on Sundays in July and August and return to the city with apples, corn, and a cider that smelled like feet but tasted like summer. Come to think of it, maybe that foot cider was a forerunner of kombucha . . .) Besides, who doesn't like a city dweller speeding down your roads, sticking his head out of the car window and yelling "FOLIAGE" at full volume? Seriously, day-trippers are always welcome; it's the people who come and stay who give locals the most grief.

Some of you may not know this, but kombucha-loving millennials are not the first to invade this once-peaceful valley. Before I moved up here, back when I was still dragging a stroller up several flights of stairs, there was an even more influential wave of urban immigrants. After 9/11, scores of city folk headed upstate and bought the first farmhouses they saw. Sure, they restored crumbling barns and breathed life into the Hudson Valley economy, but trust the Dutchess, these "cidiots" were no picnic.

According to longtimers, locals used to let their kids roam up here. They gave them space to breathe, to wander, to make mistakes. Many of the newly arriving city moms and even the Westchester moms (a very special breed who either wanted to go even farther north than they already were or who just didn't like to miss a trend) were different. They liked to hover over their kids, which meant hovering over their towns and schools. Suddenly, where there had once been the pleasant nonchalance of parenting, there were now permission slips, letters to school boards, and email chains. (And woe betide moms like me who accidentally used the back of a permission slip for a shopping list and may or may not have gotten panicked calls from school on the morning of the school field trip. Also, please don't ask me to be snack mom, because I am the mom with half a granola bar and six stale almonds at the bottom of her purse, and that's about it.) Farewell, free-roaming, mistake-making Hudson Valley childhood. Hello, hovering, high-strung parents and long, dramatic emails to the school board association.

But here's the rub: these moms don't just protect their kids. They push their kids, and they push themselves to advocate for their kids, and they do it all with one goal in mind: college.

Pour-over coffee and CBD-infused soda may be annoying, but they won't make you feel bad about yourself, and if you thought the growing number of tattoo parlors and farm-to-table restaurants was annoying, they have NOTHING on math learning centers, supplemental language tutors, and Suzuki violin studios. That's right, the striving mothers of the city have moved to points north and are not content with shaming other city parents. They are now spreading their after-school enrichment and community service requirements around the Hudson Valley, and if you're not participating, shame on you. (And by that, I mean shame on me, because the only thing enriched in my house is the flour I use to bake the cookies my kids eat while streaming endless hours of crappy TV.)

Guess what? The Dutchess sees you all, and she has heard all about life in the Valley when you could ride a scooter down the block without body armor and when high school parents didn't need support groups just to make it through the year.

City folk—come check out the foliage, please. Just make sure you don't buy a farmhouse while you're up here.

I'm kidding! Mostly.

Xxxx

The County Dutchess

~

As good as it felt to spit all of this out, I was nervous for the kids. I knew that nobody up here read the *Uptowner*, and according to my mother (who'd emailed me a list of Hudson Valley law firms looking to hire), barely anyone in the city read it, either. Still, I was writing about local moms who could make life difficult for Sam and Alice when life may have just started to get slightly easier.

I'd gotten a call from Suzy Shrub, the performing-arts faculty adviser at Pigkill Middle School.

"Alice is actually quite good," she said. I was squeezing myself into a pair of leggings when she called, and arguably not at my most charitable.

"Oh, great."

"Which is why I was surprised she wasn't enrolled in any of the after-school performing arts programs. Alice came to a play meeting, but there's so much more she could be doing."

I didn't need to ask what the other things were. I knew all about the after-school opportunities for theater kids. Alice hadn't done much more than the occasional play in the city, which may sound like a lot, but it isn't when you consider all the after-school options to improve her voice, dancing, stage presence, and so on. Those classes were chock-full of annoying stage moms ("Sing out, Mia!"), and honestly, we just didn't think Alice had the right stuff, or maybe she just didn't have the right *city* stuff. Was the bar lower here, or was Alice really better than we thought?

"I'll talk to her when she gets home," I huffed, chastising myself for my bad-mom thought while yanking at the leggings parked around my thighs.

I wasn't opposed to more after-school activities, but as it was, Alice was spending more time out of the house than she ever had in the city. I hadn't met Abigail or Courtney yet because Alice was spending time at their homes and raced out to the car when I came to pick her up. Our city apartment may have been smaller and more cluttered than many of the kids' friends' apartments (or summer homes), but it was often the hangout of choice. Sam's friends used to say that our kitchen was "cozy," which I often suspected was code for "messy." He explained that some of his friends lived in apartments with all-white kitchens, where everything had a place and a guy couldn't pour a bag of chips directly into his mouth without worrying about crumbs on the floor. Best of all, in my kitchen, with its mismatched jars and crowded counters, there was often a cake on the table and few rules about when it could be eaten, with no mention of calorie counting or ruined meals.

But even Sam was hanging out elsewhere. His two new friends were Luke, a drummer in the school band, and Saskia, a hot girl who sang with lots of boys. I know this because the three of them played a small gig at a nearby café with a few other band members. Saskia wore a tank top and no bra, and I don't remember much else. Although Sam assured me that Luke and Saskia weren't a couple, it was clear to me that both boys were desperate for her attention.

"Maybe you want to ask your new friends to hang out here," I said one night while rolling out dough and deliberately not making eye contact.

"Not happening," he replied. He looked down at his plate and shoveled lasagna into his mouth.

"Your friends in the city used to love hanging out in the apartment."

"Sorry, Mom, but I'm not bringing anyone *here*," he said, motioning to my stomach with his fork.

"I'm not asking you to invite them into the delivery room," I quipped. "Just for dinner." Because I often forget that teenagers don't understand sarcasm, at least not when it's directed at them, I was momentarily surprised when Sam abruptly dropped his plate in the sink and left the garage kitchen. I was even more shocked when he dashed back in thirty seconds later, kissed me on the cheek, then ran back out.

As for Harry's new friends, he was about to drop a bomb on me. I had just baked an apple cake and was letting him lick some batter.

"Remember how I said you didn't need to go to any faculty parties?" he asked, licking corners of the mixer paddle as I washed the batter bowl in the sink.

"Uh-huh . . ."

"I may have agreed to host the English department holiday party."

"What?" I put the bowl down but kept the water running, hoping I'd misheard him.

"I told the dean we'd host the department holiday party."

"Harry," I panted, "is this your way of getting me to socialize without making me leave the house?" I felt myself starting to sweat and leaned down and splashed some water on my face. Harry reached out and put his hand on my arm.

"No," he said, taking a step toward me and putting his other hand on my back. "It's a way for me to secure tenure."

I knew one thing for sure: hosting the party was not a way for him to secure tenure, because there *was* no way to really secure tenure. Tenure is slippery and elusive, and it's not yours until it's truly yours. But I also suspected that *not* hosting the holiday party was one way to guarantee that if Harry didn't get tenure, I'd bear the brunt of the blame.

"Fine," I said, shutting off the water and turning to face Harry. "Then we'll have a party."

I called Quick Richard.

"You need to come back," I said. "I'm hosting a party, and I need working toilets."

"How many working toilets?"

"All of them."

"You know—" he began, and I knew exactly where this was going.

"Please, not an Emerson quote."

"Actually, it's Thoreau. He didn't have working toilets, either."

"I believe that was by choice, and I'll pass. We can talk about sucking the marrow out of life when you get things flushing properly here."

"Loud and clear, Mrs. Walker."

I didn't just need toilets. For a party, I'd also need a dining room, which meant that I had to put in a call to Vivian.

"Hello, Bells," she said. "How are things?"

"Things are going so well that we are hosting the English department holiday party, and I think I need help unpacking, so could you please send Ernst to help me, thank you so much." I spat out all the information at once, before I had a chance to lose my nerve.

"A faculty party?" I could hear her wheels turning. "It would be my pleasure to send Ernst. Can I also send you some dining room furniture?"

"I don't think that's necessary," I said. "I'm sure I can buy something between now and December."

"I just happen to have a full set in storage." Of course she did. I'd kept college textbooks and photo albums in the storage locker of our apartment building. Vivian kept an entire set of dining room furniture. I thought about everything I had to do between now and the party and all the work the house needed. I could probably buy a dining room set from the comfort of the tufted couch, but there was also a good chance I'd have to go foraging for a furniture store.

"Furniture would be great, Vivian. Thank you."

"Again, my pleasure. Now," she said, pausing for full effect, "let's talk menu."

I told Vivian that although the party was two months out, her beloved son was already menu planning, and then I ended the call.

"How about mini chicken potpies with shallots?" Harry asked, holding up a brown paper bag of shallots he'd bought at a morning farm stand.

"Sounds good to me," I said, opening the fridge and wondering how much the shallots cost. "Overnight oats!" I exclaimed, showing him the blue mason jar he'd bought, now filled with mush.

"Oh, that's so sweet, but I have breakfast with the dean. Didn't I tell you?"

"Maybe, I don't remember. No worries. I'm sure this just gets better with time," I said, thinking that I'd rather eat the jar than whatever was congealing inside it.

"I'm sorry, Bells."

"Really, it's fine." The only thing moving quickly up here was Harry's social life. Maybe a baby would slow things down a bit, bring Harry back home for breakfast.

"And you can whip up something with celeriac," he said, snapping me out of my daze. "It should be in season by then."

"Huh? What is celeriac, and where was I when you turned into a gentleman farmer?"

"I'm not growing the stuff; I'm just buying it. I signed us up for a farm share! This town is a trove of produce," he said, sticking his nose in the bag and sniffing the shallots. "Oh, I forgot, I found this." He pulled a dark amber bottle out of his messenger bag and put it down on the table. "Cold brew!"

I opened my mouth to say something about the home-brew mason jar contraption he'd also just bought, but he planted a kiss on my cheek and was out the door before I could form the sentence. "Gotta run!"

Celeriac or not, if we really were hosting a holiday party, I had work to do. I had eight weeks to get Quick Richard to finish the plumbing projects and fix the banister that had recently come loose from the wall . . . and for me to find something to wear.

But first, I had a doctor's appointment.

-10-

Margaret Ross may have been a good doctor in a good hospital, but as Hanna Cohn liked to say, she had the charisma of chopped meat. She also seemed to think she was more of a large-animal veterinarian than an obstetrician for humans. On that first visit, she introduced herself and asked, "So, Mrs. Walker, is this your first AMA gestation?"

I don't think Dr. Ross knew that giving *advanced maternal age* an acronym didn't make it any more appealing, nor did she know that nobody should use the word *gestation* when talking to a pregnant woman. It got even better when she asked, "So, I see you don't wish to do any fetal sexing?" When I looked confused, she explained, "Do you wish to know the gender of the baby?"

I said no and promised myself that if she used the word *husbandry*, or even worse, *foaling*, I was out of there.

"Excellent. Why don't you hop on the scale for me?"

I wasn't hopping anywhere, and I'd begun to wish that Harry had taken a job in Scandinavia, where I'd read that doctors no longer weigh pregnant women.

She moved the weight up and down the scale, then up some more. Sweating, I forced myself to look away.

"I don't want to know," I said. "Just write it down, but don't tell me."

I heard Dr. Ross tutting, and out of the corner of my eye, I saw her shake her short gray hairdo, her craft-fair earrings swinging. But I would not be shamed into knowing how much weight I had gained eating my way through my first months in Pigkill. I thought that was the end of it, but as I got off the scale, she put her hand on my arm and said, "You know, Mrs. Walker," forcing me to look over my shoulder to see if Vivian was in the room, "with your substantial weight gain, we need to keep an eye on things." I wondered if Dr. Ross knew enough about human beings to know that her comments only made me want to go home, climb into a pound cake, and eat my way out.

When I left the office thirty minutes later, I walked a few blocks to downtown. As much as I wanted to go to The Dutchess Reads, I couldn't risk running into the PTA Coven. I walked up to what looked like a dark, quiet coffee shop only to discover that it was closed on Tuesdays, as was a bakery two doors down. Seeing me walk back and forth somewhat befuddled, a gray-haired woman in a bright-orange fanny pack stopped me.

"Dark Tuesdays," she explained.

"Excuse me?"

"From Memorial Day through the end of the foliage season, local stores are closed on Tuesdays to give their owners a break after the heavy weekend tourist traffic."

I wasn't about to get in between anyone and well-deserved rest, but my stomach didn't know about Dark Tuesdays and was barking for food. I thanked her and kept walking until I landed upon the diner. Now that it was October, there were pumpkins on the counter. There were pumpkins pretty much everywhere in town. I hated pumpkins. I didn't mind eating them, but everything else about them made little sense to me—the messy carving, the creepy faces. Still, I was surprised Harry hadn't come home with some locally sourced free-range pumpkins to adorn our front porch.

The pregnant waitress was clearing a table by the door. I was surprisingly happy to see her.

"Hey there, what can I get for you today?"

"Well, my doctor told me I needed to eat more leafy greens. Any chance you have kale cake?"

"Do you see Dr. Ross, too?" She laughed, showing me to a table and handing me a menu.

"Oh yes," I said. "I just came from there."

"She's the only gig in town. Oh, and she owns a horse farm." The waitress giggled. "If you couldn't tell."

"I knew it!" I said, opening the menu.

"Another chocolate egg cream?"

"Why not?"

"How about a butter scone to go with it?" she asked, raising an eyebrow. "No kale."

I love you. "Yes. Please." I closed the menu, handed it to her, and checked a text I'd just gotten from Alice.

Ugh. Abigail and Courtney are the worst.

I'd been playing the middle-grade-girl game long enough to know better than to ask Alice what was wrong, because in about thirty minutes I'd be getting another text along the lines of OMG! Abigail and Courtney are the BEST! Instead, I pretended I hadn't seen it and put my phone facedown on the table.

"How far along are you?" the waitress asked when she brought my cream and scone.

"Thirty weeks. You?"

"I'm right behind you—I'm twenty-six weeks along." I tried not to think about how much more pregnant I looked than she did. I hadn't looked like her since I was eight weeks pregnant with my first child.

"I'll bet *your* mother doesn't disapprove of you getting pregnant," she said.

"Don't be so sure." I laughed. "My mother disapproves of pretty much everything I do, and as far as she is concerned, getting pregnant at my age was the Nobel Prize of bad moves." I left out the two degrees I wasn't using and a lifetime of expectations. "This egg cream is seriously delicious," I said.

"How old are you?" she asked, smiling with pride and taking a seat across from me in the booth.

"Forty-three. You?"

She swallowed. "Twenty-three."

I could have been this girl's mother.

"Joey," she said, extending her hand.

"Bells," I replied. "Nice to properly meet you."

Out of the corner of my eye, I saw some moms I recognized from the PTA meeting, including the mother of the lacrosse wunderkinds. I immediately felt myself tense up. Couldn't they just leave me alone in here with my waitress friend, who didn't know any better than to judge me?

"Tell me, Joey," I said, leaning in, "is it me, or are the women in this town a little uptight for being so far upstate?"

"You mean the kind of women who order the vegan kimchi burger, hold the kimchi, hold the bun, then send it back three times because it's missing something they hadn't asked for?"

"Exactly," I said. "I was just expecting people up here to be less tightly wound. I thought it would be calmer than the city."

Joey shrugged and smiled, and I finished my egg cream and scone in silence as she bustled around the diner. I pulled out my phone, checked the blog, and discovered there were fifty more comments than when it had first gone live! Hardly viral, but more than double my last post.

Dutchess, you speak for moms everywhere! Love this!

Ha! Guess those moms are up in Dutchess County, too!

Oh no! Hate to read that the Hudson Valley is turning into the UWS.

You are one funny lady. Want to know more about you!

I sent a text to Andy, hoping he was ready to upgrade me from probationary.

Seen the blog? Getting lots of comments!

Looking good, Bells. You sure you want to remain anonymous? Looks like people want to know more about the Dutchess.

I'm good for now. Already working on my next piece! Still on probation?

For now, yes.

I had no idea what I'd be writing about next, I just needed a commitment from Andy so that I could come clean to Harry. I opened the Notes app on my phone and began jotting down some ideas. I was commenting on the **Yes, We Still Have Splenda** sign above the bar in the diner, noting the explosion of cannabis drinks and the simultaneous banishment of sugar replacements, when I got a text from Harry. He'd sent a selfie at yet another farm stand in another nearby town I'd never heard of. Did he ever have to teach? In the picture, he was holding a bundle of grubby greens. Underneath, he'd texted the word SCAPES, all in caps. What were scapes, and why did I get the feeling I was about to be googling how to prepare them?

I rushed home and walked up to the office. Harry had set up a desk and chair for me, and we'd cleaned out some of the boxes. I opened a window and faced out onto the garden with a partial view of the empty vegetable boxes. I opened my laptop and began to type.

~

Meet the Duke

The Duke is also a transplant, a city boy yanked out of his roots and replanted in the verdant Hudson Valley. At first, the Duke was antsy and out of place, willing to trade every blade of grass for a subway stop, but then the Duke discovered farm stands. In the Dutchess County of yore, farm stands were for corn, apples, and the occasional stalk of rhubarb. But the newest wave of city fleers brought obscure vegetation to the Valley, and suddenly, the Duke, a man who could once hold forth for over an hour about alternate-side parking and the correct way to order a cup of coffee, started coming home with things like ramps, which for all I knew could have been wild birds. Sometimes, he'll even send me a picture of himself clutching a newly discovered green. Last week, he sent a picture of himself holding something called celeriac. I'll let you know when I figure out what that is. Also, dandelions are now edible, so go work that one out . . .

~

I was interrupted by the doorbell before I could sign off. I didn't get many people coming to the house. In the city there had been knocks from neighbors complaining about noise (especially when the kids were small, or when Sam and his bandmates secretly practiced in his bedroom); visits from Marco, our super; and occasional requests for a few eggs or a cup of sugar from Mrs. Miller, our elderly neighbor. By virtue of our apartment living, we saw people in the hallway, the elevator, and the lobby. This house, however, was immune from visitors. I had not met a single neighbor yet, and with the exception of Quick Richard, nobody outside of the family had come by.

I opened the door to find Vivian and Ernst. He thrust a plant at me and smiled.

"It's from me," she announced.

"What's from you? Ernst or the plant?"

"Both," she joked. "He's come to deliver your furniture and help you unpack."

"I didn't realize you'd be coming, too," I said, instantly wishing I had said anything else but that.

"Don't worry. I'm not staying," she said. "I have a preservationist meeting in Cold Spring. You know, must fill my time." She forced a smile.

"You can come in, Vivian."

"I would, but I have to soldier on. All the widow books tell me I have to find my passion!" she said, throwing up her hands with false enthusiasm.

"I'm not sure people are doing that anymore."

She looked confused.

"The whole passion thing," I explained.

"What are they doing instead?"

"I think I read something about finding meaning instead."

"That certainly is a lower bar."

"You know how much I love a lower bar," I joked, hoping she'd get it.

"Don't sell yourself so short, Bells," she replied, getting nothing of the sort. "I'll join you all for a late dinner."

I let Ernst in and made a mental note to mention this to my own mother. I liked to tell her things Vivian had done for me, things my mother would never do, not because I wanted her to feel bad—at least not entirely—but because I wanted her to know that I wasn't the only mother in the world who was solicitous of her children.

It never worked.

"The German?" my mother asked later that night when I called her, shortly after Vivian had left.

"Yes. He unpacked about half of our boxes and assembled all our bookshelves."

"Are you telling me this to make me feel guilty for not bringing Germans into your home to fix things? Because Elsbeth, I'm incredibly busy right now."

Maybe by the time I am fifty, I will learn how to talk to my mother and how not to walk into traps of my own making.

As for traps, I was about to walk into the biggest trap yet: the junior-class mixer.

~

On the night of the mixer, I fed the kids and climbed into the bath. As the baby grew, my back tightened, and by the end of each day, I had to soak in a warm bath just to be able to climb into bed. There was no way I was going to be able to mix with anyone if I couldn't move. Lying in the tub, I was glad for the layer of bubbles covering most of my body. Things were happening that I worried might never be undone. I was covered in lines, splotches, and pigment run amok. I watched as my stomach rose above the bubbles, a mountain peeking through a layer of clouds.

My short-lived reverie was interrupted by a hysterical knock on the door, the kind of knock that can only be made by an irate twelve-year-old girl.

"Mom! Mom!'" Alice screamed. "It's really important."

I heaved myself out of the tub, swathed myself in a robe, and grabbed a white plastic bucket from the bathroom closet.

"I'm ready!" I said, swinging the bucket and trying not to slip on the puddle I was making. "I'm ready! I have the bucket!"

"You don't need the stupid bucket. I didn't get it."

Every time Alice let out a bloodcurdling yell, I was convinced that she'd gotten her period. Several of her friends had it already, and I was not going to be unprepared, not for this. When I read online about keeping a period bucket stuffed with supplies ready for the big day, I put one together and kept it on hand.

"What is it, then?" I asked, putting the bucket down and climbing onto my bed. I thought maybe it had something to do with play tryouts, but that wasn't happening for a few weeks.

Did something happen today in dance? Was today a dance day, or was it a voice day? Also, what day was it? I leaned back against the pillows as Alice had an epic meltdown about some Abigail-Courtney drama. The bath might have been too hot because I was having a hard time following. The drama had something to do with a math test she did badly on because the teacher forgot to give her extra time (and she was too embarrassed to ask for it), and could I believe it, "but Abigail and Courtney formed a math texting group without me."

"How do you know it was intentional?" I asked, rubbing cocoa butter anywhere I could reach. "Maybe they left you off by mistake."

"That never happens, Mom."

"Why don't you just call them? This whole group texting can be so complicated. You know how mean girls can be online."

"You don't get it!" she screamed, pacing like her father. "They left me off because they think I'm stupid and because I dress weird. These girls hate me. Everyone up here hates me. We never should have come to this crappy town!"

I started to say something but quickly realized that she needed to yell more than she needed my half-baked advice. So, I quieted my mother's voice, telling me not to be the kind of mother who lets her children yell at her and even occasionally swear, and just nodded sympathetically.

"You ruined my life!"

More nodding.

"I want to go back to the city. These girls just don't get me," she sobbed, letting me rub her back. I momentarily thought about offering her a Sophie-Tanya refresher but thought the better of it.

Alice cried for five minutes straight and then stopped to breathe. When it looked like she was done, I threw my legs off the side of the bed.

"Stay put," I said, changing the topic. "I want to try on the dress I bought for tonight." I made a mental note to call her math teacher and remind him about Alice's extra time, and I walked into the closet. I pulled a recent online purchase off a hanger and emerged moments later. I even did a clumsy twirl.

Unamused, Alice rolled her eyes. "You can't wear that. You look too pregnant."

"Alice, I *am* too pregnant."

"Fine, but that print is ugly, and why are you so bad at this?"

I ignored the insult, which I knew had nothing to do with my dress-buying prowess. "OK, why don't you help me pick something out?"

I had on a second dress when Sam walked in.

"Why are you dressed up?" Let the record reflect that I was hardly dressed up—I was just in a dress.

"Dad and I are going to a mixer for parents of juniors."

"For real? Will kids from my grade be there?"

"No, just parents," I said, reaching for my shoes.

"Nice dress, but you look sort of huge."

"Really huge?"

He shrugged and nodded slightly.

Before I could say anything, he was up the stairs to his room. I comforted myself with the thought that there was a chance he could be studying up there.

"Ignore him," Alice said, pirouetting around the pile of dress rejects on my floor. "He just wants you to look completely unpregnant. Besides, you don't look great, but you look good." And just like that, we were friends again. Alice then left, after making me promise I'd never buy anything patterned as long as I was pregnant. I agreed, checked my roots one last time in the bathroom mirror, and sat down on the edge of the bath to catch my breath while the baby kicked and clawed at my insides.

In a few months, this baby would be on the outside. I looked down at the tub and imagined myself kneeling to bathe a smiling, chubby baby, and for the first time since I'd found out this baby was coming, since I went from being a mother of adolescents to an expecting mother, I could see what life with a baby might be like. Instead of the day-by-day separation of teenagers, I would be attaching again. Instead of mood swings and shifts of anger, I would have the adoring eyes of an infant. Instead of being on the receiving end of the slings and arrows of puberty, I would have a child in the house who consistently liked me.

~

While I waited in the car for Harry to finish his own lengthy prep, I pulled down the dashboard mirror and gasped when I saw my chin. Where this morning there had been nothing (I know, because I'd checked), there was a foot-long hair hanging. I opened the car door, fell out, dragged myself up the stairs, and grabbed a pair of tweezers. Running back down the stairs, I made the mistake of leaning too hard on the banister, which fully broke off from the wall and came crashing down onto the stairs. I was cursing Quick Richard and debated having Ernst come and fix everything in the house as I climbed back in the car, where Harry sat wearing his waiting face.

"What are you doing?" he asked as I used the mirror to pluck the errant hair from my chin. I swear that thing had grown in the five minutes since I'd first spotted it.

"Avoiding further embarrassment," I said, yanking the seat belt across my expanding girth. "Let's get this over with."

-11-

In a move surprising to nobody, Cynthia hosted the mixer. I had yet to be inside any Pigkill home other than my own, and I was curious even though I suspected domestic perfection. I wasn't wrong; each room was perfectly decorated, almost too much so. This was a real home with real furniture, gleaming woodwork, oversize light fixtures, lush rugs, and matching drapes. It was also a home stuffed with random candlesticks, throw cushions, and side tables. Despite feeling like I was walking through a HomeGoods, I felt all the pangs of envy. None of the floorboards creaked under my feet, and I did not detect the stench of bad plumbing. I knew better than to test all the toilets or look for the kitchen, which at the very least was probably attached to the rest of the house. At least Cynthia's husband wasn't a professor. It would be worse if this were faculty housing.

Cynthia glided to the front door to greet us wearing a red knit A-line dress with bell sleeves. As someone who has never been able to wear red without looking blotchy, I had to give it to her—the color worked well. She looked more alive, more alert. Her layered hair was also blonder than the last time I'd seen her. "My, my, Bells, you look ready to pop," she said, her very blue eyes fixed on Harry.

I handed her my coat and headed in, letting Harry pick up the small-talk pieces. I was eating passed hors d'oeuvres when he came up behind me with name tags.

"You didn't tell me that Bill Plank was hosting this event," he said, walking over and attaching a **My Name Is** sticker to my dress.

"Who is Bill Plank?"

"Only the head of the math department. He's kind of a hotshot," Harry said, stretching his neck and straightening his tie.

This was faculty housing.

Before he could tell me more, Cynthia and the hotshot walked over. Bill Plank was almost as tall as his wife, almost completely bald, and thoroughly impressed with himself.

"Bill Plank," he boomed, extending his hand to me. "Harry, I heard you'd be here. Is your junior a boy or girl?"

"A boy," Cynthia answered. "He's already quite friendly with Luke Palma . . ." I didn't like the way she said Luke's name, but I liked the look of feigned concern on her husband's face even less. I took a stuffed mushroom from a sinewy waiter who flashed me a white, toothy grin.

"Oh, I see," Bill said. "Well—let's introduce you to some other parents. Maybe you can expand that friend circle a bit." He put his arm around Harry and led him on a tour of the room.

Now I was really ready to go home, but before I did, I grabbed a deviled egg from another equally toned waiter. Cynthia saw my eyes lingering on the waiter's back when she whispered in my ear, "Chore Donkey. It's where all the millennials look for work. You just have to sort for the ones who list yoga and spinning as their hobbies."

I raised my eyebrows. "You can do that?"

"You can do anything," Anna said as she, Peggy, and two other ladies joined the circle. "Nobody said there weren't advantages to the millennial invasion." Anna was still wearing the tiny nose ring. She was also wearing a dress that looked like the one I wore to my bat mitzvah, complete with puffed sleeves and an empire waist, but she wore it with heels and camouflage leggings. Apparently, anyone can be a hipster.

"It's true," Peggy added, cradling a drink. "My Pilates instructor just made me a frosé."

"Honey," Cynthia whispered, "we all know they are good for a lot more than making drinks." She winked at Anna, who blushed a deep frosé pink. Before Anna could say anything else, Bill returned with Harry.

"We're about to start the college-prep chat in the sitting room," Bill said. "We have a college counselor answering questions."

"College prep? I thought this was a mixer," I muttered to Harry, louder than I intended.

"Most of us have been mixing for years," Cynthia said, taking Bill's arm. "This is junior year. What else are we going to talk about?"

I followed the Planks to a room with sage-green textured wallpaper where I saw more end tables, all with gold bowls of untouched candy. A floral silk screen stood in the back of the room, thriving houseplants adorned the corners, and . . . was that an actual fig tree?

"How many APs is Sam taking?" Peggy asked as I was taking it all in.

"None." I didn't even bother looking at her.

"Ohhh," she said with a sudden look of deep concern. "Does he have . . . learning issues?"

I suppose so, if being an average student is a learning issue now. I turned to her and opened my mouth to answer, but Harry, who must have overheard where the conversation was going, grabbed my hand and pulled me down onto a love seat big enough for the two and a half of us. I could have kissed him then and there.

"Ethan and Janet," he said, motioning to an anxious-looking couple in the corner, standing a foot apart, silently staring around the room.

"Nah," I said, "he looks more like an Evan." This was the game we played where we tried to guess a couple's names. "Ethan is too strong." Harry nodded in approval. I was good at this game, with quite a few correct guesses under my belt—back when I could wear a belt.

"Ten minutes until the talk begins," Cynthia announced.

"If we are going to be comparing APs," I whispered to Harry, "then this is the perfect time for me to pee."

I launched myself out of the seat and wandered through the ground floor looking for the bathroom. I walked through rooms that flowed effortlessly into each other, each with its own distinct purpose, and stuck my head in the kitchen just for good measure. Not only was it attached to the rest of the house, but it was in the throes of food prep—complete with bustling waitstaff and kitchen crew. I took stock of the brilliant copper pans hanging over the enormous island, and out of the corner of my eye I saw Joey, the waitress from the diner, standing over the sink rinsing platters. I was surprised at how happy I was to see her—how desperate I was for a smile from a friendly face.

"Joey," I whispered loudly. "Joey!"

Joey looked up from the sink and looked around. When she saw me, she took a minute to place me and then waved a gloved hand at me. She removed her gloves and walked over.

"I didn't know you'd be here," she said.

"I think I'd rather be at Dr. Ross's," I laughed.

"You were so right! These parents are no joke." She lowered her voice when she realized she might have offended me. "I mean, this just seems like a lot of freaking out for college."

"Don't worry," I said, raising an eyebrow. "Not all of us are freaking out." *Although some of us occasionally freak out because we haven't freaked out enough.*

"Joey," someone called from the back of the kitchen, "are the platters clean?"

"Gotta run," she said. "I'll see you at the diner. Good luck!"

The Planks' powder room was a pink palace. The walls were blush, and the ceiling was covered in rose-gold wallpaper, giving the whole room a warm glow. While I was washing my hands with pomegranate soap, my phone buzzed. Alice. I dried my hands on a pink towel.

How bad is it?

Pretty awful. I'm hoping I can get Dad to leave soon.

Good because Sam just left and I don't like being in this big house alone. I miss the apartment.

(Talk about burying the lede.)

WHAT? Where is he?

He said to tell you he went to Luke's to study for a physics test.

I was willing to bet my unattached baker's kitchen that there was no chance Sam was studying for a physics test.

Out of the corner of my eye, I saw Meegan-rhymes-with-vegan making the rounds in a pink shift dress that could have come directly from Vivian Walker's closet. I eventually found Harry, who had abandoned our love seat and was talking to a gaggle of adoring mothers. All I heard were the words *artisanal* and *antiquing*.

"Can we go?" I whispered.

"Don't you want to stay for the Q and A?" asked a woman with a few hundred extra eyelashes and dark lip liner. "It's about to start."

No, thanks. I'd rather give birth in the kitchen.

"Just a few more minutes?" Harry asked.

Meegan and the man attached to her walked over to Bill Plank, and from the slaps on the back the two men gave each other, I assumed that like Cynthia, Meegan was also a faculty spouse. Watching her beam adoringly while her husband spoke, I couldn't help but think that it wasn't just the dress that Vivian would have endorsed. While I was looking for an exit, Meegan was also doing what faculty wives should be doing according to Vivian—shining a bright light on her husband.

I turned my back in defeat and went in search of a drink. Standing at the bar, waiting for my cranberry and seltzer, I heard voices behind me. These people wasted no time.

"He's so much more social than she is."

"Yeah, you can tell she really doesn't want to be here."

"If you were the mom of a kid like theirs, would you want to be here? I hear he's hanging out with Luke Palma."

"And what's wrong with Luke Palma?" I asked, whirling around, my cranberry and seltzer shaking with the rest of me.

A woman in a pair of fabric clogs (hard to miss those) shot a surprised look at her friend, then smirked at me. "Let's just say that if they gave out grades for mediocrity, Luke Palma would be valedictorian."

"Yeah," chimed in a woman with dyed-too-black hair, "he's the kind of kid who plays at the Hovel on a weeknight. Oh, and I see your son is on some kind of guitar."

She thrust her phone at me. Sure enough, there was Sam playing his bass, wearing a black leather jacket I'd never seen before, rocking out in a dark corner of what was presumably a dark bar. Luke drummed behind him as Saskia crooned in front, her eyes dark and narrow. She was wearing a black low-cut jumpsuit. Hovel, indeed.

"What is this?" I stuttered, backing away from the woman and her phone.

"It's Luke Palma's Snapchat story," she said unapologetically. Not one of the women seemed nonplussed that a fortysomething was following a sixteen-year-old, let alone on Snapchat.

"You don't even know Sam," I said, fully understanding that at that moment, I wasn't sure I did, either.

"That's right," Cynthia said, joining the conversation, nodding sympathetically. "None of us do. Because he's not in any of our kids' classes." She made a sympathetic face and then rested a hand on my arm.

"There are basically two tracks at the high school," explained the dyed-too-black hair. "The honors track and everyone else."

"I'm sure he's a great kid," said a woman whose face made me think of vanilla pudding.

"It must be a relief for you," the fabric clogs said. "You know, because you really don't have to think about competing on this level." She spread out her arms to include the other women, all of whom nodded as though they reluctantly accepted the burden of high-achieving children. "I almost wish Hayden were in all regular classes," she added. More nodding.

I was squeezing the cranberry juice so tightly I almost cracked the biodegradable plastic cup. These women could make fun of me all they wanted. They could call me old, fat, and ugly. They could wonder how I managed to land a guy like Harry in the first place. But Sam was mine. He may have been in all the wrong classes and mixing with all the wrong kids, but he was my baby, my boy, and he was untouchable.

I marched across the room and found Harry. "Now," I said. I watched as he momentarily considered the hit he'd take by leaving this party, calculating the opportunity cost of missing an event that could help him. But I didn't have to pull him away from his admirers. He knew by my tone that we had to go. He also knew it was Sam related.

"What's he done?" he asked as I cried in the car. It was freezing, a million times colder than fall in Manhattan. I pushed some buttons and prayed that for once Fulbright's heat would kick in quickly.

"Nothing," I said. "And that's the point." I didn't know what happened to kids like Sam in high school, but I was beginning to see how they got flushed out in the college process.

Harry opened his mouth to speak, but I interrupted. "He told Alice he went to Luke's to study for physics," I said, rubbing my hands together and blowing into them. "But he wasn't studying for physics because he was playing a gig with his friend Luke at a bar called the Hovel. And I know all this because one of these awful moms showed me a video of him on her phone." With that, I leaned back in my seat and closed my eyes.

"Do you want to come up with a plan of action?" Harry asked, using the windshield wipers to remove the tree's worth of leaves that had fallen on the car. "So we know what to say to him when he gets home?"

"Not yet," I said, eyes still closed. Harry obeyed, knowing me well enough to give me the car ride home in silence. Harry's problem often needed to be dissected and discussed in the moment, and then over and over again until there was nothing left to say. Because I was the one who'd found out Sam was lying and because the task of defending Sam's lack of drive often fell to me, this was my problem, and my problems needed to marinate. They needed to stew.

We pulled up to the house and sat in the driveway, just in time for the car to start heating up. I didn't want Alice to know I'd been crying, so I pulled down the mirror to check my makeup. As I wiped mascara off my face, I tilted my chin and saw it: another foot-long hair that had grown right next to the one I'd plucked only hours before. If nothing else, I'd given the vipers at the mixer something else to talk about. Old, fat, pregnant . . . and bearded.

Harry texted Sam and ordered him to come home, then went to make some tea. I told him I needed a few moments to gather my senses—as if they were sheep that had wandered off. I walked upstairs into the office, cranked up the two space heaters under the desk, and opened my laptop. Bells Walker may not have had the guts to confront the chatter at the party, but the Dutchess definitely did.

~

The Viper Moms of the Hudson Valley

Who hasn't had a run-in with a helicopter mom? She's the mom who shamed you for not breastfeeding and a few months later shamed you for failing to puree your own baby food. She's the same mom who packed her little darlings bento boxes for lunch (animal-shaped rice mounds, anyone?) while you were sending in a cut-up apple, six pretzels, and a cheese stick. She's also the mom who then shamed moms everywhere by posting her lunch creations online.

The Dutchess has met her fair share of moms and can report that while these moms are desperately whizzing over their offspring just about everywhere, up here in the Valley the moms are more of the *viperous helicopter* variety. It's not enough for them to push their own kids—they need to take your kids down to do it. These moms fled the dangers and maybe the rigors of the big city, but they brought all of that big-city nastiness with them and then watched it grow in the fertile Hudson Valley soil. You can buy as many farmhouses as you like and stuff them with half of HomeGoods (the Dutchess moms are especially partial to the end table), but trust me: *mean* travels.

Maybe the moms of the Valley just aren't busy enough. Maybe there aren't enough fairs and fests in their schedules. (I don't know how that is. Just last week I had to decide between the Sheep and Wool Fair and something called Felt Fest.) Maybe they're so tired of competing with the swarms of hip, toned, and impossibly aloof millennials. Maybe it's all the kombucha. (Just last week the Dutchess accidentally drank two cups in a row, got a little bit drunk, and couldn't pick the kids up from school.) Whatever the reason, Dutchess moms have enough time to form college-application support groups—for *themselves*—and have hours a day to one-up each other with how many AP classes their kids are taking, all in the form of the age-old humblebrag—POOR CINDY IS SO STRESSED OUT BECAUSE SHE IS TAKING TWO HUNDRED AP CLASSES! And out of the corner of their pinched little mouths, they need to tell you that you must be so relieved that your own underperforming child is still counting on her fingers, and mustn't it be lovely to get to parent an unassuming underachiever?

You'd think a mom who uses goat-milk soap, knows the difference between an apple betty and an apple crisp, and felts her own purses might not have this much mean in her. You'd be wrong, dear readers. Very wrong.

-12-

An hour later, Harry and I were sitting in the garage kitchen across the table from Sam. In a move of contrition, he pulled his hoodie down off his head.

"Why would you tell Alice you were out studying for a physics test?" I began. "Even better, why wouldn't you check with me first before going out on a school night?"

"Oh, so now you're one of *those* moms?" he asked, looking right at me, which threw me off.

"You mean a mom who doesn't like being lied to?" I asked, leaning in my seat.

"I didn't lie to you."

"No, you didn't tell me you were going out, and you lied to your sister," I retorted. "Why do that?"

"I don't know." He shrugged, then looked away. "Sometimes it feels good to be doing something you don't know about. Besides, you probably wouldn't let me play a gig the night before a physics test."

"I actually had no idea you had a physics test tomorrow," I said. "I'm not that kind of mom." I sensed Harry shifting uncomfortably next to me.

Out of the corner of my eye, I saw a text pop up on my phone from Andy.

TERRIFIC. Posting immediately.

I quickly flipped my phone over, but I had nothing to worry about; Harry's mind was elsewhere, and Sam had no interest in the workings of my phone.

"In addition to lying to us," Harry said, "there's the matter of your friends." *Oh, Harry. Why do you sound like you're proctoring an exam?*

"What about them?" Sam charged.

"We think you could be choosing more wisely," Harry replied, shooting me a look.

"Choosing more wisely?" Sam asked, his eyes narrowing. "What does that even mean? Luke and Saskia are good friends, and I didn't know a person up here a few weeks ago . . ."

"They may be good friends," I said, "but they are also the kind of friends who would encourage you to sneak out and play in a bar. Is that what the Hovel is? A bar?" Why hadn't I bothered to google it, and why was I hungry again? I got up and grabbed two bananas from a wire basket on the kitchen counter. I peeled one open and took a bite.

"It's a restaurant. No bar is gonna let us play if we're under eighteen."

"Oh, and where'd you get that biker jacket?" I asked.

"It's Luke's," Sam said, looking down at the coat as though he'd just remembered he was wearing it.

I filled a glass with water and handed the second banana to Sam. He took the banana and kept talking.

"And for your information, I met Luke because he's basically in all my classes. If you want a kid with AP friends, maybe the next one will make you happy." He pointed to my stomach with the banana.

"You know very well that I don't think there's anything special about AP classes, or AP friends," I said. "I'm genuinely happy you are making friends; we both are." I looked at Harry, who had walked over to the fridge and come back with a blue glass bowl full of grapes. "We just want you to make good choices, and sneaking out to play in a restaurant with a name like the Hovel is not a good choice. That's all."

"That's actually not all," Harry said, mouth full of grapes. "There has to be some sort of consequence for lying to us."

"You know what," I said, getting up and deliberately not looking at Harry, "let Dad and me talk, and we'll get back to you about those consequences." I smiled, and to my surprise, Sam smiled back. He walked to the door, turning back before he left. "Thanks for not totally flipping out, and I'm sorry, Mom. I'm sorry I lied."

When he was out of earshot, Harry finally spoke. "And you wonder why he doesn't bother to try?"

"Why?" I asked, turning to look at him. "Because I don't think that right now is the time to talk about consequences?"

"No, because he knows that you'd do anything in the world to avoid turning into your mother, including undermining me and letting him do whatever he wants and then smiling when he does it."

I had always known that the Walkers worried when Harry brought home a girl from a broken home—a girl with an absent father and a mother whose answer to that absence was self-involvement on speed. I knew because they did nothing to hide it. Vivian drilled me for information on my upbringing—was I really home alone from three until seven? Did I really do all my homework in front of the television? Was I kidding when I said that my babysitters were Oprah and Carol Burnett? (No. My TV shift started with Oprah and ended with reruns of Carol.) I knew that Vivian was really asking, How could I possibly be a good wife and mother if I'd never seen one up close? Although I could handle the Walkers and their Chappaqua judgments, I couldn't handle Harry blaming me for Sam.

"What if we were harder on him?" Harry persisted, taking advantage of my speechlessness. "What if he's capable of more, and we'll never know because we aren't pushing him, because you don't believe in pushing?"

"You're right," I said. "I didn't want to turn into my mother, and now your son is mediocre." I got out of my chair and marched over to the sink. "Do you really think if we kept pushing he'd be on the chess team or the yearbook or in AP bio?"

"I never said that," he said.

"No, you said something worse," I said, walking to the door. "You said I'm a shitty mother because I had a shitty mother, and now all these really shitty women are talking about me."

"I just don't like the idea of him sneaking around and lying about it."

"So tell me what you want to do."

"I think we should ground him for two weeks."

"Fine," I said. "I'm sure that is going to fix whatever is going on with him."

"That's not why we're doing it," he said. "We're doing it to make a point."

"*We* aren't doing anything," I shot back, walking to the door. "But *I* am going to bed." I didn't wait for him to respond.

~

I may have stormed off, but Harry nodded off way before I did and then proceeded to sleep right through the night. Once he fell asleep, I plodded into the bathroom to check my phone, congratulating myself on waiting this long. Everyone else may have been asleep, but the house and I were wide awake. I perched on the toilet, listening to the creaking and groaning, and unlocked my phone.

I had a text from Suki, in caps. She had forwarded me the Dutchess's post.

> DO YOU KNOW THIS LADY? SHE'S A RIOT! SOUNDS LIKE SHE IS ALSO ON THE FAIR AND FEST CIRCUIT. SHE DEF NEEDS TO BE UR FRIEND.

Andy texted me a series of exclamation points and then the words PROBATION OVER. I rushed to the blog. There were hundreds of comments and likes, and scores of shares. People were sharing the post on their pages so other people could like it and share it, and on and on. I was sitting on a running toilet, listening to my old house moan itself to sleep, and the Dutchess had launched.

I took a deep breath and began to read the comments.

> You are hysterical. Want to know more . . .
>
> Come on Dutchess, who are you?
>
> Viper Moms—love it! But seriously—those moms are EVERYWHERE.
>
> College support groups for moms? For real?
>
> Dutchess—do you live in Rhinebeck? Red Hook?
>
> Didn't I meet you recently at the Waffles and Wings Fest in Beacon?
>
> What IS the difference between and Apple Betty and an Apple Crisp?
>
> What if the Dutchess is really a 300-pound Russian guy dishing on fake people?!
>
> Be careful Dutchess, vipers bite back.

I gasped when I read that last comment, so loudly that I was sure I'd wake Harry. Then I realized that nothing wakes Harry. I read through every last comment, combing for clues that someone in Pigkill had read the post—but found nothing more than that one comment.

I stood up and stared at myself in the bathroom mirror. It would soon be time to cover my roots. I had dark, deep circles under my eyes, two random zits on my jawline, and a splotch of angry pigment on my neck. I looked like a woman too old and too tired to be having an unplanned baby. I looked more like the mother of a teenage son who was keeping her up at night. No, I didn't look like royalty, but thanks to the hundreds of people who were reading my words, a small piece of me felt like royalty. I squared my shoulders, lifted my chin, and turned off the bathroom light. I walked into the bedroom and climbed in next to an ever-sleeping Harry.

The Dutchess needed to sleep.

~

I lay awake for most of the night. I had a vivid memory of my grandpa Sam, my mother's father, who died six months before Sam was born. He wore false teeth for as long as I could remember, and every night he'd take them out and put them in a glass of water next to his bed. On the nights my mother had to study late or work, I'd sleep at my grandparents' apartment, sometimes right in between the two. I could still see those teeth, sinking to the bottom of the glass (often a jam jar), the small bubbles rising to the surface. On nights like these, when problems that seemed manageable in daylight were suddenly mammoth, I wondered what it would be like to pop my brain out, like a set of Grandpa Sam's teeth, and plop it into a jar next to my bed.

At six I called Suki from the bathroom. I knew she'd be up doing Pilates in her living room before her girls were up.

"Are you OK? Is the baby OK?" she asked, huffing and puffing.

"I'm fine," I whispered. "The baby's fine."

"Thank god," she said. I heard the background noise shut off. "What's up, then?"

I opened my mouth to tell Suki about Sam but couldn't get the words out. They got stuck somewhere in my throat. As much as I wanted her to reassure me that Sam was exactly where he should be and that this would all work out, I was ashamed. Harry had shamed me. What if he was right and everyone saw it, too—even Suki? Was Sam where he was because I wasn't diligent, because I didn't hover? Was I failing him because Hanna had failed me? I had called my best friend at six in the morning, freaked her out, and had nothing to offer her.

Unless I did.

"I'm the Dutchess," I blurted.

"The what?"

"The Dutchess. The County Dutchess."

"Are you kidding?"

"No, it's me. I'm writing the blog posts."

"Hell's Bells!" she screamed, then suddenly lowered her voice to a whisper. "What were you thinking?"

"I was thinking that you told me I was funny and that I should write it all down."

"I was envisioning more of a fictionalized short story, or maybe even an article. I didn't mean start an anonymous blog to trash the women in your town!"

"Suki . . ."

"And more importantly, why didn't you tell me?"

"Because until now I was just writing on a trial basis, and I wanted to wait. Nobody knows other than Andy," I said, moving from the edge of the tub to the closed toilet.

"Not even Harry?"

"Not even Harry."

"Wow," she breathed.

"At first I didn't tell him because I didn't think it was going anywhere, and he thinks blogging is frivolous. He's also so invested in me succeeding up here that I didn't want to get his hopes up. But as of last night, I'm no longer on probation."

"And now you don't want to tell him because you don't want him to be mad that you're the anonymous town gossip."

"Exactly."

"Crap."

"Suki, I know I'm an idiot, but the Dutchess gives me some room to breathe up here."

"I thought the air is better upstate," she quipped. "Don't respond. I know what you mean."

"Maybe I couldn't breathe in the city, either, and I just didn't know it. But the Dutchess is mine," I whispered. "I'm writing, and people are reading."

"I get it," she whispered. "I just wish you'd have told me sooner."

"I miss you," I said, standing up and stretching.

"One more thing," she said. "Did you really get drunk on kombucha?"

"Sort of. I tried it for the first time, and after my second glass, I got a little too buzzed for the middle of the day. I googled it afterward and learned that it's not only hip, but it's also unpasteurized. So no more kombucha for me."

"That's probably a good thing," she said. "And don't go native on me and start brewing your own when the baby comes. My neighbor did that and gave her whole family food poisoning."

We said our goodbyes, and I lumbered downstairs, grabbed my coat and boots, and trudged in the dark into the garage kitchen in a light but freezing rain. By the time the kids and Harry were up and ready to eat, I'd already consumed two breakfasts and four cups of creamy decaf. Quick Richard miraculously appeared, shrugged apologetically, and made a beeline for the basement before I could shower him with praise just for showing up. I heard him banging around and hoped this meant that all the toilets would be up and running soon.

Nobody spoke much that morning. Sam came down late and ate without making eye contact or saying a word to any of us. Alice had that astute yet off-kilter middle school radar by which she could pick up any changes in the force yet be completely unaware of her own behavior, and she wisely ate in silence. As we were leaving for school, she ran back into the house because she forgot her phone, then back again thirty seconds later to grab her homework off the kitchen table.

I was driving home from school when Harry called me.

"Are we going to talk about this?" he asked.

"You know I need time to cool off," I said.

"I know," he said. "Can I make a request for sooner rather than later?"

"I'll see what I can do." I ended the call, and I realized I wasn't ready to go home yet. I went to the only place I could think of—the diner.

~

I didn't even know for sure that Joey would be working, but she was behind the counter, pouring coffee. I plopped down on a cracked red pleather barstool. Joey took one look at me and whipped up an egg cream, sliding it in front of me.

I took a silent gulp and looked up.

"That bad?" she asked.

"Sort of." I took another gulp. "Got a minute?"

She looked around. Nobody seemed to need her. "What's up?"

"What's the Hovel?"

"It's a restaurant in New Paltz. It's a thing now to open a shiny new place and give it a grungy name. Why?"

"Oh, my son lied to me and went and played a gig there last night."

"It's cool that he's good enough to play gigs," she said, reaching over to a cake dish stacked with scones, taking one for each of us.

"I guess so," I muttered.

"Whatever," she said, taking a bite out of a scone and swallowing. "According to some of the women around here, I'm not really a good role model." She pointed to her stomach with her scone-free hand.

"Why?"

"Because I dropped out of college and then went and got pregnant."

"What school were you at, and why did you drop out?"

"Albany," she said, stopping and taking a sip of water. "At first, I dropped out because my mom got sick, and I wanted to help my parents out until she got back on her feet. And then this happened." She placed both hands on her stomach. "So I stayed dropped out."

"I'm really sorry to hear about your mom," I said, not wanting to press her for any information she didn't want to give me. "And one day I'll tell you more about my own mother, who only came into her own when my dad left us."

"Really?"

"Yeah, she eventually went back to school, and now she sits atop her corporate perch and judges me and my life choices." I laughed and pointed to my own stomach. "You're not the only one with an unplanned pregnancy."

Joey smiled.

"And, Joey, there's going to be a lot more to your story than you think."

Joey smiled and someone waved her over to a table. She returned a few minutes later and handed a ticket to the kitchen staff. "How did you find out about the Hovel?" she asked, changing topics and refilling my water.

"I heard some moms talking about him at that stupid grade mixer, and then one of them shoved her phone in my face, and there he was on his friend's Snapchat feed."

"Ha!" She laughed. "Some mom follows a random high schooler's Snapchat stories?"

"Thank you!" I said as we high-fived.

"People here can be pretty judgy," she remarked. "Especially Cynthia Plank and her squad."

I nodded.

"Whatever," she said, grabbing a grilled cheese from the kitchen window. "I don't know how a woman like her can talk smack about anyone."

"What do you mean . . . a woman like her?"

"She's sleeping with her yoga instructor." Joey delivered the grilled cheese to a man at a booth and came back.

"Do you know her yoga instructor, too?" I asked, trying to mask my desperation.

Joey looked around and her voice dropped. "Yeah. Drew Crawford. He was a year ahead of me in high school."

A crew of people walked in and sat at a large booth. "I gotta go help them," she said. "I can tell by looking at them that they came for the tempeh buffalo wings."

"What are tempeh buffalo wings, why are you selling them, and how can you tell?" I asked.

"That's a lot of questions." She laughed. "All I know is that it's not a great time to be a greasy-spoon diner." She shrugged. "Anyway, they're not as bad as they sound." With that, she walked over to the table of hipster beards and man bags.

I finished my coffee and left money on the counter. Thanks to Joey's yoga remark, I knew where I had to go next. I had more to write about. That comment came back to me.

Be careful Dutchess, vipers bite back.

-13-

Fortunately, I was no stranger to yoga. At one point I'd even gone twice a week, which for me constituted a solid exercise regimen. Before the IUD decided to go on strike, I was going to yoga about three times a month, maybe four, which meant I knew enough to fake it.

Although there was only one obstetrician in town, there were two yoga studios and a third opening in a few months, possibly with alpacas—to compete with the goat yoga two towns over. It took me several minutes of online searching to find Drew Crawford and his studio.

Two hours after my chat with Joey, I walked into Breathe and approached a skinny girl in a high blonde ponytail behind the counter.

"Hi," I said to the high ponytail. "I'm here for the ten o'clock class."

"Oh!" she chirped, handing me a flyer. "Pregnancy yoga meets on Friday mornings."

"I've done yoga before," I said. "I think I'll check out the next class if that's OK."

"Sure," she said tentatively and handed me a set of forms to fill out. I took a pen and filled out the paperwork. (*Are you pregnant?* MOST DEFINITELY.)

"I need to borrow a mat. We just moved here, and I can't find mine," I overexplained. The ponytail was not buying any of it, but she directed me to the rental mats hanging on the wall. The truth was that

I did once own a yoga mat, but it was not in a single box Ernst or I had opened, leaving me to suspect it may have been culled along with a giant exercise ball and some stretchy bands.

Realizing I could not do yoga in a muumuu, I also needed to buy something to wear. I paid for the class and walked around the selection of clothes on sale. I had on a pair of maternity leggings, but I'd tried on every top in my closet and could not bring myself to show up at the studio in a stained, misshapen T-shirt. I grabbed an XL stretch tank top off a hanger, paid forty-nine dollars for it (one-third of a messenger bag, thank you very much, Harry), and wandered into a miniature dressing room. The ribbed tank stretched over half of my stomach and a third of my backside. I yanked it down one more time for good measure, threw my giant purse into a locker, and forced my hair into the submission of a giant bun.

Cynthia was the first person I saw when I walked back out into the reception area.

"Bells! Was there a pregnancy class this morning?"

"No, I have a regular yoga practice," I said, more firmly than I intended. Cynthia just smiled awkwardly and walked into class.

While I placed my mat down near the back of the small, sunny studio, Cynthia positioned herself front and center and began doing some pre-yoga. I sat cross-legged on my mat and stared down at my belly button, which had popped out like the timer on a turkey. When I looked up, she was upside-down on her head in the middle of her mat.

As soon as Drew entered the room, all chatter ceased. At least Cynthia had good taste. He was tall and tanned and totally gorgeous, with a mouth full of very white teeth. He was also a good twenty years younger than we were. While I was trying to figure out if he'd been one of the waiters I'd noticed at the grade mixer, Drew glided to the front of the class, inches from Cynthia and her leopard-print yoga mat. I scanned the room and saw Anna and a few other Coven members. I got forced smiles from all of them.

I was not the only pregnant woman in the class, but I was definitely the oldest. A pair of moderately pregnant early-thirtysomethings were in a row in front of me, both in leggings with large mesh panels, a trend I'd spied in the city. I looked down at my legs shoved into maternity spandex and winced at the thought of them peeking out through squares of mesh. At this point in my life, the goal of my clothes was conceal, conceal, conceal. The Pregnants turned and smiled at me with faint recognition, but we weren't really on the same team. They barely looked pregnant from behind; I probably looked pregnant from space. I remembered what it was like when I was expecting Sam, when I had the time and energy to do hours of yoga. At the end of class, I would sit on my mat, my hands on my belly, and talk to him. I don't think I'd said a word to this baby, and as for Sam, he was moving further away all the time. I put my hands on my belly and closed my eyes. *Hello, Baby.*

"Let's do this," Drew announced. He fiddled with his phone, and before I knew it, I heard the sounds of pulsing music from the speakers in the ceiling. Maybe yoga was different in the Hudson Valley, but I wasn't sure how hip-hop music was going to help me find inner peace. I looked around to see what people were doing and got on all fours just like the women in front of me.

Following Drew's commands, I arched and bent and even managed to lift one leg in the air. When I tried to raise the opposite arm at the same time, I wobbled and came crashing down on the mat. Drew glided over to me.

"OK, everyone, now alternate sides!"

"Hi, honey," he whispered. "Kerry said you'd done this before."

"I have," I said, getting back on my knees. "It's just been a few weeks." I watched as the women in front of me rolled onto their sides and did something with their legs that I knew I could no longer do.

"OK, then," he said, not sounding at all like he believed me. "Just remember power yoga can be a little intense, so take it slow and stay off your back."

"Got it." I smiled. *Power yoga? How did I miss that on the schedule?*

Drew instructed us to stand at the tops of our mats. I kept staring at the row of Pregnants who may have had the smallest backsides I'd ever seen on pregnant women. I watched as they placed their legs in a wide squat, although not as wide as Cynthia, who seemed to be made of Silly Putty. Drew amped up the music, and the next thing I knew, everyone in the room was squatting and pulsing. I tried to squat and pulse, but I did two squats and realized that unless I wanted to pee all over the mat, two was probably my limit.

The pulsing continued, but now everyone had their hands up in the air. This part I could handle. But when everyone stood up straight, got on one leg, and grabbed an alternate foot with their free hand, I took a pass. I faked my way through a series of warrior poses, none of which we had to hold for very long, and didn't even try to touch my toes in the forward bends, partly because I could no longer see them. After a series of hip openers, I realized I'd sweat through the new tank top and these maternity leggings, which I had purchased in the workout section of the online maternity store and which were seeing their first actual workout. As much as I wanted this class to end, I wondered if maybe a little more exercise wasn't just what I needed. When the time came to lie on our backs for the next portion of the class, I rolled onto my side and rested my sweaty head in my hands. The lights dimmed, and the music slowed.

I woke myself up with a snore. I looked around to see if anyone had noticed, and of course Cynthia, her Coven, and the three Pregnants were looking right at me. Drew appeared behind me.

"Honey, I think you took a little nap," he said, running a hand through his shiny hair. I waited for him to walk away so I could lift my head out of the pool of tacky drool that had amassed on the mat. I rolled over, got up on all fours, and brought myself to a sitting position.

I was getting tired, light-headed, and hungry. Certain that class must be almost over, I glanced at my watch without obviously glancing at my watch—an old yogi trick. We still had twenty-five minutes left. I put my hands on my belly and whispered, "You're right, we need a milkshake, and we need one now."

I looked around the room. Just like in the cartoons when the ravenous coyote looks around and everything starts to look like a chicken drumstick, everyone in that yoga studio—gorgeous Drew and the Pregnants included—looked like a malted milkshake to me, and I knew I could not be in that room for another minute. In between poses, I got up, rolled up my mat, and snuck out the back door.

If I wanted a real milkshake, I needed to walk three blocks to the diner, but I wasn't sure I would make it. I took my chances and tried the smoothie place next door, which had just opened in what used to be a general store and had kept the vintage signs and exposed brick of its earlier incarnation. I looked at the menu on the chalkboard. In a sea of carrot, beet, kale, and ginger, I chose the cocoa banana coconut cream smoothie and prayed for the best.

"Do you want a hemp boost?" asked the millennial behind the counter in a tight, faded "Got Milk?" T-shirt. He had long hair and a tiny goatee, and the Dutchess and I both wondered why Jesus was making smoothies in Pigkill.

"I don't know what that is, but I don't think so," I said, smiling to myself.

"Green superfood?"

"No, thanks."

"Maca root?"

"I just want a smoothie," I begged. "Please, just give me my smoothie." The poor boy looked scared and scrambled to make it for me. I was ready with an unpeeled bamboo straw when the smoothie appeared.

My smoothie tasted like a coconut had been rolled in dirt and sprinkled with cocoa powder, but I gulped it down. I thought about ordering a second, but I wanted to get back to the studio for the end of class, and there was only so much dirt I could swallow.

I must have lingered longer than I thought, because when I walked back to Breathe, class was long over and the studio looked empty. My car was on the street, but I stuck my head around the corner to check out the parking lot and saw Cynthia and Drew standing in front of an SUV adorned with honor-roll stickers. (I'd be damned if Fulbright ever looked like that, even if my children were honor-roll darlings. I did make a mental note to sign Sam up for an ACT class and tell him about it later.) They were only inches apart, her hand on his chest. I wrapped my coat around myself and held back, shielded from their sight by an abandoned storefront holding its breath until it became a coffee shop or ironic hat store. They talked for a few minutes, and then he ran his hand through her hair.

Then Cynthia pulled out her phone and, with Drew watching, typed something in. They both laughed. Drew was still laughing when Cynthia popped the trunk of her car and revealed eight Whole Foods grocery bags—by my calculations an easy $350. I had no idea what was going on, but I had even less of a grasp on what happened next. Drew popped the trunk of his car, a not-at-all surprising Prius. (Bumper sticker: **I Brake for Shiva**. My mother would have a field day with that.) He took the high-end groceries and put them in his trunk.

Cynthia leaned in, whispered something in his ear, and then climbed into her honor-roll SUV. I waited a few more minutes until Drew had also left and then got into Fulbright to drive home.

~

That night, I jotted down some notes on what I'd seen in the yoga parking lot, trying to make sense of it all. Andy had also sent me a string of texts asking where my latest blog entry was.

Anything new for me?

I wasn't sure I had anything to write about, other than the fact that the PTA president was probably sleeping with her yoga instructor. That was news to me, but I didn't think it was newsworthy, at least not yet. By the time Harry got home, I was eating brownies in bed and reading Meegan's latest blog post, where I learned how to make a cornucopia centerpiece out of cornflakes, leaves, and spray-painted Oreos. I scanned pictures of her still-tan, towheaded "babies" gluing, painting, and mostly smiling. They were all wearing shades of oatmeal. She posted a recipe at the end of the blog post. Apparently for every mom making quinoa bowls for dinner, there are twenty moms just looking to serve meat loaf made with onion-soup mix. Meegan was both of the moment and a throwback at the same time, and it worked.

I snapped my computer shut and put it on my nightstand next to a half-eaten brownie. Harry lay down next to me and put his head in my rapidly disappearing lap.

"I'm sorry," he murmured into my belly. It took me a moment to figure out he was talking about the fight we'd had the night before. In the past twelve hours, I'd attended my first power yoga class and spotted a hookup in the parking lot.

"Are you apologizing to me or the baby?" I asked, running my fingers through his glorious, glorious hair.

"Both. I was mean to you, and that's not good for either of you." He raised my shirt and placed his lips on my stomach. He looked up at me. "This has nothing to do with your mother."

"I forgive you," I said, not wanting to tell him that everything has something to do with my mother. "And maybe you're right. Maybe we should push Sam a little more. Maybe *I* should push him a little more."

"How about we start with just being slightly less forgiving of the lying and sneaking around?" he asked, looking up at me.

"Fine," I said. "But when he hates me, it'll be your fault."

"Nobody could possibly hate anyone who makes brownies like this," he said, his mouth full.

He leaned in, and I kissed the crumbs off his lips. Alice and her new platform sneakers bounded in from play tryouts.

"I got the part! I'm Edwina!"

"You mean you're the Edwina in *Dear Edwina*?" Harry asked.

"Yes! I am the *actual* star," she announced, taking a bow in the center of the room.

"That's amazing," Harry said, sitting up and giving me a maybe-this-kid-has-actual-talent look.

"Take that, Kayla Lewis," I laughed.

Alice narrowed her eyes at us, realizing she'd just seen us kissing in a bed. "Really? You guys are already making more babies?"

"Alice, you know that's not how it works," Harry said, pulling down my shirt. "You know that a woman can't get pregnant while she's pregnant, right? It's like God's birth control." He laughed at his own joke.

Alice just flashed us a perfected eye roll. "I just came to give you the good news," she said, "and to tell you that I kind of like it here." She blew us a kiss, then left us alone with the rest of the brownies and what I assumed were the muted pings of the Dutchess's incoming comments.

~

Harry was wrong about the power of my baked goods. I offered the brownies to Sam for breakfast, but they failed to work on him. He was about to take one when his phone buzzed.

"Luke and Saskia are outside," he said, wearing the leather jacket again. "They want to know if I want a ride to school with Luke's older brother."

"You know we can't let you do that," Harry said. "You're still grounded."

"This sucks. I can't wait for Albany, just to get away from here." The high school rock band was headed to Albany in December, which I knew because I'd already gotten about thirteen hundred emails about it.

"Why not have a brownie?" I slid the plate over to him.

"You think you can buy me with brownies?" he asked, pushing them away. "You guys grounded me right when I finally made some friends."

"Hopefully, this will be the first and the last time," Harry said, reaching out and helping himself.

Sam shot him a look that he did not see.

~

Suki gave me twenty-four hours' notice.

"I'm covering VegFest," she announced one night. She'd called while I was scrubbing a pie dish.

"A festival for vegetables? That doesn't sound very original."

"It's a festival for vegans," she said. "The pitch is fun, activism, and food."

"In that order? I think I'll pass." I rinsed the dish, flipped it upside down, and set it down next to the sink.

"It's also a zero-waste event. The entire thing is compostable."

"Are you trying to make sure I leave town so you can't drag me?"

"Not only am I dragging you, but I'm dragging you tomorrow," she said. "I'll pick you up at ten." Vivian wasn't the only one who didn't like to give me advance notice.

When Suki showed up at 10:45 (she may have used her techniques, but Suki did not have Vivian's punctuality), I was already dressed and ready to go. I gave Suki a quick tour of the house, and she made all the appropriate noises about the giant, albeit unattached, kitchen and almost wept with joy when she saw the vegetable beds.

"I'll come back in the spring and help you plant," she promised. "But first, vegan wares await us."

I gave her the least enthusiastic smile I could muster.

Suki and I had always had a food friendship. Even before I began testing her earliest recipes, she took me to little places around the city nobody else knew about, then taught me how to find my own haunts, including a place with carrot cake in the Bronx and our favorite Koreatown restaurant, which served steaming soup in hot stone bowls. Food was our love language, and when we sat down at VegFest and found a table filled with animal-free wares, I realized how lonely I'd been.

"I need to go easier on vegans," I said with a mouth full of coconut flan. "This stuff is awesome."

"Don't look now," Suki said, looking up from her cashew frappé (old habits die hard), "but there are three women walking over here—it looks like they know you."

I swallowed and looked just in time to see Cynthia, Peggy, and Anna headed our way. My god, these women also loved their groups of three. As always, Cynthia and Peggy were almost matching, and Anna looked far too glamorous for a vegan food fair. I prayed, for her own sake, that her cropped fur jacket was faux.

"Hey, Bells." Cynthia forced a toothy grin.

I forced one back, minus the teeth because I suspected mine were still gummy with coconut flan. "Hi, guys."

Cynthia shifted her gaze to Suki, who'd just had her highlights done and was looking pretty terrific. If I couldn't have my game on, at least she did. "Are you new to town, too?" she asked.

"No, she's just visiting," I answered. I hadn't seen Cynthia since I'd spotted her canoodling with Drew in the parking lot. I felt like I was seeing her naked and averted my eyes, wishing she'd cover herself up. I also knew I had to make some introductions. My eyes fixed on Suki, I said, "Suki, this is Cynthia, Anna, and Peggy." I paused but kept staring at Suki. "And this is my best friend, Suki. She's visiting from the city."

"Are you a vegan?" Anna asked.

"No, just a food person," Suki explained, thankfully leaving off that she was a writer. I didn't need these women making any Dutchess connections.

We all smiled at each other for a few more heavy moments, and then Anna raised her right arm and showed us a metal bucket. "I just came to pick up some composting worms," she explained. It took a lot of guts to wear fur, faux or otherwise, just to forage for composting worms.

"That doesn't seem very vegan," Suki joked. The women laughed. I shifted in my seat.

"OK, so we better move on," Cynthia finally said. "Nice to meet you, Suki."

"Likewise," Suki said, and then, as soon as they were out of earshot, she muttered, "Why were you so awkward? Are these the moms you wrote about?"

"Yeah, that and the fact that I just don't like them. Or at least they don't like me." I took a bite of cheeseless cheesecake.

"How do you even know that?" she asked, reaching over for her own taste. We nodded at each other. Very good, even if cheeseless. "Don't you remember how you thought Jen and Melissa hated you?" Jen and Melissa were my friends from law school, both of whom had long since left the city, and yes, I was convinced they hated me until we got assigned to the same first-year study group and quickly bonded over playlists and a shared office-supply obsession—a fondness it turned out many law students shared. (Jen was always one step ahead of us when it came to the newest Post-it Notes. Melissa liked a scented highlighter. Naturally, I was often in charge of snacks.)

"This is different," I said. "And these women are not Jen and Melissa."

"Bells, you thought I didn't like you, and I basically asked you out to lunch on the first day we met."

"I thought you felt sorry for me because I was sitting on the steps alone."

"It's not like you made any mom friends in the city," she said, finishing the cake. "Maybe this is just your default setting."

"Maybe, but it's probably too late with these women. I promise to be more open to the next new group of moms I meet."

Suki rolled her eyes and took a big slurp of her drink. "If you don't want to make friends, that's your choice. Just don't go making enemies up here."

I fought her for the last bite of flan. She won.

-14-

Quick Richard had disappeared, leaving us with a room full of his supplies. His giant toolbox was in the potbelly room with a Post-it Note attached: *Back soon. Making jerky. (Do you have any idea how much those city people will pay for rabbit jerky?)*

This would have been tolerable had my oven not crapped out.

I was happy to share one toilet with three other people (even if two of those people were teenagers, and even if only one of them was talking to me), and I could overlook drips and leaks, but if you take away my oven, you are also taking away my middle-of-the-night anxiety baking, not to mention the eating that came with it. (I had rolled out dough for a midnight babka and preheated the oven while I puttered. The oven was stone-cold twenty minutes later, so I cranked up the heat, then turned it off and on again—nothing. I contemplated throwing the dough in the potbelly, but I had a feeling that a babka would come shooting out of the chimney. When I tried to bake it in the toaster oven and almost set fire to the garage kitchen, I realized I needed help.)

Harry must have told Vivian about the oven because she showed up one afternoon bearing two rotisserie chickens and a tray of Ludmilla's kielbasa fried rice.

"Vivian, thank you. I—"

"Don't worry, I'm not staying."

"I wasn't—"

"I'm coming from prison, so I really must get home to shower."

"Prison?"

"The Junior League decorates the visitors' center at Bedford Hills. I've been hanging fall decorations for three hours."

"Is this a new thing?"

"Volunteering? Hardly."

"I meant the prison."

"Just keeping busy," she said, forcing a smile and walking back down to her car. "Busy, busy, busy," I heard her murmuring.

I hadn't joined any of the local email lists and didn't feel like reaching out to the Coven for advice. I had nowhere to go for a handyman recommendation, and Richard was off making jerky.

Unless I went on Chore Donkey.

I thought back to Cynthia's grade mixer and to the comments about using the app to hire worked-out waiters. Maybe there was a blog entry in it for me. Maybe I could get my oven fixed and finally send Andy the post he'd pressured me to write.

I created a profile and sent in an urgent work request, typing Cynthia's name in the referral box.

Minutes later, I had a response. Lance would be at the house in thirty minutes.

Thirty minutes? I looked down at myself. I was wearing a pair of Harry's sweatpants, an old hoodie that Sam had long since rejected, and a stretched-out, stained V-neck underneath. My hair was untamable, and I hadn't washed my face or brushed my teeth yet. I unzipped my hoodie and released a wave of fumes that were wafting up from inside my V-neck.

I don't want to say that all millennials look the same, but I had a hard time distinguishing Lance from Drew, Cynthia's yoga instructor of choice. Both were young. Both had broad shoulders and were in great shape. Both had very white teeth.

"You a friend of Cynthia's?" he asked as I led him through the yard to the garage kitchen.

"Yeah," I said, zipping my hoodie as high as it would go.

"Great." He smiled, following me.

"Do you also know Anna?" he asked as I opened the kitchen door and showed him the stove.

"Sort of," I stuttered. "I'm new here." I bent down to open the oven door, to show him all the parts that were no longer doing their job, when I felt a hand on my lower back. I wondered if he was just being friendly or if he thought I'd fall over if I bent too far forward.

"Then I get to be one of your first friends here," Lance said, now putting a second hand on my lower back and starting to massage me. I jumped a foot into the air, or at least as high as you can jump when you weigh five hundred pounds and pee every time you move too quickly.

"Just being friendly." He grinned, lifting his hands to where I could see them. "Besides, plus-size ladies are kind of my thing."

I momentarily contemplated crawling into the oven.

"I'm sorry," I mumbled, "but this isn't really *my* thing."

"I'm pretty flexible," he said, his voice lowering. "I'm willing to try *lots* of things." He took a step closer to me and I inhaled, breathing in his scent. Lance looked like a millennial Ken doll and smelled like vanilla and sugar.

"You smell like a baked good," I whispered. Before I could retract the words, Lance leaned in and placed his lips on my sweaty neck.

"Well, you *taste* good," he murmured.

I was pretty sure nothing could have been further from the truth. I snapped out of whatever cupcake reverie I was in and pushed Lance away.

"You misunderstand me," I said, marshaling my most direct Hanna Cohn voice. "Sex is not my thing. I mean, sex is my thing, obviously. I mean, how else would I have ended up this way?" I laughed at my own joke, but poor, confused Lance certainly wasn't laughing. "But sex with *you* is not my thing. I mean, you seem nice, you certainly are good-looking, and you smell really, really good."

"You said you were a friend of Cynthia's," he said, looking no less confused.

"I am . . ."

"And you also know Anna . . ."

I nodded.

"Then what did you think this was?" he asked, a baffled look spread across his pretty, pretty face.

"An oven repair?" I suggested hopefully. I really did need my oven back.

"OK, I get it," he said, picking up his messenger bag. "Sometimes the timing is off."

"So that's it?" I asked, my stomach barking for a loaf of banana bread and a tray of muffins.

"Well, you don't want what I'm offering. So yeah, that's it."

"What about my oven?"

He cocked his head to the side and said, "You know I don't really fix ovens, right?"

I was tired and hungry, and now I was going to have to wait even longer for a muffin. I led Lance to the door and opened it. Before he stepped into the garden, he stopped at the counter and stared down at a brown, nubby root Harry had brought home the day before.

"Celery root," he said, lighting up. "That's totally my jam."

I picked up the root and turned it over in my hand. For me, the best vegetables are ones that can also be served as a cake—zucchini, carrot, even sweet potatoes. There was no way this thing was going to end up as dessert, oven or no oven.

"Here," I said, handing him the root. "It's all yours."

He took a small step closer and raised an eyebrow. "These things are pretty pricey. Are you sure I can't give you anything for this root?"

"Yes, Lance. I am one hundred percent certain that there is nothing you can give me in exchange for this root, but things are starting to make sense."

~

The Unspoken Perks of Millennials (HINT: IT HAS TO DO WITH SEX)

I've been going on and on about all the hipster millennials up here in the county and the tension between them and the viperous helicopter moms from the city and its environs. I'd been so distracted by body art and piercings and college support groups for parents who have already applied to and attended college that I'd failed to notice something that had been right under my own unpierced nose. It turns out that the fortysomething crowd may not resent all those twentysomethings after all. In fact, there seems to be some generational cross-pollination happening, if you get my drift.

I learned from a group of local parents that when your husband starts to look like he's losing the war with middle age, and you just want a break from hovering over your children and monitoring their many, many accomplishments, you can dip your toe in the sweet sea of millennials. Let's just say that a certain woman up here, I'll call her V (for Viper), is part of a gaggle of gals who uses certain apps to hire twentysomething fitness instructors who are looking for extra work. Some of these sculpted youngsters make balloon animals for the under-ten set, some pour drinks at middle-age cocktail parties, and if what the Dutchess recently learned is true, that's not all these twentysomethings are doing.

Looks like millennials are good for a lot more than reintroducing fashion from the 1980s.

You might wonder why a twentysomething with abs of steel, a collection of ironic T-shirts, and copious amounts of free time wants to hook up in the back of an SUV covered with honor-roll stickers. Here's the thing about most millennials: they don't want commitment, they don't think long term, and they have *very* expensive taste.

In some ways, they couldn't be a more perfect match for moms too stressed out by prepping for standardized tests and "editing" their high schoolers' essays. These moms may have a lot on their minds, but they also have disposable income.

I'd heard some rumors of May–September dalliances, and desperate to get to the bottom of it all, I decided to go undercover. I installed Chore Donkey on my phone, put in an order for a leaf raker—listing a local mom whom I happen to know is a frequent flier as a reference—and waited. (While waiting, I may or may not have thrown on some lip gloss and gone overboard with a pair of tweezers, even though I swore off home grooming after I once bikini waxed myself to the kitchen floor and had to wait for my roommate to come home and unstick me. That, however, is a story for another time.)

Thirty minutes later, I opened my front door to a beautiful young man who didn't know a rake from a salad fork. The rakish raker put one too many hands on a body I have already pledged to the Duke, and I quickly sent him on his way, but not before he tried one last time to offer me his services in exchange for an overpriced vegetable the Duke had procured in his farm-stand wanderings.

So this is how it works, eh?

How nice it must be for these millennials, so strapped for cash in between teaching yoga classes, plant feeding, and dog walking, to have extra money for some of the things that middle age can buy—like overpriced kimchi and perishable probiotic shots. Are millennials really offering up their extra services so they can buy fresh zoodles and organic maca root? (Also, what does one do with a maca root?)

Stay tuned while I keep digging, and in the meantime, *namaste*.

Xxxxx

The Dutchess

~

I was proofreading the piece on the tufted couch when my mother called. My mother never called.

"I'm coming your way," she said. "Trust-and-estate conference at Vassar."

"Great," I said, feigning excitement and saving my blog draft.

"How far are you from Vassar?" she asked.

"I'm not sure."

"You do know where Vassar is, don't you?"

At this point it was clear to me that my mother was trying to say "Vassar" as many times as possible because she believed that hearing the name of the most prominent university in the region would be hard for someone whose husband was only able to get a job at a second-rate college.

"Yes, Mother. I know where Vassar is, and I'm sure you'll have a wonderful time at Vassar, which is in Poughkeepsie." Two can play at this game, Hanna Cohn.

"Can we have dinner while I'm up? I won't be seeing you for Thanksgiving because I'll be in London." My mother found a way to miss Thanksgiving at Vivian's every year, without ever offering to make the meal herself. This was probably for the best. Hanna Cohn never learned to cook because, ten years younger than Vivian, she was born to a generation of women who believed that if they learned to cook, someone would make them do it every night. (She may not have been wrong.)

"Sure. You'll still make it to see the last blasts of the foliage." Did I really say that? "Tell me when you're coming, and I'll put it on the calendar and make sure everyone is home for dinner."

"Great, and you can pick the restaurant," she said.

Hanna Cohn was also born to a generation of women whose daughters rebelled against eating microwave pizza while their mothers worked late by insisting on cooking everything from scratch. It pained my mother to watch me cook and serve food, so much so that on the rare occasions when we ate with her, we did so in a restaurant.

"I don't know the restaurant scene up here so well yet, but I'll do some digging." Once again, I knew the mistake I'd made before I had finished making it.

"Elsbeth, please tell me you haven't cooked dinner every night you've been up there."

"OK, I won't." *I* have *cooked dinner every night I've been up here. And for Sam, sometimes twice.*

"We need to have a talk about what you are going to do with your life after this baby."

"Mother, I have to go."

"The clock is ticking, Elsbeth."

"Who even says that?"

"Mothers of women who fritter away their lives."

Fritter away? I didn't know what she was talking about. I read the piece one more time and sent it to Andy. The Dutchess was about to have her most productive day to date.

~

Andy texted me within minutes.

> Let me get this straight. Women are meeting these guys on Chore Donkey, then they pay them extra for sex?
>
> I think so, yes.
>
> You think??

Sex is definitely happening, and local women confirmed the Chore Donkey detail at an insufferable party.

Andy sent me two emojis—a thumbs-up and a pair of fingers, crossed.

~

That night, with Lance on my brain, I couldn't make eye contact with Harry. Unfortunately, Harry was in the mood for all sorts of contact. He had just been asked to represent the English department at an upcoming conference in Chicago and was in an especially buoyant mood. I thought I had rewarded him with dinner and soup, but soup was not enough for him that night. I lay on my side in bed, two pillows wedged in between my legs and one shoved under my lower back.

"Harry," I said, trying to resist without actually pushing him away, "how about we do this another night? It's only been a couple of weeks."

"It's been a lot longer than that," he said, running his hand up my thigh.

"Can you at least run your hand up the leg that still has sensation?" I asked, shifting in my pillow fortress.

Harry complied, but then let his hand wander up to my underwear. Before he went any further, I clamped my hand firmly on his.

"There are things in my underpants that would keep you up at night."

"Try me," he murmured, trying to lean over the divide and find my neck.

I put a hand firmly on his chest. "Look at me," I begged him. "I'm veiny, completely misshapen, and seriously gross stuff is happening down below. I know it's been a while, but wouldn't you rather wait?"

"I think you're sexy," he said, undeterred. I could hear the cranked-up amp coming from Sam's room.

"Let's be honest," I said. "You think I'm sex. There's no way any of *this* is sexy." I waved a hand over myself, as if showing all of it to him for the very first time.

He finally relented and rested his head in his hand. "I'm a big boy. How about you just tell me that you don't want to do this, and I'll be fine. Just don't try and tell me what I think is sexy."

"Are you mad?"

"No. You're pregnant. You're tired. And sure, you're a little . . ."

"Fat?" *Plus-size ladies are my thing.* I shuddered and tried to move the thought of Lance and his vanilla scent out of my mind.

"I was going to say cranky."

Poor Harry. I could make buckets of soup, but Harry wanted something else. What if the men of Pigkill also used Chore Donkey? If I kept turning him away, would Harry have no choice but to turn to a twenty-five-year-old with a flat stomach and half a dozen tattoos?

"Fine." I relented. "But I want total darkness."

"Done!" he said, leaping out of bed and turning off the light.

"That, too," I demanded, motioning to the corner of the room with my head.

"The night-light?"

"All of it."

Harry obliged, which made two of us.

~

In the middle of the night, I woke up to pee and maybe bake a sour-cream coffee cake. When I remembered I couldn't bake, I ran myself a bath. According to my online wanderings, just about all of my miserable conditions could be solved by sitting in a bath of very warm water, which was fine with me as long as I didn't have to see myself. Waiting for the tub to fill, I looked down at my body and added bubbles. Then I added some more.

I thought back to Lance. If I'd been game, I could have given him what I'd just surrendered to a very grateful Harry. But there was no room dark enough or cloud of lavender bubbles thick enough to make that palatable. I could not imagine showing any of myself to a man other than Harry, let alone a millennial, and I could not for the life of me imagine any millennial being hard up enough for cash that he'd be willing to see a naked fortysomething in her twentieth month of pregnancy.

-15-

The day the Dutchess began her flight through the stratosphere was also the day that Hanna Cohn paid her first visit.

I suggested Joey's diner, just to show my mother I'd eaten out in Pigkill, and because I'd seen Joey that morning for what was rapidly becoming my daily egg cream. But Harry took us all to AIX, a farm-to-table restaurant in Beacon, and told the maître d' we didn't need menus. The temperature was dropping quickly, and I appreciated the woodburning stove in the middle of the restaurant. We sat in the least comfortable steel chairs in North America at a long wooden table that ran the length of the restaurant, which we shared with two other parties. Edison bulbs hung everywhere, and I held my breath until I saw a mason jar. Seven seconds.

"You don't order off the menu here," Harry announced to us all. "You order *off-menu*."

"I have zero idea what you are talking about," Alice said, momentarily putting her phone down. I saw an Instagram selfie of her and Abigail and Courtney, all puckering up at the phone.

"Ordering off-menu means you don't need an actual menu because there are a select number of dishes only available to people who know to ask for them, and Alice, no phones at the table, please," Harry explained.

"But I only have a hundred and twenty likes, and I posted the picture an hour ago," she protested. That didn't sound too shabby to me.

"You have four likes right here at the table who would love the pleasure of your undivided attention," he replied, and I nodded in agreement. Alice rolled her eyes, slipped her phone into her tiny, impractical backpack, and began doodling on the back of a brown-paper, presumably bamboo, napkin.

I opened my mouth to tell Harry that off-menu or not, I still wanted a menu, when a waitress appeared with a small plate of food.

"The chef knows how much you like the beet chips, Harry," she said, flashing some perfect teeth at all of us, but mostly at Harry. "They're on the house."

Harry beamed at the plate of beet chips, my mother dry coughed, and I stared at the waitress.

"I'm Colleen?" she said, ending the statement like it was a question. Colleen had dirty blonde hair, enormous dimples, and no wrinkles. Also, she wasn't twenty months pregnant and cranky. I refused to make eye contact with my mother, for whom Colleen's perky arrival was suddenly Christmas and her birthday all rolled into one—not that she celebrated either.

"Oh, you've been here before, have you, Harry?" my mother asked.

Harry nodded, his mouth full of beet chips.

For a smart man, this husband of mine was walking into every possible trap. Harry continued to beam and nibble on chips as Colleen told us the specials on offer. He may have been happy, but his children did not look so thrilled at the thought of chanterelles, quail eggs, and grass-fed, free-roaming ducks.

Then Harry did his off-menu thing.

"So, Colleen," he began, "do you have anything with . . . squash blossoms?" He lowered his voice at the end of the sentence, sounding like he was on the hunt for a Cabbage Patch Kid circa 1983.

Colleen smiled a secret smile. "Why, yes. We have ricotta and squash blossom pizza, and roasted poblano and squash blossom tacos."

Alice, speaking for the rest of us, asked, "What's a squash blossom?"

"Any pasta?" I blurted, not waiting for the answer. I didn't know what a squash blossom was, but I was way too hungry to eat a flower for dinner. Also, my mother was enjoying this too much, and I needed to stop the showcase of Harry, Colleen, and their squash blossoms.

"Um, let me think," Colleen said, resting her pen in one of the dimples and striking a pensive pose.

"Yes!" she exclaimed. "We have sweet potato ravioli in a mascarpone truffle sauce."

"Any mac and cheese?" I asked, rubbing my hungry belly.

"Bells," Harry interrupted, "I've had the ravioli, and it's excellent. It's the dean's personal favorite."

"Is it now?" muttered my mother, when Sam suddenly slammed his fist down on the table. I followed his glare to the door, where Saskia, in her braless glory, walked in hand in hand with Luke, who was back in possession of the leather jacket. It took me a few minutes to recognize them, which made me flush with the realization that I'd kept Sam from his only two friends in town. The couple walked over to the musicians in the corner, exchanged pleasantries, then picked up a take-out order from the bar. They left before they saw Sam, Luke's hand planted on Saskia's back. For the rest of the meal, Sam refused to do much talking and kept his gray hood up, even though I kept muttering requests for him to take it down. Although Harry kept himself busy by offering a running commentary on everyone's food, and my mother kept her Vassar mentions to a minimum, the meal could not end soon enough.

"This is all your fault," Sam spat as we walked to the car.

I stopped to look at him, but he shielded his face from me.

"You basically kept me locked up after the Hovel," he said. "And then it was just the two of them, without me. What else were they supposed to do?"

Part of me was so happy that he was confiding anything at all in me, but the rest of me was confused. Was that how it worked? If two boys and a girl hung out and one of the boys got grounded even though his mom didn't want to ground him, did the other two naturally become a couple? And did the boy who won the girl get to wear the jacket? But the biggest question of all was: Had I tried to protect Sam but ended up hurting him even more?

I was contemplating all of this and wedging myself into Fulbright when my phone began to buzz with texts from Andy.

Holy shit. Just posted and you're getting real traffic.

What?

Yup. Check it out!!!!

Andy was not one for exclamation points, let alone four. If the Dutchess really was taking off, it was just a matter of time until the Coven were onto me, which meant that Harry would know soon, too. At the same time, I had traffic, actual traffic. I needed to breathe. I tugged at the collar of my coat, undid the top buttons, and slid my window down, letting in a blast of cold air.

"You OK?" Harry asked.

"Uh-huh," I said.

I speed walked up the stairs to my bathroom and sat on the closed toilet, still in my coat, and went straight to the blog on my phone. Hundreds of people were talking about it, tweeting it out, and sharing. The comments went on for pages.

> It's not just up in the Hudson Valley. Come to Brooklyn. Half the moms here are doing a lot more than just flirting with their baristas and dog walkers.

Is this the new version of sleeping with your pool boy?

I'm so lame. I was only using Chore Donkey to have someone actually rake my leaves.

My mother always says: don't say anything about someone you wouldn't say to her face.

The Dutchess is the best thing I've read in ages. Keep it coming!

Do you teach English at Rhinebeck Middle School? I'm sure I know you!

Of course these hipsters are having sex to pay for fancy groceries! Who else can afford WHOLE PAYCHECK?

Ha! Gives new meaning to high-end poke bowls!

Hmm. Sounds like the Dutchess may have to relocate if she keeps dishing on her friends.

Whoa. Are you sure you meant to publish this?

The last two comments threw me. I felt a chill even though I was bundled up. I got off the toilet, peeled off my support hose, and texted Suki.

Me: I think I've gone too far.

Suki: I saw. I can't believe you brought up the bikini wax! I remember having to chisel you off that ugly linoleum!

Me: And I remember having to wait for you to get home. Ugh. What am I gonna do when Harry finds out?

Suki: I don't know what to tell you.

Me: Now is the part where you encourage me anyway.

Suki: The Dutchess is so good and so funny, but why aren't you writing about YOU? Much less dangerous, no risk to Harry, and honestly, an even better story.

Me: I am currently staring at a six-foot-long varicose vein. I can promise you, nobody wants to read about me.

What I couldn't tell Suki was that even if I wanted to ditch the Dutchess and start writing about something else, even myself, I couldn't stop now. Each of these comments was from someone I didn't know and would probably never meet, someone who'd read my words and cared enough to post. My writing was resonating, and I just couldn't let that go.

-16-

Andy called first thing the next morning while I stood on the front porch drinking coffee. A few neighbors walked past, looked at me, and neither waved nor smiled. I can't say I blamed them. I had neither waved nor smiled at any of them, either.

"They want to know who you are."

"Who?" I asked, looking around.

"Your readers! This is the most traffic we've ever had! A bunch of other blogs have run it, and we just picked up five new advertisers."

"What?"

"You're a big deal, Bells. People aren't just reading you; they're talking about you."

They're talking about you.

I felt myself grinning, something I hadn't done much of lately—my smiling muscles were tight and unused.

"This is wild," I said, walking back into the house with some firewood for the potbelly. I'd been planning on a midday nap to make up for another sleepless night in which the baby did calisthenics while I tried to rest.

"Everyone wants to know more about the Dutchess!"

"How much more?"

"Maybe just a couple of details—which town you live in, how many kids you have—enough to keep them hot on your trail, and to keep our numbers up."

"Absolutely not."

"I thought you might say that," he replied. "How about *New York* magazine?"

"What?" I dropped a piece of wood and stared at it, contemplating whether it would be worth the energy I'd need to expend to pick it up.

"Yup. They want to include you in their special edition on the Hudson Valley. It's called 'Hipsters on the Hudson.'"

"Oh my god," I said, plopping down on the tufted couch, realizing, not for the first time, that this room needed more furniture. "I can't. I can't go public—not now."

"I get it. Besides, I think it kind of adds to the mystery. How about this—I'll keep running whatever you send me, the juicier the better, and you promise not to forget about the little guys when you have a book deal."

A book deal? Would the Dutchess be the talk of the town? Would everyone forget Meegan, her six little blessings, and whatever marshmallow craft project she was shilling?

"Got it," I said, finally speaking. "I'll have something for you soon."

Easier said than done. I'd written a bombshell but had no follow-up, at least not yet. I didn't let that bother me, though. In the following days, as more and more people read and commented on the blog, and as Andy sent choice comments my way (We want more of the Dutchess! More!), I felt more awake and alert than I had in months.

"You're in a good mood," Harry said as I filled out forms for Sam's Albany trip and read over what felt like Alice's thirteenth essay on colonial farming.

"Huh?"

"Yeah, lately you're either smiling or laughing," he said. "It's like you just heard a joke you don't want to share."

"Really," I mumbled, swallowing. "I hadn't noticed."

"Well, I have," Harry said, swooping in and planting a kiss on my crumb-covered mouth. "And I think it's fantastic. It's good to see you settling in."

Is that what I'm doing? I smiled lovingly at him, marinating in the lie I had told him, a lie I was only making worse each day that I kept the Dutchess to myself. I was dying to tell Harry about the blog, imagining the comments he'd make in the margins: *You forgot a comma, you're sexy when you're snarky.* I so wanted him to see that even though I spent most of my days holed up in our house, I had a productive life. I was a writer—a writer with readers, and lots of them. I had something I'd wanted for as long as I could remember, but that something could threaten the one thing that Harry wanted.

"Absolutely," I said, getting up and shielding my now-worried face from him. "I'm taking a cue from you. I'm learning to love Dutchess County."

~

Love it or not, I needed the county. I needed more dirt so I had something to write about. When I wasn't obsessively checking the blog, counting the number of views I was getting each hour, reading and rereading the comments, I was scouring websites for local news and even fell down the rabbit hole of the school-district forum, desperate to find a story. It got so bad that even Alice told me I might have a screen problem.

"Seriously, Mom," she said, trying to get my attention one afternoon, "since when are you super addicted to your phone?"

Since I became an internet sensation. And since I realized that it could all come crashing down unless I find something else to write about.

"I'm just trying to find someone to come and fix the oven," I lied, reclining on the couch. "There's only so much baking I can do in the toaster."

"Maybe we just need a new oven," she said, finishing a sandwich, then checking her teeth with the camera app on her phone.

"What?" I said, looking up from my phone. Two brand-new comments had just come in.

"Are you even listening to me?" she asked. "We need a new oven."

"Oh," I said. "Maybe we do." I had left a panicked message for Quick Richard, begging him to come fix the oven, after several other handymen had flaked on the job.

Please come. You can quote all the Emerson you want.

Alice gave me a fed-up shrug and walked upstairs to her room.

Alice may have been right. We may have needed a new oven, but I needed something more than an oven. I needed a story. I needed dirt.

What I really needed was a stakeout.

-17-

There are few things more obvious than a very pregnant woman in a minivan on a stakeout. Obvious or not, I was happy to have something to do over the next few days, and I'd be lying if I said that the snacking involved was not a serious incentive. While Harry, Sam, Alice, and I had breakfast in the garage kitchen, I did my best to feign interest in their conversation when all I really wanted was to get out and start digging.

Our conversation went something like this:

Harry: "Sam, I saw on the test calendar that you have a math test tomorrow. How do you feel about it? Are you ready?"

Sam: "Are you really checking the test calendar? Don't you make fun of those parents who check the test calendar?"

Me, to self: *Yes. Yes, I do.*

Harry: "If they didn't want us to check the calendar, they wouldn't send it out. Besides, there's nothing wrong with me asking you about a test. Right, Bells?"

I nodded, contemplating whether a hat on a stakeout was too obvious.

Alice: "Don't you notice that you never ask me about how I'm doing in school, but you guys are kind of obsessed with Sam's grades?"

Sam: "That's because they're scared I won't go to college."

Me: "That's not true."

Sam: "Fine. Then I'm not going to college."

I did my best impression of a mom keeping her cool and finished my oatmeal. (Let the record reflect that I was eating oatmeal because we still did not have a working oven. Oatmeal is what you eat when you can't bake your breakfast.)

Alice: "You still haven't asked about me."

After I'd made all the right noises and convinced Alice that she mattered, I dropped the kids at school. I drove a different way through town to avoid some roadwork, past piles of fallen red and orange leaves, and spotted Cynthia and Peggy at a café I'd never seen before. I squinted without slowing down too much and saw that it was called Roast and Reefer and advertised "the county's best pour-over CBD coffee!" I guess this is where they headed after drop-off when I went to the diner. Whatever. Those moms needed all the help they could get.

I drove two towns over to a bakery Suki had recently alerted me to and asked me to check out before she came up to review it. Who knows, maybe there was also a story lurking among the baked goods.

I walked in and was immediately blanketed by the warm smell of baking butter and flour. Lance may have smelled good, but this place smelled fantastic. I closed my eyes and did some deep yoga breathing, letting the scent fill me up. *Namaste.*

"Ma'am?" said the studded twentysomething behind the counter, yanking me out of my butter trip.

"I want some of those," I said, pointing to a row of round, crispy things I'd never seen before.

"The bisnuts?" she asked.

"Excuse me?"

"Bisnuts," she explained proudly. "They're a cross between a biscuit and doughnut."

Naturally, I'd discovered the Cronut only when Suki told me about it, and by then the lines were so long that I never bothered making the trek downtown. I had to wait for Suki and the Cronuts to travel up to me.

"Great," I said. "I'll have three."

"Are you on the wait list?"

"Come again?"

"I can only sell you a bisnut if you're on the bisnut wait list," she said, puffing out her chest and raising her chin.

"I don't understand," I said. "Why would you have them out if I can't have one?" This girl, and I say this because she was getting younger by the moment, had never learned not to come between a pregnant woman and her trendy baked good. She gave me a bored blink, and I knew she was hoping I'd leave soon so she could check her phone.

"It's the store policy. Would you like something else?"

I looked around and saw a chalkboard sign with the day's specials and an announcement: **ABSOLUTELY NO CAKE POPS. EVER.** In the end, I took several chocolate croissants and a latte. As I was paying, I saw a familiar woman out of the corner of my eye. Like seeing a teacher out of school, I knew that I knew her, I just couldn't place her.

"Hello, Bells," she said, her felt owl earrings dangling.

"Hello, Dr. Ross." I grabbed a fruit cup and added it to my order, hoping she hadn't noticed that I had also purchased pastries for five. "Picking up some food for a meeting," I announced. "A big meeting."

"That's nice. I'll be seeing you soon, then." She turned to the loaves of hearty bread and began to place an order.

As I was leaving, I heard the girl behind the counter call out, "Ma'am, if you come back next week, you can be the first to buy our Cragels!"

I didn't want to ask. I pushed open the door and let in some young new moms, all wearing babies swaddled up in a variety of wraps and slings. I was sure that when these mothers looked in the mirror, they saw sleepless nights, but all I saw was youth, lots of springy youth.

~

I was eating a croissant and walking down the block (ignoring my mother's voice in my head chastising me for eating and walking at the same time) when Alice started firing texts at me.

You should've asked me about math this morning.

Wait for it.

Just failed another test. May get cut from the play. GPA too low.

I shot back, Failed another math test??! and then wished I had texted just about anything but that.

Can I get a tutor? Will do anything to stay in play.

I promise we will work this out when you get home. Will find you tutor. xxxx

I hoped that was the end of it, at least for now, and kept walking. I passed the same mix of stores I saw in Pigkill—older stores that sold a combination of items that never seemed to belong together (guitars and antique desks, milk glass and vacuum cleaner parts) as well as bleached-wood boutiques that seemed to sell only seven or eight overpriced items, one of which was always a glass water bottle you carry around to broadcast to the world that you've forsaken plastic. Harry had three.

I stopped short in front of a boutique called Artisanal Wares with wooden shelving and about one item on each shelf. I leaned into the window and saw a rosemary-cassis candle for forty-eight dollars. I wondered what made a candle artisanal and leaned in a little closer. There was a **6/6** handwritten on the candle's label. I was wondering if only making six of something made it artisanal when a twentysomething in a knit cap with very broad shoulders and perfect skin pulled the candle off the shelf and walked to the register. He then handed it to Anna, whose hair and eyebrows I instantly recognized. She was once again in a boho-chic outfit of a long breezy blouse, ripped jeans, and studded booties, which would have made me look like an aging hippie, but which on her looked on point. I watched her pay for the candle, an ecru handmade sweater, and yes, a glass bottle. When she'd signed her name and put her credit card back in her purse, she handed the bag and the receipt to the millennial. I ducked into a coffee shop before they could see me and congratulated myself on a successful start to my stakeout. I watched Anna and her young friend linger outside the shop for a few moments, then climb into two different cars and drive away. When they were out of sight, I decided I'd seen enough here for the day. If I'd been this lucky a few towns over, who knew what I'd spot in downtown Pigkill.

I drove over to the river and parked underneath a tree whose red leaves would inevitably end up stuck under my windshield wipers. I opened a bottle of seltzer, slunk down in my seat, and checked my phone to see if by any chance Alice had gone quiet.

She had not.

Why are you ignoring me?????

Mom? Mom?

MOOOOOM????????

"Bells?"

I dropped my phone into my lap and looked up at Joey standing at my window. She was wearing an orange woolen trapper hat and purple mittens.

I waved and rolled the window down. "Oh, hey, Joey," I said.

"You just hanging out?" she asked, her eyes on the croissants resting in the passenger seat, perched next to a supersize bag of Twizzlers and some barbecue potato chips.

"Yeah, just taking in a view of the river." I looked out at the river side of the car. Trees and a public bathroom blocked my sight. "What are you up to?" I asked as casually as I could.

"Walking." She sighed. "I have gestational diabetes, and Dr. Ross wants me to get more exercise. So, here I am." She held her arms out by her sides. "Wanna come?" I glanced over at the uneaten food and figured some exercise might not be such a bad thing. Besides, I would look a lot less obvious walking with a friend than I would sitting alone in the car in front of a public bathroom.

I climbed out of the car, and we began to walk.

"Wow," I said as we passed a mom and a set of twins in matching hats, gloves, and jackets. "I haven't taken a walk like this since we left the city."

"Why did you leave the city?" she asked.

"My husband got a job at Dutchess College."

"What does he teach?"

"English, which means good jobs are hard to find, and when you get one, you move, even to Pigkill."

Joey smiled awkwardly.

"Oh, I didn't mean that it's a bad place," I said. "It's just different."

"I've been here my whole life," Joey said. "You don't have to apologize. Anyway, I'm learning to be who I am. And right now I'm a twenty-three-year-old pregnant college dropout." She shrugged and added, "Almost twenty-four."

"If it makes you feel any better, I'm a fortysomething who got pregnant accidentally and am eating my way through the stress of a move, raising teenagers, and preparing for a baby I'm not sure I'm ready for."

"Aren't you scared?" she asked.

"About which part?"

"All of it, but mostly the labor," Joey said.

"In my experience—and it's been about twelve years since I did this—the labor is the least of it, and the part you can't really plan for. Your job is just to get that baby out safely, and then the hard work begins." I stopped and took a deep breath. "Sleep while you can, Joey."

"It's that bad?"

"For me it was," I said, using a bench to stretch out my hips, which had started to seize up after this sudden spurt of exercise. "There were days when I was so tired that my face hurt, and there was always a mom in earshot claiming her babies slept through the night before they even got home from the hospital."

"Those are the moms in my birthing class who say they've never felt better in their lives than they do now," Joey said as we started walking again.

"Yup, the exact same ones." *And they will continue to shame you, well into your child's teenage years.* "But you're young, which means you can weather the lack of sleep a little easier and your boobs will bounce back." I looked down and examined my own boobs, which were sagging beneath the weight of layers and years. "I'm a lost cause."

Joey laughed and reached out to put her hand on my arm. I know she wasn't what Suki had in mind when she said I needed to find my people, but Joey was the closest thing I had to people up here.

"Let's walk back closer to the stores," I said, hoping to see something, although I still wasn't sure what. We passed Green's, a local high-end grocery store. Once again, in the parking lot I saw Anna and her friend in the knit cap from the candle boutique. Just as I was congratulating myself on my instincts to come back to Pigkill, Anna and her young man walked through the lot, looking around as they made their way to a Prius with an **Eat Local** bumper sticker, the same car her friend had parked outside the candle store. He popped the trunk and helped her load the groceries from her cart into his car. I squinted at the grocery bags, all of which looked like they'd just been purchased at the store. I saw that two of the bags had clothes inside. You had to be willing to drop a lot of cash if you bought locally sourced hemp clothing at Green's.

"Tell me, Joey," I said, "why would a fortysomething-year-old woman be buying pricey groceries and artisanal candles for a guy twenty years younger than she is? Also, what is an artisanal candle?" I laughed at my own joke.

"Easy," she said. "You can't keep paying for sex with money, because at some point your husband will notice."

"OK . . ."

"But you can have higher grocery bills and charges from fancy stores, because that's easier to explain."

"That's crazy," I said. "That's really crazy."

"I know, but do you know how much a gallon of that pricey oat milk costs?" she asked, grinning.

I didn't know how much a gallon of oat milk cost, but I did know what the Dutchess could do with information like this.

We walked back to Fulbright. Joey headed to the diner, and I climbed into my seat and saw even more texts from Alice. She seemed to have moved on from the math test.

What are we doing for Dad's b-day tomorrow?

We rly need to shop.

Usually Harry didn't have to drop hints because birthdays were my thing, but I'd been so wrapped up in the Dutchess that I'd lost track of the date. I knew it was November, but that was pretty much all. If you'd have asked me what day of the week it was, I would have had to look at my phone. With no oven, I couldn't run home and bake a cake. Even worse was the realization that if I'd known tomorrow was Harry's birthday, I would have punted this morning's sex to the next day.

With no cake and birthday sex I didn't even get credit for, I sat in the car and racked my brain. What do you get for the man who buys himself loose-leaf tea and glass water bottles?

The man needed a candle, and an artisanal candle at that.

I looked at the time and raced back to the candle boutique, parking right in front. The store was empty, but there was another candle on the shelf near the window. I picked up what I thought was the new candle and saw that it was also rosemary-cassis with a **6/6** on it.

"Oh, you're in luck," the woman behind the counter said. "Those are a limited edition—only six were made, and someone just returned this one."

I stopped for a moment.

"Did the person who returned this also return a sweater and a glass water bottle?" I asked.

"Yes," she said seriously. "He did."

I knew two things for sure: the millennials were cleverer than I thought, and the Dutchess had to get home and write about it.

~

Quick Richard was fixing the oven when I got home. I heaped praise and gratitude on him and ran up to my office before he could launch into a recounting of his rabbit-jerky adventures. I cranked up the space heater and began to write.

~

Sex and Artisanal Candles: Life in Dutchess County

I told you I would do some digging, and people, I dug.

You see, even though Chore Donkey is an easy way for fortysomething moms to find *household help with benefits*, their husbands would become suspicious of work orders for problems that do not exist and large weekly cash withdrawals or checks made out to "cash." (Besides, how many times can you pay someone to rake your leaves or fix your oven?) What husbands might *not* notice are larger grocery bills or fifty-dollar charges from a fancy new store in town—even if that fifty bucks was for ONE SINGLE CANDLE. (I wish I were kidding about this.)

Even better, the right purchases can then be returned for cash, which is all anyone really wants, and the circle of life, or at least the circle of sex, is therefore complete.

The Dutchess did a little snooping and couldn't figure out why the ladies of the county were buying overpriced groceries and artisanal candles for men twenty years younger. (A real tip-off was bagfuls of clothing purchased from said grocery stores—if you've ever wondered who outfits themselves in all the overpriced hemp clothing at Whole Foods, now you know. Also, where did the word *artisanal* come from, and how do we send it back?)

Dear readers, one at a time, the Dutchess observed these not-so-desperate housewives buying bags of the stuff and handing it over to incredibly attractive younger men. The men then go back minutes later and return the pricey items for cash.

That's right, the Dutchess has stumbled onto a sex-for-groceries-for-cash scheme, which was right under her very own nose. And because life up here is getting crazier by the day, I also now know that a Cragel is what happens when a croissant and a bagel have a baby.

I just don't know how you milk an oat.

Send help,

The Dutchess

~

This year, inspired by his recent fetish for chia pudding in little glass jars, I baked a chocolate chia cake for Harry's birthday. I never usually premiere a cake on a birthday, but I also never usually write blogs under a secret persona or accidentally get pregnant.

I still don't understand what I did wrong. Maybe I misread the instructions and left out an ingredient, or maybe I was distracted and repeated a step without knowing it, but instead of the moist and fluffy confection promised by the vegan baking website to which many in the online baking community had recently pledged their allegiance, the cake was nothing more than a chocolaty, gelatinous mush. Actually, it was cacao, which I know some people find to be the superior version of cocoa, but which I find tastes more like cold-processed dirt. I piled the heaping mound of chia onto my favorite milk glass cake stand, but it collapsed and began to ooze down the sides within seconds. We ate quickly.

Harry was a terrific sport and gulped down the goo with a smile on his face. The kids were less generous but did a good job celebrating their dad despite the fact that the cake gummed up their mouths. We all washed it down and sang a loud "Happy Birthday" to Harry, and for a few moments, everything felt normal, almost easy.

Quick Richard, who appeared midcelebration with a part for one of the toilets, declined to partake when he heard the word *chia*.

"Last time I heard that word was on a middle-of-the-night infomercial for something shaped like a porcupine. I think I'll have to pass, but thanks."

"I'm just happy the oven is back," I said, soaking the gummy cake pan.

Richard smiled proudly. "Now you can bake as many pies as you want for Thanksgiving."

Even though he'd just said the word *pie*, my stomach sank. Thanksgiving did not mean unlimited pie. Thanksgiving always meant one thing: the Walker compound.

-18-

Suki was the one who first dubbed it "the compound." Everything about the Chappaqua situation was different from the way I had grown up in a series of small prewar apartments. My grandparents lived ten blocks away, and none of us owned anything; we all had landlords. In Chappaqua, not only did Vivian own her home, but years ago she and Harry's father had bought up the lots surrounding their property. She offered a lot to each of her sons. Harry's other brothers and their families both lived next door. Harry's parents had offered us a plot of land, and when we turned them down, they went and built an enormous pool, complete with a pool house that the three families shared. It wasn't that we intended to reject them by living in the city, in a world they did not control, it was just that we wanted to live in the city, in a world they did not control.

Despite my sisters-in-law, I do not enjoy spending time in Vivian land. In the early days of my marriage, before I had my sisters-in-law as committed allies, I counted the minutes not just until we were out of the house, or even in the car, but back in the city, where I felt enough distance from Vivian and her impossible standards. I would always open the car window, gulping breaths of air as we rode over the Henry Hudson Bridge into Manhattan. This year, though, the thought of Vivian did not inspire terror—after I'd written about the sex-for-candles scheme, I was desperate to get out of Pigkill and away from the fear of being uncovered.

Andy published the piece the day after I sent it to him (This is your best piece yet!), and the comments came swiftly and fiercely.

> Who said millennials aren't ingenious? This is hysterical!
>
> This is really hard to believe, and kind of obnoxious.
>
> Lol! I thought my teenagers were sneaky . . .
>
> Something about this doesn't sit right . . . who are you?
>
> Hey Dutchess—WE ARE WATCHING YOU, TOO.

I spent several nights wide awake, waiting for more comments to come in (and watching the number of views climb higher and higher). Then they took an even nastier turn.

> Hey bitch, we said we are watching you, and guess what? WE WILL FIND YOU.
>
> CHANGE YOUR LOCKS.

Andy must have read my increasingly addled and panicked mind because he sent me a late-night text pretty quickly after that:

> Took down those nasty comments, and please, ignore the crazies.

That's easy for you to say, I wrote while lying in bed next to a sleeping Harry. You aren't living among the crazies.

> You don't know where these people live. Besides, nasty comments are the hallmark of a great blogger.

> What if they really are watching me?

> How about a Q and A, in character, as the Dutchess? It's a great way to cool things down and remind people that you're a real person . . .

> Um, I may be real, but the Dutchess is not.

> You know what I mean—be your usually chatty and friendly self and people will calm down.

Chatty and friendly? Had he met me?

> Can it wait until Thanksgiving? I think I need a few days off.

> Sure, and in the meantime—take it easy. You're fine. Nobody is coming after us.

Maybe nobody was coming for Andy, but I was convinced that it was now just a matter of time until people started watching me back. In the days before Thanksgiving, I all but refused to leave the house—for any reason. I couldn't risk saying something to someone and unintentionally revealing myself. What if one of the people I'd written about had read it and recognized me? Worried that Harry and the kids might grow suspicious, I took to my bed and faked a virus until it was time to hit the road.

We drove down to Chappaqua after dark, avoiding parts of the highway and driving down surface roads and winding lanes, stopping far more frequently than we had on our first drive to Pigkill, which made sense given that my bladder was probably the size of a dime.

As we drove down through Dutchess County, then Putnam, and finally into northern Westchester, I watched the houses change. The plots of land may have grown slightly smaller, but the houses grew bigger and better tended. In Dutchess and Putnam, there were pockets of blight and void, but northern Westchester gave off the aura of towns blessed by wealth.

Vivian's home rose from the fields and fences of Chappaqua. She described the style as "European-inspired country," but to me the style was more "enormous-inspired rich." In addition to the pool they all shared, the house was on a small lake, complete with a pair of aluminum rowboats and a weathered canoe, because anything motorized would have been gauche. Vivian's taste stayed within the bounds of large and stately but always in the realm of what she considered tasteful (my mother liked to call this "gentile taste," but we won't go there now). We drove past the lake and the boats and up the long driveway to the front door under a sloping roof. Vivian had a simple wreath on the front door. (I chuckled when I thought about Meegan's latest blog entry: a wreath made entirely of Ziploc bags.) I knew better than to expect Christmas lights. Instead, Vivian adorned each of the first-floor windows with an antique candle. (I was never more grateful for this sparseness than the one and only time my mother had come up for Christmas. It was bad enough that she glared at the giant yet simply decorated fir and muttered, "Nice tree.")

When we arrived, the house was already full. On the night before Thanksgiving, Vivian always served grilled cheese sandwiches and tomato soup on her mother's china. She presented the soup in a giant pink tureen, which sat in the center of the table on a pressed tablecloth.

Harry's brothers and their wives sat at the table, the walls behind them covered in pictures of the boys at all the stages of their lives.

"Bells! Look at you!" Molly jumped out of her seat and put her arms around me, then rested her hands on my heaving middle. "You're beautiful."

I really did love her. I slipped off my shoes, hung my coat in the closet, and kissed Alex, whom I loved a little less.

"Damn, Bells. You look like a barge! Any day now!" He grinned, knowing there were many more pregnant days ahead of me. Luckily, Alex was distracted by the presence of both of his brothers in the room at once. He looked over at Mark, the oldest of the three boys, and the two of them pounced on Harry, dragging him into the living room. Their interactions followed a similar pattern. They began by roughhousing—Harry was currently pinned to Vivian's Oriental carpet while his brothers mauled him. This would soon be replaced by verbal ribbing and jokes ("Sleeping with any of your nurses yet? How many hedge fund managers does it take to sink the economy?"), which would then be replaced by the age-old debate about who was their parents' favorite child—all the while gingerly skirting the fact that Harry was still reaching for professional validation as both his brothers had long grasped it. There were no tenure jokes.

"This makes me really happy I only had one boy," laughed Jess, Mark's wife, when she saw Mark had Alex in a headlock. She pulled up a chair, and I sat with Jess, Molly, and the giant pink tureen.

"Where is she?" I whispered, looking over my shoulder.

"Vivian? She went to the attic for some decorations she wants to give us," Molly said as she ladled some soup into a china bowl.

"Mercy!" Alex called from the rug as Harry pawed him. "That's my operating hand!"

Alex, like Molly, was a doctor, as were all of their friends. I knew this because they tagged their friends by their professions. I had heard all about Jack the nephrologist and his wife, Jennifer, the radiologist; Dylan the urologist and his wife, Nancy, the cardiologist; not to mention Jake and Susanne, the married gastroenterologists who were the craziest of the crew. Any annoyance I may have felt was quickly tempered by the pleasure I derived from watching Vivian squirm when Molly, pediatrician to New York's A-list, had to work late or be on call during family vacations, or even better, had a speaking engagement, forcing Alex to be on sole parenting duty. A surgeon son of hers on sole parenting duty with an even more successful wife was the stuff of Vivian's nightmares. Still, Vivian got the daughter-in-law of her dreams in Jess, who was married to Mark and his hedge fund. The two met at Princeton, and Jess decided against law school in favor of full-time mothering and volunteer work. Her own mother disapproved (sound familiar?), but Vivian could not have been happier.

Molly poured red wine, even for me, and the three of us sat and compared notes. I heard all about Jess's twin son and daughter, who were both awaiting their college early-decision letters, if they even sent letters anymore. I heard about Molly's three little girls, who were all born in rapid succession. Being married to a Walker boy meant that even though we were each so different, we all had Vivian and her beautiful, clever sons in common. Inevitably, any time I spent with my sisters-in-law left me wondering why I wasn't living closer to them, and inevitably, that question was answered.

"Hello, Bells," Vivian said as she walked into the room carrying a clear plastic container neatly marked **Christmas Decorations**. "Where's Harry?" Realizing she had to pretend to be interested in me, she looked me over.

"You look exhausted."

I wondered: Did I really look more exhausted than a woman with a full-time medical practice and three children under the age of five, and a woman with over-programmed twins, who tended to her husband's career like it was a hothouse orchid, sitting on all the right boards, as well as planning dinner parties and group vacations? It didn't matter.

I knew what Vivian was saying. She put the box down and went in search of Harry.

"My boy," she said when she saw him. "My beautiful, clever boy."

The actual Thanksgiving meal was relatively easy, if only because Vivian had what she most wanted—all three of her sons at her table. She looked so happy and full up, sitting at the head of the table in a pale-pink wrap dress with a scarf knotted at her throat, in a way that only highlighted how deflated she was in all the days in between these visits. We all knew to dress for the meal, and Jess even thought to wear pink, clever girl.

I had tried to prepare Sam for the barrage of rapid-fire questions—mostly centered around college. Fortunately, Jess's kids bore the brunt of the questions, but they lived nearby, which meant that Vivian knew all the answers. She hadn't seen Sam in a while, and frankly, he was less known to her. She pretended to be interested in his music, but his lack of what she considered direction made him seem like an exchange student from the land of the less motivated.

"Are you taking the SAT or the ACT?" she asked as Harry filled all our water glasses, her eyes hovering on the longish hair that Sam was currently refusing to cut.

He looked at me. "ACT," he answered, seated to my left.

"How's the prep going?"

"Fine," he and I both said at the same time.

"Have you made a college list?"

"Why does he have to go at all?" Alice asked, expertly reading the room, or at least her brother, and probably whispering a secret prayer of gratitude that Vivian was too focused on Sam to ask her about her own classes. "He just wants to play music."

I reached down for Sam's hand and squeezed it in solidarity. He squeezed me back. In that moment, I would have held his hand forever, protecting him from other people's expectations.

"Music is a hobby," Harry said, echoing words my mother said about writing twenty years ago. "He can be a music major in college, he just has to go to college." He paused, looking at Vivian for approval. "It doesn't matter which one."

I heard Vivian draw breath. Poor thing. I doubt that Vivian Walker would ever have adorned the back of her SUV with college stickers ("Tacky," I imagined her saying), but for her, a "second-tier college" was a communicable disease. Now, her bright and beautiful son had been shunted to one, and his own son didn't even want that for himself.

Knowing the pangs of parental disappointment all too well, Molly came riding to the rescue.

"Bells!" she declared, serving herbed rice to her impeccably behaved girls in their matching frocks. "Have you heard about the County Dutchess?"

My mouth fell open, and half a leg of turkey tumbled out. "Excuse me?" I asked, retrieving the food from my lap.

"Oh my god, there's this blog on the *Uptowner*. It's hysterical."

I tried swallowing what was left in my mouth, but the food moved down into my esophagus and lodged itself there. I tried coughing it up.

"*You* read the *Uptowner*?" Vivian asked.

"Nice, Mother," Mark said, turning to me. "Everything OK, Bells?"

I nodded silently.

"I read it when Bells wrote for it," Molly explained. "I must have signed up for updates, because I started getting this blog in my inbox, and my god, this woman is a riot."

"People still read blogs?" Alex smirked.

"Who is she?" Jess asked, ignoring Alex and pouring more wine. I slid my glass forward for a second glass, and she filled it with a raised eyebrow.

"Nobody knows. She's anonymous," Molly said, taking a sip of wine. "She calls herself the County Dutchess. Get it?"

"That's cute," Harry said. "There's a lot happening in Dutchess County. You'd be surprised."

I gulped down wine and looked over at the kids. Sam was engaged in what looked like a deep conversation with the twins, and Alice was gleefully belting out a song about forks and knives to the younger kids. (Thankfully, I signed her up for after-school math help, and her role in the play was secure.)

Molly kept talking. "Seriously, though, this Dutchess totally dishes on the people in her town. She just hasn't told us which town it is."

Jess jumped a little in her seat. "It could be Pigkill! You could know her, Bells!"

I saw Jess reflexively reach for her phone to pull up the most recent blog, but then she glanced at Vivian and thought better of a phone at the table.

Molly's girls asked to be excused. Alice shot me a "Who does that?" look, then did the same and followed them to the next room.

"Tell us more," Alex said, his eyes widening. As much as I was enjoying the Dutchess's fame, I was also praying Vivian's hardwood floor and heirloom Oriental rug would open up and swallow me whole.

"OK, it's MILF-millennial hookup heaven," Molly said.

Vivian looked puzzled. "Molly, are you speaking English?"

"You know—it's like the Real Housewives of the Hudson Valley."

"Come again?"

"The ladies are hooking up with yoga instructors," she explained. "You know, sleeping with them."

"Oh, please," said Vivian, folding the napkin on her lap. "That's not a new thing."

"Mother!" Harry gasped.

"Well, it's not," she said, looking not at all unpleased with herself for having something to contribute.

"Yeah, well the catch here is that the age difference is about twenty years. All the moms who escaped the city fifteen years ago after 9/11 are now hooking up with the millennials who just escaped Brooklyn. And they're using handyman apps to do it," Molly explained.

"Again, apps aside, not news," Vivian commented.

"Here's the rub, though," Molly said, pressing on. "They find these guys on the app, and they have them do random chores and serve food at parties. If they want to do something more, it gets hard to hide. I mean, how many times can you pay someone to rake your leaves?" She chuckled to herself, and for a moment, I basked in the glow of being quoted. "These moms have to find other ways to pay these guys without looking suspicious. The Dutchess thinks the moms pay for sex in high-end groceries and pricey home goods, which the millennials return for cash!"

"What?" just about everyone at the table asked.

"Yup," Molly said proudly, as though she herself had come up with the idea. "Who knew these hipsters had it in them?"

"I need some air," I announced.

"It's freezing out, Bells," Vivian warned.

"The baby's kicking, and I'm in pain," I said, getting up and pushing in my chair.

"Contractions?" Harry asked, his voice shaky.

"I could deliver the baby right here!" Alex announced as I put on my coat.

"That's gross," called an ever-eavesdropping Alice from the next room. She was creeped out by all middle-aged men who were not her father. Admittedly, the thought of Alex poking around my pelvis creeped me out, too.

"Not contractions," I said to Harry. "It's more of a shooting pain from my hip to my foot."

"Sciatica," said Molly and Alex at the same time.

"Sciatica just sounds old," I said. "Can't they call it something else? Like hot-lady leg."

"Whatever," Molly said. "I have moms in my practice way older than you. Besides, you look terrific."

"I'll tell Ludmilla to clear so we can have coffee," Vivian said as she rose and walked into the kitchen, probably to breathe into a paper bag.

"I'll be back," I said. I walked out into the yard and stared at Vivian's winterized flower beds and the spots where her roses and trellises stood in the spring. I sat down on a stone bench and closed my eyes, trying to clear my mind. If I was going to do a live Thanksgiving Day chat with my readers, I needed someplace nobody would find me. I knew Harry would come up to our room in search of a tryptophan nap, so I walked in through the back door and grabbed my laptop. I headed up a flight of stairs and down the hallway to Vivian's room. I pushed open the bedroom door and entered her enormous closet. Surrounded by a sea of pinks, with the odd beige or gray thrown in for good measure, I sat on a blush ottoman in the center of the closet and looked around at all of Vivian's clothes, shoes, hats, and purses, and then I saw it. Perched on a shelf above a row of block heels was the tiara Vivian wore to her wedding. I slid over the moving ladder, tested my weight on the bottom rung, and climbed to retrieve it.

Once back down, I grabbed a mink stole that Vivian still insisted on wearing, wrapped it around myself, and placed the tiara on my head. I looked at myself in the triptych mirror. I assumed Vivian's posture, squaring my shoulders, raising my chin slightly, and putting my right foot forward. I was pretty sure the Dutchess did not wear stained UGG boots, or any UGG boots for that matter, so I slipped them off and walked over to Vivian's shoes. Her feet were smaller than mine, but not so small that I couldn't squeeze myself into a pair of her gold boudoir slippers with a white marabou tuft in the front. With the slippers on my feet, I smiled at myself in the mirror. The Dutchess smiled back at me.

I sat on the tuft, opened my computer, and saw an email from my mother. She had attached a picture of herself in front of Big Ben under a surprisingly blue London sky. Not long ago, I'd thought that kind of travel wasn't far off for Harry and me. Now, I wasn't so sure. Europe and childless voyages would have to wait. Speaking of which, I rubbed my belly and shifted the baby's leg off my pelvis. I reread the email from Andy with chat instructions, then logged on to the *Uptowner* site and opened the Q and A.

> Greetings, readers, the Dutchess here! Looking forward to answering your questions!

There was already a list of questions in the queue, the first of which were pretty dull.

> Jenny: What's your least favorite thing about living in Dutchess?
>
> Dutchess: Easy. KOMBUCHA.
>
> MimiR: When is the best season to visit?
>
> Dutchess: Anytime but winter. It's cold, bare, and unless you like mulled cider, snow drifts, and competitive wreath hanging, it's also pretty boring.

(I obviously had no idea what winter in Dutchess was like, not having lived through it yet.)

> Layla: What are your favorite local eateries or coffee shops?
>
> Dutchess: Eateries? Who even uses that word? I'm a diner coffee girl all the way.

At some point, I worried that this chat was going nowhere fun, but after a few more innocent questions, the tone shifted.

> Ginny: Is it just the women sleeping around in Dutchess? What about the men? Has the Duke drifted?
>
> Dutchess: Darling, that's three questions, but I'm in a generous mood. Maybe, maybe, and absolutely not!
>
> Denny: Just how many of your friends are sleeping with their yoga instructors and paying for it with candles?
>
> Dutchess: I know better than to implicate my friends! Trust me, nobody in the Dutchess's inner circle is doing anything like this.
>
> AnnieG: Have you ever cheated?
>
> Dutchess: Not interested!
>
> NYCMickey: Well, assuming you did, would you go younger?
>
> Dutchess: I'm not sure I could get naked in front of a man with fewer wrinkles and less body fat than I have.

I had to laugh as I typed, because I was pretty much doing that on a regular basis.

BrooklynSuki: Switching gears—if you could eat any dessert made in the Valley, which would it be?

Nice, Suki. Way to cool off the conversation. I was listing a few desserts she'd told me about, in addition to a couple of the vegan delicacies we'd sampled together, when I saw another suspiciously familiar name pop up.

PigkillPeggy: Do you have any kids? How many, and how old are they?

Dutchess: Without going into too many details—yes, a few of them, and some of them are old enough to read this.

I hoped this would throw the Peggys of Pigkill off my trail and made no mention of the accidental baby currently lodging its feet in my ribs. I stood up and swiveled my hips, hoping for some relief. As I sat back down, another round of questions popped up.

NancyInNYC: Do you worry that you're ruining people's reputations just for a laugh?

MomUpstate: Who's the prime Chore Donkey offender? Are her initials CP?

I flinched in shock and missed the ottoman entirely, landing on the closet floor. Sprawled next to the ottoman, I panicked. Who was this? Was it one of the Coven, or even worse, Cynthia herself? Reaching over to my computer, my hands shaking, I typed: No names, sweeties! Then I began to scroll through some questions looking for something milder.

"Bells, what on earth are you doing?"

I looked up and saw Vivian. Even worse, she saw me, sprawled on the floor of her closet. My heaving belly was wrapped in her fur, my swollen feet squeezed into her shoes, and my enormous hair shoved under her wedding tiara.

"I'm writing."

She took a step closer to me. "What are you writing?"

"A blog." I rolled onto all fours and pushed myself up to standing. I faced Vivian and wiped sweat off my forehead.

"Why are you writing a blog in my closet? Better yet, why are you writing a blog in my closet wearing my clothes?"

"Because I'm supposed to be royal."

"Why are you supposed to be royal?" Her voice softened into an unfamiliar tone. "What's going on, Bells?" She motioned, and we both sat on the ottoman.

"I'm the Dutchess," I whispered. "I'm the County Dutchess."

"You're the woman they were talking about? The blogger?"

I nodded.

"You write about the women in your town? Your friends?"

"They're not my friends, and yes." I heard new questions pinging on my computer.

"Does Harry know about this?"

"No."

"None of it?"

I shook my head.

"Are you planning on telling him?"

"Yes, I'm just waiting for the right time."

"I see," she said, smoothing out her hair and surveying the mess I'd made in her closet.

"It's really still pretty small potatoes . . . ," I said.

"Well, I suppose it's not a bad thing to have something for yourself, no matter how small it is."

I nodded.

"And those baby years are long and lonely."

I nodded some more.

"Besides," she went on, "you don't want to find yourself years from now with nothing to do but attend irrelevant meetings and worry about your children."

"I wouldn't want that," I said. I thought about her appearing on my doorstep on her way to meetings she did not want to attend, committees on which she did not want to sit, volunteer work that did not seem to inspire her.

"Who would?" she whispered. She opened a drawer, took out a jeweled brooch, and pinned it to my collar. "There," she said. "Now you look like royalty."

We sat in silence, staring at each other.

"I'll bet you're good at it," she added. "Funny."

"I am."

"And now you get to be a real writer."

"I do."

"And you get to prove your mother wrong." She smiled. We both did.

Vivian got up and walked to the closet door.

"If it's yours," she said, "if it's all yours, keep it."

I nodded some more.

"Be careful, though. Harry really needs this tenure."

"I will be," I promised.

"Oh, and hang up the mink when you're done."

-19-

Hudson Mom of Six: Counting My Blessings, Ten Toes at a Time

WHO IS THE COUNTY DUTCHESS?

I don't usually comment on other bloggers here, unless I'm reposting their adorable family pics or sharing household tips I wish I'd thought of myself. Also, having six kids (#blessings!) keeps me too busy to read lots of other blogs, especially gossipy ones.

But this woman is on my turf.

We don't know who the County Dutchess really is. We just know she's a gossipmonger who claims to live up here in the Hudson Valley and blogs on the website of some big-city paper. (Not *that* big-city paper. It's one you've never heard of, and not that there's anything wrong with it, but it's *free*.)

She delivers all the usual stereotypes about life in the Valley: food fairs, farm stands, helicopter moms (guilty as charged!), and trendy people moving up from Brooklyn. (Which she could totally be making up from her living room in the city—cliché much?)

What does she write about? Good question.

The County Dutchess doesn't post useful cleaning tips or easy and cheap recipes, and she doesn't share supercute craft projects.

This woman, who may or may not be real, is gabbing about all the dirty things she says moms are doing up here in Dutchess. *Really* dirty things. The kinds of things that should never be happening, and should definitely not be blogged about by someone else.

I won't post a link because I don't want to give her the satisfaction of a trillion of my followers heading over to her mean-spirited blog. You guys are just gonna have to trust me.

As for trusting the Dutchess, if she's fake, she's lame, and if she's real, this woman should be ashamed of herself. There's enough nastiness out there in the world. We should be putting the goodness back in.

That's what I try to do each and every day—with my DH, my kids (blessings!), and my community—which includes all of you.

Who is the County Dutchess? I don't know. But we don't need more toxic web drama in our lives. Tune her out, my dear followers, and choose light, goodness, and homemade cookies instead.

#blessed,

Hudson Mom of Six

~

New York Magazine, Hudson Valley Edition

Local Woman Dishes on Life in Dutchess

Just when you thought blogs were passé, a woman up in the Hudson Valley is putting them back on the map. You can find the County Dutchess on the *Uptowner*'s website, where a Dutchess native is scooping out local gossip. According to the Dutchess, local moms are hooking up with millennials using task apps. Andy Garfinkel, the *Uptowner*'s editor, is closely guarding the Dutchess's identity but says she was born from a "great interest in all the Hudson Valley." True, the Valley is all the rage for foodies, day-trippers, and city people with cash to summer somewhere other than Central Park. "Still," he says, "we never expected it to take off the way she did. Our web traffic has gone through the roof." When pressed, Garfinkel admits that while the blog was born from a desire to read about life up in Dutchess, its popularity is really fueled by an interest in "all things mommy wars." He adds, "At the end of the day, people like to read about the mean girls who grew up and became moms behaving badly—wherever they live."

~

To: Bells
From: Suki
Subject: You showed up on a foodie blog!

The Dutchess Eaters

There's More Than One Kind of Dish in the Hudson Valley!

Folks, I know we usually limit our discussion to in-season eating and farm-to-table living, but there is something we need to discuss: WHO IS THE COUNTY DUTCHESS?

A mysterious woman is blogging right here in Dutchess County, and she's not blogging about chanterelles. The County Dutchess, as she calls herself, is doing a different kind of dishing. We heard that the women of her town (we don't know which one yet, but we have our suspicions) are using the Chore Donkey app to find hot, younger men under the guise of needing help around the house. When these ladies want extra help (wink, wink), they pay for it in high-end groceries and artisanal wares, which the young men can exchange for cash. That way, everyone's tracks are covered.

Are we surprised this happens? Not really.

Are we shocked someone had the nerve to go public? Kind of.

Who are you, County Dutchess? And if you're feeling brave, we'd love to have you guest blog and tell us what food fuels you!

—Cathy and Eve (The Dutchess Eaters, www.DutchessEaters.com)

~

Suki: YOU NEED TO GO ON TWITTER RIGHT NOW. #WhoIsTheCountyDutchess

Me: Please tell me you're kidding.

Suki: No! GO!

Sure enough, there I was trending, albeit at the bottom of the list. People were retweeting the *New York* magazine article, Cathy and Eve's post, Meegan's blog, and blogs I hadn't seen yet, all with the hashtag #WhoIsTheCountyDutchess.

What if it's my wife? #WhoIsTheCountyDutchess

Who knew all the action was happening upstate? #ILoveNY #WhoIsTheCountyDutchess

Come for the apples, stay for the illicit sex. #WhoIsTheCountyDutchess

I feel so boring. I just use Chore Donkey to assemble Ikea furniture. #WhoIsTheCountyDutchess

Will definitely be trading in my overpriced artisanal candle for hot millennial sex. #WhoIsTheCountyDutchess

~

Statement from Shayna Ewing, CEO of Chore Donkey

While we are more than happy that men and women nationwide are using Chore Donkey to improve the quality of their lives, we do not, in any way, condone the use of the app for any sort of sex.

~

The *New York Post's Page Six*

Chore Donkey CEO Shayna Ewing steps down when affair with neighbor is revealed, especially in light of the app's recent implication in a Dutchess County affair scandal.

-20-

It's hard to describe exactly what it feels like to be terrified of recognition and at the same time slowly begin to crave it so intensely that you can think about nothing else. If only I had been willing to stop at that point. If only I had been willing to hide out at home and wait for this storm to die down. But that small taste of recognition had fed something in me, and instead of filling me up, it only left me ravenous for more. I spent several nights googling myself, and the only results that came up for "Elsbeth Cohn" were my wedding announcement and some articles from the *Uptowner*, which a total of thirty-six people had liked. (I had written for the *Uptowner* using both my full first name and my maiden name on the off chance that my mother would approve, but I don't need to explain how well that worked out for me.) The Dutchess, however, was another matter. I downloaded an app that kept track of my social media mentions, and when I saw a graph with an upward-surging arrow, I concluded that if the Dutchess wasn't blogging, neither Elsbeth Cohn nor Bells Walker counted.

~

A few days after Thanksgiving, I dropped the kids off at school, then parked in front of Joey's diner. I walked a few streets over to Roast and Reefer, where I confirmed my hunch. Cynthia, Peggy, Anna, and Meegan sat crouched around a bleached-wood table by the window.

They looked like they were deep in conversation but also wore the comfort of women who sit in the same seats around the same table almost every day. My first reaction to the whiff of exclusion was to run home and stay there, my head buried deep in a recipe for cinnamon buns. But instead, I closed my eyes and reminded myself of the mission: information. The cinnamon buns would have to wait.

"Hi, guys," I said, feigning surprise when I walked past their table.

"Hello, Bells," drawled Cynthia, looking genuinely surprised to see me. "We haven't seen *you* in here before. What's the rule on pregnancy and CBD coffee?" She smirked, looking around the table for approval and getting it quickly as the other women grinned their support and devotion.

"I'm pretty sure it's a no go. But I'm here for the . . . croissants," I said, praying that this place actually sold croissants. I scanned the pastry shelf and saw four on a white cake stand.

"That's nice," Anna said. "When you're on the other side of this pregnancy, make sure you try the coffee. It's the best in town."

I looked on the specials board, squinted, and saw **Flights of Coffee** written in chalk. I had no idea what a flight of coffee was, but I made a note to find out.

"Would you like to join us?" Cynthia asked in a way that made it clear to me that she could think of nothing less pleasing than the thought of me joining them.

"No, thanks. I'm more of a diner coffee girl myself," I said, suddenly remembering that this was something the Dutchess had said in the Q and A. I felt my face prickle with panic and strained to examine their expressions—were they doing the math in their heads? Had they already figured me out?

Given that not one of them offered to pull up a chair for me, I wasn't about to wait around to find out.

"Enjoy your day," I said. I bought a croissant (I suppose every cloud has a silver lining) and walked out. I popped into the diner, had an egg cream with Joey, who still did not look anywhere near as pregnant as I did, then walked back to Fulbright, pulled out my phone, and googled "flight of coffee." I learned that a flight is a sampling of something, usually served on a wooden tray that looks like it's made from a piece of driftwood. Flights started with whiskey and then wine, but you could now get a flight of salami, olives, cheese, and yes, even coffee.

Sometimes this stuff just wrote itself.

~

Flights of Fancy

Sometimes I have to wonder if we Dutchess denizens want people to make fun of us. While out for dinner with the Duke last week, I asked for the daily specials and was offered a "flight of cheese." I was once again reminded that I am just about the last person to learn about food crazes because a flight of cheese is not what happens when a dairy product goes airborne. No, a flight is what happens when you want to eat something but can't decide exactly what you want, and moreover, you're convinced that the best way to consume that thing is to only have two small bites of it. Oh, and you'd like it presented on a large piece of tree bark.

People, it's a sampling. It's what Costco has been doing for free since forever. But up here, a sampling of salami just doesn't have the same je ne sais quoi as a flight of cured meats.

And speaking of flights or flying high, you may not be able to find any Splenda in the hipper corners of the Hudson Valley, but if you are looking for a bevy of beverages infused with CBD—which the locals assure me is not marijuana, only marijuana adjacent—then you are in luck. You can't throw a stone up here in the Valley without hitting a CBD-infused tea, coffee, or energy drink. The locals and the recently arrived can't stop touting all the many health benefits, and as much as I'd love to rid myself of hay fever, anxiety, lower-back pain, and ten extra pounds, I think I'll have to pass for now. Come back to me when you can put it in a milkshake, or better yet, a malt, and then I may be interested.

~

I stared hard at the third paragraph and considered deleting the entire post. I felt myself flying too close to the sun, dropping in facts and hints that could eventually be traced back to me. If I published it, I was playing with the worst kind of fire—the ire of women scorned by other women. But if I hit the brakes and didn't publish it, I risked having the Dutchess slide off into the sunset, read by nobody, discussed by nobody, tweeted by nobody.

Looking back, I want to be able to say I wasn't thinking straight, that my brain was a dangerous combination of pregnancy and middle-aged addled, a mixture that does not make for sound decision-making. But I knew what I was doing. I closed my eyes, and I saw the way those women looked at me, how they dismissed me. I saw the kids and all they had at stake, and Harry and all the things he so desperately needed to happen, and I still did it. I did it because I was so hungry for significance. I was starving to matter, and that outweighed any consequences I could contemplate.

~

A few days later, I met Suki at Ferment, a new place she was reviewing dedicated to all things pickled. I gazed at the parchment-paper menu. I would have much rather eaten burgers and fries or just about anything, but her schedule was tight, and I took what I could get.

"I think I need some help," I said, scanning the restaurant for anyone I knew. "Why would anyone eat a pickled egg?"

"Open your mind." She laughed and called the waitress over.

"We'll have one of each of the appetizers," Suki said to the young woman with a pixie cut and obligatory tiny nose ring, "as well as a kimchi burger, the beet lasagna, and the sauerkraut fajitas."

"Yum," I muttered. The waitress shot me a confused look.

"It's fine," she said. "Just so you know, everything here is pretty much pegan friendly."

I cocked my head to the side.

"That means it's paleo and vegan," Suki whispered, handing the waitress our menus and shooing her away before I could do anything else that screamed middle-aged and out of touch.

I typed some notes into my phone—*ALL THINGS PICKLED.* While I had my phone out, I did a quick scan of Twitter and the blog. Not much activity. The flight piece had not taken off.

"I know you're checking your stats," Suki said, taking a sip of the kombucha martini she'd ordered as soon as we sat down. "Stop shielding your phone from me."

"I know," I said, taking a sip of a very boring sparkling water with lime. "I can't stop myself. It's like for a few minutes I feel calm and content, but then it wears off and I need to check it again. The worst part is that there's not much to check—I'm barely registering right now." I threw my phone down in disgust.

"Bells, you need to listen to me. You can write a snappy send-off if you want, but you really need to walk away from this thing."

"Walk away?"

"When your identity comes out, and it eventually will because everything always does, you will have an army of really pissed-off women up here."

"I know you don't think these women are that bad, but trust me—they're pretty awful. They have this coming."

"Do you really want awful women gunning for you?" she asked.

I shrugged.

"Here's the thing," Suki said, not giving up. "Being friends with the moms of your kids' friends and classmates may not always be fun, but it's necessary." She paused and put down her fork. "Compulsory, even."

"Maybe," I agreed, "but if you tell me that it takes a village, I'll walk—even if it means missing the opportunity to eat a sauerkraut fajita."

As if on cue, the waitress showed up with armfuls of tiny plates. I glazed over while she described the differences between the appetizers, which all seemed to be variations on a dill pickle.

"Fine." Suki relented. "But that baby is coming soon." She looked right at my heaving middle. "And you're gonna need all the help you can get."

I took a bite of a pickled radish. "The Dutchess is the only thing I have that's mine, and I'm not sure I can give her up," I said. "Especially not if I'm about to descend into the fog of a newborn."

"And Harry?"

"I haven't even told you the worst part," I said, feeling all the vinegar in my pores, as if I myself were starting to pickle. "Some of these women . . . are married to professors."

"At Dutchess?" she whispered, looking a lot more alarmed than I was hoping.

I nodded.

"Bells . . ."

"I know."

"You know what? That this could hurt him?"

"Of course I know that," I said. "But I need this more than I thought I did. There has to be a way for me to keep writing and at the same time make sure Harry doesn't get hurt."

"Then you have to dial her down. Keep focusing on food trends, tourists, things like that. Just stay away from mommy gossip."

In the days that followed, I watched my blog stats fall off a cliff. I checked my mentions app, and even though the Dutchess had been riding high a few weeks ago, I wasn't getting anywhere near the amount of attention I got when I was dishing on sex, candles, and middle-aged moms—what Suki called "mommy gossip." It was becoming clearer to me that while poking fun at hipster eating was good for laughs, it was not driving big numbers for me.

I thought hard about Suki's advice to stick to focusing on food trends and fun facts about the Hudson Valley. I knew she was trying to help me, and a part of me knew she was right. But Suki already had a writing career—people read her work and genuinely wanted to know what she thought. She mattered. It was easy for her to tell me to dial it down from her perch above the food world.

As for the Coven figuring out I was behind this, when nobody put two and two together after the flight piece and came up with me—even though a modicum of research would have revealed that I used to write for the *Uptowner* and stopped right when the Dutchess sprung to life—I took it as a sign that taking risks was just what good writers do, or at the very least, it was what the Dutchess needed to do.

All I needed was a story.

~

I told Harry about our meal at Ferment, which he took as a cue to come home with a bag of winter vegetables and a dozen canning jars. Always a team player, I was stirring a mixture of vinegar and sugar on the stovetop while he stood at the island thinly slicing the vegetables.

"This will be an excellent way for us to continue eating fresh vegetables well into the winter," he said.

I shot him a look.

"Joe Phillips, over in the German department, was the one who first told me about pickling. He's been doing it every year since he was a kid."

I heard the ping of an incoming text and reached into my cardigan pocket for my phone. A reminder from Dr. Ross's office. While I had the phone in my hand, I checked my Google Alerts to see how the Dutchess was doing. A food blogger in Wisconsin was quoting my piece on flights. I felt the momentary warmth of recognition.

"Bells, are you listening to me? Have you heard anything I said?"

I looked up. "Were you saying something?"

"Joe Phillips? German? The pickled apple joke?"

I gave him an apologetic smile.

"Are you even paying attention to me?" he asked.

"Yes, of course," I said, putting the phone facedown on the counter.

"Sometimes I wonder," he said.

"About what?" I asked, not wanting to know the answer to the question. I had zero desire to go down the rabbit hole of my failings as a wife, especially my failings as a faculty wife. I did take a moment to note the irony of the situation—Harry was asking me to take more of an interest in his work, and I was intentionally keeping him in the dark about mine.

"You're right. I'm distracted," I said, picking up the spoon and looking straight at him.

"And you know how important this is, right? You know what tenure would mean to us, to me, to my family?"

I thought about Vivian, who worked so hard to be enthusiastic, struggling to smile when she said the words *assistant professor*, and Harry's brothers not making the kind of jokes about professors they would have made if Harry already had tenure, especially the right kind of tenure, and I wondered if Harry should have reversed that order of importance.

"Harry, I care about your work, and more than anything else, I want you to get tenure. I want the dean to show up with a marching band and place a great big tenure crown on your head." I walked over and wrapped one arm around his waist while running the other hand through his hair. "I don't know what my problem is. Can I blame it on pregnancy brain?"

He looked at me and thought for a moment. "Only if you get a note from Dr. Ross," he finally said. He reached behind him and grabbed a chocolate chip cookie off a plate, offering it to me. "And please don't eat all the cookies."

As for Dr. Ross, I now had an OB visit every two weeks. A few days later, when the doors of Fulbright were frozen shut and I wanted nothing more than to climb under the covers and stay there, I tried to convince her that I was a perfect candidate for bed rest.

She was having none of it.

"What makes you think you need bed rest?" she asked, wrapping a measuring tape around my girth (her word, not mine).

"Look at my ankles," I replied, swinging an engorged leg in her direction. "Have you ever seen anything like this?"

"Actually, I have," she said. "Bells, you're almost at calving season. Swollen ankles are perfectly normal."

I opened my mouth to speak, but she wasn't done yet. Besides, the constant comparison to a farm animal was less offensive now that I was starting to resemble one.

"Not only is bed rest unadvisable, but the best thing you can do is keep moving. And when you're ready to bring on labor, there's nothing like intercourse and a long walk."

I left her office with a prescription for long walks, making sure to keep the intercourse solution to myself. When I told Joey about this, she just smiled and shrugged.

"At least you have someone to do it with," she said, slicing me some rhubarb pie.

I didn't tell Joey that I was having enough sex in my sleep to make up for the drought in my waking hours. That night I woke up from a dream that I'd had for five nights straight. It involved me and Lance, the stove-repairing millennial who knew nothing about stoves but everything about the workings of a pregnant fortysomething body, and it also involved the baker's island. In each dream, I'd responded in kind to Lance's advances, and the next thing I knew, we were getting busy on the giant slab of marble. At some point, we'd pause, take a bite of something I'd baked in the oven (which dream-Lance actually managed to fix), then we'd resume. The dream varied slightly—what I was baking (one night it was a pear-cranberry pie, which I thought might be a good addition to the holiday party menu) and what Lance was wearing (in one dream he was wearing Harry's favorite blazer, after which I could not make eye contact with poor Harry for a full twenty-four hours). I was all but certain that in one of the dreams we did something with the celeriac. In all of the dreams, I was pregnant, which only seemed to add to the heat in the kitchen, and I was doing the sorts of things I had hitherto thought impossible for pregnant women.

I awoke from a particularly saucy dream one night with back pain and climbed out of bed a little after midnight, slightly guilt-ridden and relieved for a moment that Harry was in Chicago at the conference and not gently snoring next to me. I splashed cold water on my face, and knowing that I wouldn't be going back to sleep anytime soon, I checked my stats. They were trending low and getting lower. The only mention I could find of myself was in the comments on Meegan's blog. In response to a piece she'd written on do-it-yourself farmhouse decor, someone had written:

> Love these ideas, especially the vintage laundry signs! And I'm so glad you managed to shut up

> that nasty Dutchess!!! She's gone back to being boring and cliché.

I scanned the local blogs as well as the online *Gazette* for a story—any story—that I could write about. Surely something salacious was happening up here. Someone must be doing something with someone else that would have all the makings of a good post. The only trips of note I'd made were dropping off Sam at his ACT classes, conveniently held in the high school gym, and a simultaneous outing to the Poughkeepsie mall with Alice in search of a onesie. The middle school was about to be in the throes of something called Spirit Week, and Monday was Onesie Day, followed by Camo Day, followed by please help me before I die from this stupidity. Alice, Abigail, and Courtney had decided to go as a zebra, panda, and flamingo (that is, until Abigail and Courtney presumably decided to change it up last minute and forget to tell Alice). To my great surprise, we found both a panda onesie and a camouflage sweatshirt dress all in under thirty minutes, which just goes to show you that good things can happen in Poughkeepsie.

We swung back to the high school and sat in Fulbright while we waited for Sam. I glanced over and saw a picture that Alice had just posted of herself trying on the onesie. She already had seventy-five likes (how was that?) but wore a look of panic as she waited for more to come in.

"You may want to obsess less about how much approval you're getting from people who don't know you."

She glanced up from her phone and looked at me blankly. We heard some noise and both looked out the window to see a small cabal of mothers descending on the picnic tables out front. I'd seen this group before, often helmed by a particularly petite mother with a head of very long, very curly hair. This mom, who liked to dress like a teenager, was wearing sparkly sneakers and was chewing gum ferociously while she gesticulated to the group around her.

"I don't understand," I said. "Who are these moms, and what are they doing?"

"Those are the Extra Moms," she said. "They're always together."

"What makes a mom an Extra Mom?"

"It means they do all the extra stuff. In middle school, they decide on the themes for spirit days and come in early to decorate the school. In high school, they're probably the ones who send all those emails you complain about."

In addition to all the band emails, I'd just started getting emails asking me to vote on ways to honor Sam and his soon-to-be senior classmates next year. There were questions about band banners for each senior and requests for baby pictures. (Sam had been born at the time when many of us were still taking pictures with cameras and printing them out, which meant that his baby pictures were in a box in a closet somewhere, and I had a better chance of being on the cover of *Vogue* than I did of finding that box.) The worst email I got was one about something called a Mom Prom. I'm not kidding when I say it would involve me and Sam and a school dance. Delete, delete, delete.

"Oh," Alice said as if suddenly remembering, "the Extra Moms also buy their kids the new phone models as soon as they come out."

"Nice try, sister," I said. "What are you if you're not an Extra Mom?"

"I dunno. Basic?"

Sam climbed into the car, his hair tucked behind his ears.

"How was it?" I asked.

"Average," he said. Alice winked at me.

~

Extra! Extra! Get Me Out of Here!

Dutchess County is home to some of the best egg creams in the state, micro-batch ice cream, something called bean-to-bar chocolate, and the Extra Mom.

The Extra Mom helms all the detritus that comes with having a child in school. I'm not talking about packed lunches, school supplies, or even field trips, which I previously thought of as the extra stuff of school. No, up here, the Extra Moms do things like coordinate Spirit Week, which is no more than five days of theme dressing, complete with Onesie Day, Camo Day, and Crazy Hair Day, and which forces a certain mom (ahem) to drive several towns over for an animal onesie because she forgot about Spirit Week and it's too late to order one online. These moms are also behind the mid-December emails asking other moms to sign up to decorate the gym for Spring Fling because "spring has a way of creeping up on us." (I really don't know where I was when it was a parent's job to do anything in a gym other than show up and occasionally clap.)

The zeal of the Extra Mom reaches a fever pitch senior year, when grown women can be found ordering matching T-shirts and helping their children decorate their cars for Senior Drive-Around Day. Every time I think about this, my head hurts. It hurts so much that I don't think I'll tell you about the Mom Prom, which is a senior-year dance for mothers and sons. There's also the Pop Hop, so daughters and dads don't feel left out in the cold, and if this is all a little too *Flowers in the Attic* for you, you can take a seat next to me.

I know I've written about the college-frenzied moms and the dust cloud of panic that follows them around. But the Extra Moms, dressed like teenagers and perpetually energized, are something else. With the college moms, there's an endgame—an overhyped and overrated endgame, but an endgame. What's in it for the Extra Moms? A solution to boredom, a need to feel needed, included? A desire to relive high school, or maybe live it better this time around?

To use the lingo of the young people around me, if you're not an Extra Mom, you're a Basic Mom, and frankly, basic sounds just fine to me.

Basically yours,

The Dutchess

~

I proofread the entry a few times, sent it off to Andy, then got down on all fours. I arched and rounded my back for some relief. At some point, I climbed back into bed, hoping to avoid another dream that would have me naked on the island with Lance and some micro-sprouts. I needed to get Lance and his sprouts out of my head, and if I was being perfectly honest, I needed to briefly forget about the Dutchess. In a matter of hours, some of the women I'd been trashing online would be eating sugar cookies and pear-cranberry pie in my home. I had bigger, more terrifying fish to fry.

-21-

Vivian always said that when throwing any party or event, you have to know that three things will go wrong. The trick was to keep calm and count them off.

The first thing happened the day before the party.

Harry came back from Chicago buoyed by his success.

"They loved me," he said, hanging up his shirts. "I got several RFPs." (Requests for publication. Basically the academic's version of crazy online stats.)

"That's great," I said, sitting up in bed and scanning my own numbers on my laptop. My Extra Mom piece had been just the boost I needed, and my numbers were climbing. Andy told me that *New York* magazine had contacted him again and asked if I'd guest-write a column on competitive parenting. #WhoIsTheCountyDutchess was back up and running amok on Twitter. Even Meegan's minions had noticed. One tagged both of us in a tweet: Looks like the Dutchess is at it again, trashing moms who pick up the slack for lazy moms like her. @ HudsonMomofSix @TheCountyDutchess

"And I've been asked to speak at other conferences."

"Wow."

"Two in Europe."

"Amazing."

"And one on Mars."

"Nice try," I said, looking up at him. "I'm listening."

"You may be listening, but you don't sound interested."

"Aren't we about to have half the college in our home? How much more interested could I be?"

"Why do you say it like that?"

"Like what?"

"Like you don't want to have this party."

"Because I don't want to have this party." The words got out before I could even register them, and they hung over me.

Harry didn't look anywhere near as surprised as I thought he'd be. "Bells, weren't things supposed to be different here?"

"What are you saying?"

He sat on the edge of the bed and looked straight at me. "I'm saying that this wasn't supposed to be like the city. You were going to make an effort here." *You weren't going to fall suddenly ill an hour before a cocktail party or get there and stand in the corner and talk to the one person you know. You weren't going to forget the names of the people I work with or look visibly bored while I talk about the politics of my job.*

I opened my mouth to ask him if he really blamed me for what happened in the city, if he truly believed that I was the reason he hadn't gotten tenure. But I wasn't sure I wanted his answer, and even more, I wanted to play it safe. I knew that any minute now Harry could find out about the Dutchess's blog. I was counting on his well-established self-involvement to keep him away from a mommy blog about the housewives of the Hudson Valley, because as soon as Harry read a few entries, he'd know I'd done something a lot worse than be apathetic about a holiday party.

"I'm doing the best I can, Harry," I said—words that may not have been that far from the truth. "Even if my best isn't always good enough."

And because Harry Walker is a good, albeit slightly self-involved, man, he knelt in front of me, took my hands in his, and accepted my apology.

~

The second thing that happened was my dress. I had an outfit picked out—the only dress in which I felt somewhat human. The night before the party, I tried to squeeze into it and was sure there must have been some mistake. Only days ago it had fit, even if snugly. I was sure my weight had finally plateaued, especially because for the first time in months I wasn't ravenous (probably because my stomach was now the size of a dime). I wrapped the dress around my midsection and tried to cross it, but the panels would not stretch over my stomach or boobs. I tried on two more dresses and then collapsed into a sobbing heap.

I was still crying in the ill-fitting dress when Sam walked in.

"Mom, are you OK? Are you having the baby?" he asked, panic rising in his voice.

"I'm fine," I said, wiping snot on my sleeve. "I just can't find anything to wear."

And then this boy, this boy who had just spent months pulling away from me so that I'd presumably miss him less when he inevitably left me, this boy lowered his lanky frame down next to me and rubbed my back.

"You know you look great in anything," he whispered.

"We both know that's not true," I sniffled.

"What does it even matter?" he asked. "You've worked so hard for this party. Why don't you just throw on a hoodie and enjoy it?"

"A hoodie?"

"Yeah, I'll lend you a big one, and you can wear it over your dress. Nobody will notice."

I looked at him and cried even harder.

"What's wrong?" he asked.

"It's easier for me when you're being obnoxious," I said. "Then I don't worry about missing you when you go."

Sam just smiled. And the three of us sat there on the floor in front of my closet—me, my first baby, and the baby who was getting ready to make an appearance. That appearance would be the third thing that went wrong.

-22-

Sam was right. I could have worn a gingham tablecloth to the holiday party and nobody would have noticed. Harry invited about forty faculty and spouses, mostly from the English department, but he'd also invited faculty who lived in Pigkill, which meant the Planks and Peggy and her husband, Kevin, a sociology professor with an unsettling mustache. It also meant Meegan and her husband, Alec, a historian who specialized in the Gilded Age, before there were Ziploc bags and giant store-bought marshmallows.

Alice and Sam swung into a rare, helpful gear. I must have really freaked Sam out the night before, because he and Alice were falling all over themselves to pass trays and pick up empty cups. I watched them float in between the guests and basked in the glow of their helpfulness. My kids may be mediocre students who do very little around the house when nobody is watching, but look at them now!

I had also hired Chuck, a last-minute bartender, hours before the party. He may have been the strangest-looking person I'd ever seen—which made me sure I'd spooked the hot millennials on all the task apps. Each time I booked someone, a few minutes later I'd get a cancellation. When Chuck agreed to bartend, I was too excited to look at his picture. If I would have looked, I'd have seen that Chuck looked like a human goat, and not in a hot Narnia way—more like a large, hairy beast come to life as a twentysomething with ill-placed facial hair.

With Chuck behind the bar and the kids circulating with the food, I was able to spend my time hiding in the garage kitchen, making sure the baked goods were coming out on schedule. In addition to everything I'd put out on Vivian's shabby-chic dining room table, I also planned a series of circulating desserts, ending with small pots of molten chocolate, which may have screamed 1995, but which kept me in the kitchen until they were ready to go—a good move given that every time I emerged from the kitchen, I had the telltale sensation that everyone was talking about me.

The room was swimming in what I was sure was nervous chatter. If I listened to the whispers, I swore I could hear the words *the Dutchess*. Cynthia and Peggy were conspicuously huddled in the corner between the tufted couch and the potbelly stove, their drinks resting on one of the three midcentury teak end tables Harry proudly brought home from an antique store in Beacon. (He'd marched each one into the house, discussed its provenance, and polished it with a mixture he'd made in an amber glass spray bottle I'd never before seen.)

I floated past Cynthia and Peggy once or twice, but each time they dropped their voices and smiled weakly. As was their practice, they were dressed in almost matching outfits, Cynthia's always slightly more fabulous—her jeans a little skinnier, her heels a little more kitten. They were both sporting shirts with the shoulders cut out, a truly unfortunate trend I was ready to see go the way of peplum, which I assumed both these ladies were wearing a few years ago.

I was nervous, but I also felt strangely powerful. These people were chattering, possibly about me—the incredible growing woman who'd holed up in this rickety house and eaten her way through an interminable pregnancy. It didn't matter that I was so large I had to tape my dress shut and wear my teenager's hoodie over it. I counted. I mattered.

Halfway through the party, after consuming what I assumed were a few snowballs (Harry's cocktail of choice, in a move he considered both hip and retro and partly inspired by his precious end tables), Cynthia pulled me over to her corner.

"Nice party," she slurred.

"Thanks," I said, trying to think of a reason to extricate myself and suddenly wishing I was wearing something other than this enormous gray hoodie with a giant fist on the front.

"Have you heard?" Peggy asked, cradling a drink. "Some bitch is blogging about all of us, which is probably why you could only get the hunchback of Notre Dame to bartend for you."

So I hadn't gone mad. People really were talking about the Dutchess. "Come again?" I asked.

"You haven't read her?" Cynthia asked, eyeing her husband, who was only a few feet away.

I shook my head, too afraid to open my mouth. I didn't have to say anything because Cynthia nudged me and winked in the direction of Cathy Moore, head of the creative writing program, who was engaged in a full-on make-out session with her husband.

"Look at them," she said. "I don't know why they bother leaving the house."

"My mother always told me that couples who make out in public don't go anywhere near each other at home." I laughed.

"Or maybe they have something to hide," Cynthia jeered. "Nobody will suspect Cathy Moore of sleeping around if she's all over her husband in public."

I was dying to ask them both a million questions: How had they first heard about the Dutchess? How many people in Pigkill were realistically reading her? But what I really wanted was their list of suspects.

"I'm not much of a blog reader," I said, bringing the subject back to the Dutchess. "So I haven't heard of her."

"We thought it was Lacrosse Mom at first, but she's just as mad about it as we are. Anyway, whoever she is, she's a terrible writer," Peggy said. "Don't bother."

"Unless you want to read a bunch of trash talk about half the people in this room," Cynthia said, taking a gulp of her drink. "She just made fun of the moms who show up and do all the extra shit that nobody else wants to do. But that woman is playing with some serious fire—those moms are fierce. Let's just hope she or her spouse don't have any college affiliation, because if so, they're going down."

I opened my mouth to say something but thought better of it and popped a cheese puff inside. I mumbled something about ice buckets and rushed back through the house. I walked through the yard and felt a few snowflakes fall. For a moment I envisioned all the guests getting stuck here in a storm and thought about jumping into Fulbright while I could and getting far away.

I was in the kitchen, both wondering what Lacrosse Mom had that I didn't (had I even been a suspect?) and trying to convince myself that I had not gone and firebombed Harry's career. My back started to hurt again, so I took a seat at the kitchen table and was plating some more cheese puffs when Harry walked in. He didn't look happy.

"Why are you in here?" he asked.

I felt a jolt of pain surge down my right leg. "I'm in here because we're hosting a party, and the hostess is often in the kitchen. It's not my fault the kitchen is on the other side of a snowy yard." I breathed through the pain.

"I'm confused," he said, not looking at all confused. "You say you spent weeks, almost months, preparing for this party—and yet you still have to spend most of the evening in the kitchen?"

"Why are you so upset?" I asked, wondering for a moment if Harry had sensed the tension in the room. I quickly reminded myself that reading a room accurately was not Harry's thing.

"Do you really not know?"

"Let me plate these puffs and I'll come out. I'll mingle, I promise." I took a few more deep breaths and stood up, stretching out my lower back by bending over a chair.

"You make it sound like it's a chore."

"Harry, it *is* a chore. You know that about me. It doesn't mean I don't care. It doesn't mean I'm not making an effort." Damn, this pain was intense.

"And that sweatshirt?" he asked, his hands planted on the table.

I looked down at the giant fist.

"Harry . . ."

"You're trying to tell me that you want to make an effort. That you know how important this is to me, and even though you've known about the date for months, you decide it's OK to host the party wearing Sam's hoodie?"

"I'm hot, my back hurts, I have no clothes that fit, and I'm plating cheese puffs, which I really want to eat more of but which gave me indigestion, because just about everything gives me indigestion."

"I don't want excuses, Bells, I just want you to care."

Just then, a spasm of pain shook me. I gasped. "Are you for real?" I asked when I could get the words out. "How much massaging could you possibly need?"

"What?" Harry looked stunned. "And are you OK?" He made his way over to me.

"This is rich," I said, moving away from him. "I've been baking and freezing round the clock. But all you see is this hoodie, a hoodie I have to wear because I don't have any clothes that fit me. Have you even noticed that? Do you notice anything that has nothing to do with your precious job?"

"I want us to be partners, Bells, and right now it feels like I'm out there hustling alone. And you know how it works. You know you have a part to play."

"Is this you talking, or your mother?" I asked.

"Funny, I could ask you the same thing," he snapped.

I wanted to tell him that I wasn't my mother. Hanna Cohn would never have thrown a party like this for people she didn't like, and she certainly wouldn't have spent months prepping for it while her husband swanned around buying useless end tables and overpriced, obscure vegetables he then expected her to cook.

I would have told him all of this. I would also have told him that I loved him and that I knew I could do better, even if socializing was so much harder for me than it was for just about everyone else in that room, but I couldn't say anything because at that moment, I felt the mother of all back spasms, and my water broke all over the garage kitchen.

-23-

Harry Walker likes an eventful birth. He got the Sturm und Drang of a long, drawn-out, several-days-long labor with Sam and an overdue Alice, who seemed so firmly lodged inside of me that I all but shook her out. In a similar fashion, Steven Theodore Walker, already an eventful baby, came into the world with a dramatic rush of broken water, followed by the longest car ride of my adult life.

While I threw towels down in the garage kitchen, Harry ran through the house until he found Sam and Alice and instructed them to stay calm and help the guests find their coats when they were ready to leave. He then stood in the front hall and announced to everyone that my water had broken but that people didn't need to rush out because there was plenty of food and drink.

I walked around the back of the house and met Sam and Alice by Fulbright. Alice was holding my quilted overnight bag.

"I didn't pack this," I said.

"I know. I did." She smiled. "I figured one of us needs to be prepared." She handed the bag to Harry and hugged me.

"OK, we have to run," Harry said, looking up at the falling snow.

Sam bent over me in an awkward boy hug and whispered "Good luck, Mom" into my ear.

Harry opened the door and heaved me into Fulbright. "I'll see you guys soon," I said, breathing through my first full-on contraction.

Poor Harry was so nervous that he drove through the increasing snowfall apologizing over and over.

"Harry, you didn't do this—you don't need to apologize. I was probably already in labor before the party," I said, remembering the nights of back pain.

But Harry couldn't hear me. He was now repeating "Stay calm" to himself as he missed the exit for the hospital and I winced as another contraction came barreling toward me.

"I really don't want to have this baby in the car," I wailed, worrying that I'd have to tell my mother that we couldn't even get a baby born at the Vassar hospital.

Harry gripped the wheel, turned back, and made the exit. By the time we pulled up to the hospital, I was clinging to the inside door handle and screaming in pain. Harry leaped out of the car and ran around to help me out, not realizing that the keys were in the car and that the car was still in drive and had started to roll forward. I howled until he ran back, put the car in park, and looked around for someone to park the car.

"What are you doing?"

"Looking for a valet!"

"Where do you think we are? There is no valet. Get me inside!"

Harry nodded, ran back around to my door, and with his arms around my middle, pulled me out of the car. At the intake desk, I was shoved into a wheelchair as Harry grabbed a clipboard of forms and followed directions to the delivery room where we were told by a bored-looking receptionist that a nurse would meet us.

Harry eased me out of the wheelchair and onto a bed as I screamed over the pain. "This baby is coming! I need an epidural!"

"There's nobody here yet!" Harry cried, ducking out of the room and coming back in. "You just have to wait a few minutes. Hold my hand and keep breathing. The nurse is on her way."

In that moment, I knew one thing for sure—if I wanted help, I was going to have to scream for it. I rolled onto all fours on the hospital bed and barked at the top of my lungs, "I NEED A NURSE!"

Sure enough, one appeared—a red-headed nurse named Sheila, who called for the anesthesiologist and helped me into a gown. When I was on my back, she promptly checked me and called the anesthesiologist again. "You have to hurry," I heard her say. "She doesn't have much more time."

I breathed and moaned through the contractions until a tall, thin anesthesiologist showed up and helped ease me out of my misery. When I felt like I could see straight, I leaned back in the bed and held Harry's hand.

"Dr. Ross is on her way," Sheila said, checking me again, but when I was ready to push, Dr. Ross was nowhere to be found.

"It may be a while," Sheila said, wincing. "Dr. Ross is delivering a foal on her . . ."

"Oh, for god's sake," I screamed. "This baby is coming! I'm ready to push!"

Sheila motioned for Harry to grab one of my legs while she took the other, at which point Harry Walker, who hitherto had been clutching my hand and apologizing at the side of the bed, realized he was about to fulfill one of his lifelong dreams.

He was going to help deliver this baby.

He looked at me. "You've got this," he said, grinning, wearing an enormous this-is-my-moment expression.

When the time came, I bore down, and a few pushes later, Sheila, Harry, and I delivered an appropriately surprised-looking baby boy with a shock of the Cohn hair, and just like that, Steven Theodore Walker made his entrance. Harry cut the cord and then burst into tears.

I held the baby on my chest, looked down at his dark hair, and for what felt like the first time in almost nine months, I exhaled.

~

Two days in the hospital turned out to be just what the doctor ordered. I basked in the glory of forty-eight hours off my feet, a cold drink, and a bowl of oatmeal only a nurse's call away. Also, if I can ever afford it, I will buy a big boxy machine that churns out nothing but crushed ice, the kind of ice I've only ever had in the hospital after giving birth, and the kind of ice that would—almost—make me want to do it all over again.

The children made an appearance the morning after I delivered.

"What kind of name is Steven?" asked Alice, taking a variety of selfies, most of which only featured the baby in the background, and none of which featured me.

"It was my father's name, and you know it," said Harry, gazing at a swaddled Steven, whom he had picked up and refused to put down, only relinquishing him to me for feedings.

"Yeah, I knew that," she said, puckering for another picture. "But isn't it super old-fashioned?"

"Yes, and we like that," I added, chewing a mouthful of ice. "Besides, Alice and Sam aren't exactly hipster names."

"I guess so, but Steven seems so . . ."

"Weird," Sam remarked, fiddling with the remote to the large hospital TV fixed to the far wall of the room, a room I had to share with absolutely nobody. Sam was present but refused to make eye contact with me or the baby. Mostly, he was terrified that by looking at me, he ran the risk of seeing an enormous nipple, or even worse, that at any moment I'd spread my legs and squeeze out another baby.

"We can call him Stevie," I said, watching Sam flip through the lunch options and click on his choices—a chicken Caesar salad and sweet potato fries. (The last time I had a baby, I was given a piece of paper and a golf pencil and told to circle my meal choices.)

"We will absolutely not call him Stevie," announced Vivian, who'd materialized within hours after I delivered wearing a lilac cashmere twinset and bearing several personalized outfits for a baby whose gender she'd only just learned.

I wasn't sure what we were going to call him, but it was hard not to feel something each time Vivian choked up saying the baby's name. It was entirely possible that I had made Vivian truly happy, and I wasn't going to risk it by calling the baby Stevie, at least not in front of her.

I'd texted some pictures to Suki and my sisters-in-law. I sent one of the baby to Joey with the words YOU ARE NEXT! She responded with an emoji I'd never seen before and didn't really understand, but I suspected it may have been a nervous face.

My mother texted from San Francisco, where she was attending a conference, probably for women in their sixties who openly disapprove of their daughters:

> I won't make it to the hospital. I'll see you when you get home. Mazel tov.

Once Harry left to drive Sam and Alice home, rejecting Sam's request to drive because he was all of two weeks into driving school, Vivian walked over and sat next to me. I wondered if this was the moment she'd take me in her arms and tell me that if only she'd had a daughter like me, her life would have been complete, or that out of all her daughters-in-law, she loved me best of all.

"I have to go, too," she said. "I just wanted to say one thing while I have you alone."

I smiled and gave her my hand to hold.

"You need to stop the blogging," she whispered.

"But I thought you said . . . in the closet?" I stammered, pulling back my hand.

"You said it was all just small potatoes, Bells," she replied. "These potatoes don't seem very small anymore. By offending the women in your town, even the annoying ones, you're putting Harry's job at risk. Do you want to be responsible for derailing his career when he's finally so close to tenure?"

I shook my head.

"You can still write, Bells. You just need to write about something else." Vivian paused, as if thinking for a moment, as if she hadn't rehearsed this entire conversation twenty times on her drive up. "Maybe you can write about being an older mom with teenage children and a baby? That could be funny."

Having Suki and Vivian give me the same advice for the first time in my life should have been something of a sign. But what both women didn't know was that nobody wanted to read about the harried reality of midlife parenting. They didn't want to read about invisibility, self-doubt, and comfort eating. They wanted saucy, interesting, and sexy.

They wanted the Dutchess.

-24-

In the city, I had babies in isolation. The Upper West Side may be a neighborhood, but it is not a community—at least it wasn't one for me. When Sam and Alice were born, my mother sent me some of her favorite take-out meals, all of which had scant fat content and absolutely no taste. Vivian sent Ludmilla over with a batch of Polish food, which seemed to be about 80 percent potato. Other than that, I was basically on my own.

In Pigkill, I was expected to board something called the meal train. Days after my return home, the emails and texts and then the calls started coming in.

Cynthia: Bells—Congrats on your newest addition. The PTA would love to organize meals for you! Any allergies? Dislikes? Preferences?

Peggy: Bells—the DCSA (Dutchess College Spouse Association) is planning on sending you some meals. (See the meal train login info.) If you have any allergies, please let us know by 5 p.m. tomorrow, and CONGRATULATIONS from your Dutchess family!

I didn't respond to any of the emails or texts, and the meals arrived anyway. Apparently I had been living under a very large urban rock when the casserole upped its game, because we were suddenly awash in one-dish suppers, many that involved quinoa, farro, wheat berries, and yes, the occasional chanterelle.

One afternoon, I opened the front door and found Cynthia standing in front of me, a casserole in one hand and a tie-dye tote bag in the other. She was wearing a thick down coat, a red hat with earflaps, and fingerless gloves. Her nails were done.

"I brought you some new-baby goodies." She smiled, offering up her wares and stepping inside. She put down the tote and, with her spare hand, offered to swap me her casserole for a baby. I made the trade. The dish was still warm.

"It's one of Meegan's recipes," she said, cradling Steven.

I wondered which of Meegan's most recent posts this could be—the mac-and-three-cheese, the Chinese chicken bake she'd made with frozen Birds Eye vegetables, or the curry made with whatever coconut milk she'd been promoting.

"I just love a new baby," she breathed, leaning over and inhaling.

"It's very nice of you to bring me food," I said, counting the seconds until she left. If only I'd been hungry enough to eat any of it.

In the first days of Sam and Alice, I'd been ravenous. Never one to suffer from a small appetite, breastfeeding ignited a hunger in me that was virtually impossible to fill. But with Steven, I could barely bring myself to start, let alone finish, a plate of food. After a few bites, my throat would close, and I fought to swallow. I threw out so many uneaten plates of food that at some point I shoved the incoming casseroles into the fridge and left it to Harry and the kids to eat them, fueling myself with the occasional protein bar.

But it wasn't just the lack of appetite that marked those first weeks with Steven. All new mothers are told to sleep while their babies sleep, and although I'd initially been unable to sleep with Sam, spending hours staring at him while he slept, marveling at my good fortune, eventually

I'd pass out when the exhaustion washed over me. Now, I lay awake, but it wasn't my good fortune that kept me up; it was everything else.

I'd nurse and hand the baby off to Harry for changing and burping and then watch them both sleep soundly while my mind whirred. I stared at the ceiling, making lists of things I should have done but had forgotten, as well as things I anticipated needing to do in the next few weeks—the costume for Alice's play, endless forms for Sam's trip to Albany. I also replayed conversations, mostly with Sam, and chastised myself for not being more relaxed and at the same time more motivating. I even fell back on a favorite middle-of-the-night pastime and imagined fights with my mother.

Mostly, though, what I did was worry.

Stevie was an easy baby, or at least easier than I remembered either Sam or Alice being. Once fed, burped, or changed, he found his thumb and soothed himself back to sleep—an entirely new experience that didn't require me to keep a stash of pacifiers on hand, or reach over and offer him one in the middle of the night. Still, I worried about how I'd integrate him into a life I already felt spinning out of control, about how my other children would react to this new demand on my time, and about what kind of mother I could be to this baby when I'd be in my sixties while he was in college. The whisper of college would lead me straight down the mineshaft of Sam worries, because as much as I told anyone who would listen that I thought we'd all gone nuts about college and that it was only hurting our children, I still worried about what was going to happen to him next, especially when he seemed so unable to engage. Then I'd slide into Alice worries and how I was making her a middle child when she'd already felt so neglected. When all was said and done with them, I'd move on to Harry, who wanted tenure more than just about anything, and who, when he found out what I'd done, would pick up and leave me.

If I managed to fall asleep at all, I woke up, not because Steven cried out, but because my heart was threatening to burst from my chest, and I'd sweat through whatever I was wearing to bed, even though it was midwinter in the Hudson Valley and the heat on the second floor was sporadic and temperamental. I'd find myself drenched and out of breath, and the only things I could think to do to steady myself were walk around, slow my breathing, and remind myself that everything seems worse at 2:00 a.m.

Most nights, I'd roll out of bed, check the baby, grab my laptop, check the baby again, and head for the bathroom. I logged countless hours sitting on the closed toilet seat (which had recently come loose—Harry would have to figure out how to replace it because without a super, these were the kinds of things we were expected to do on our own), and I had nowhere to go but online. In my day-to-day life I was an anxious nobody, worrying in circles and drowning in anonymity. I was both worried about everyone and unable to connect with them.

Online, I was still a somebody. I had a voice. When I felt that all was lost, that I had failed as a mother and was about to do it again, when I was certain that I had wasted a decade and a half of my life parenting children who would fail to live up to their potential, I heard my mother's voice and told myself that the Dutchess would sustain me. It was just a matter of time before someone offered to syndicate me or gave me a book deal. I'd patch up the inevitable bad feelings and be on my way to stardom by Steven's first birthday. People had a better sense of humor than I gave them credit for, right?

But the Dutchess was of no use to me. My Extra Mom piece was still getting traffic and comments, but because I'd done nothing but nurse and change a baby for almost two weeks, I had nothing new to write about. I started and deleted at least ten posts, none of which made any sense to me and all of which screamed of desperation. Andy had sent me a text when the baby was born and told me to take all the time I needed, but I didn't need time. I needed a topic.

To make matters worse, Meegan's book was about to hit the shelves, and she had published her book-tour dates. Book tour! That was supposed to be happening to me, not some mom who made crafts out of Oreos and was completely dishonest about what it was really like to be a wife and mother.

Her most recent post was particularly painful.

~

Christmas Blessings

I'm counting mine this year. I love a decorated house, a roaring fire, and the scent of a real tree, but best of all, I love that my children are all home, safe and snuggled, where they belong. I don't know what you guys are doing, but our vacation days are full of craft projects, winter walks, and as of today . . . technology-free activities.

Yes, for Christmas this year we are abandoning presents, with the exception of anything homemade (click *here* for a list of my personal favorites, including one for homemade soap made with Crisco), and are gifting ourselves a year of screen-free living. As a mother of six, I know how hard it can be to keep a kid busy without the easy crutch of your phone or whatever screen you have lying around. But as a mom, I also know that kids need to play and be bored and then play some more, and screens just get in the way of that.

So, I'm asking you to join me. With Christmas days away, won't you commit to a year of screen-free living?

Love and blessings,

Hudson Mom of Six

PS: I'll be guest blogging on a whole bunch of parenting-magazine websites as part of my book tour, and I'll also be talking about my crafty, tech-free life on TV. (*Click here for schedule.*)

~

To this already nauseating post Meegan had attached a picture of her six little moppets, backs to the camera, facing a roaring fire. They were all wearing oversize sweaters in various shades of cream and had all presumably scrubbed themselves clean with soap made from Crisco.

It seemed pretty rich to me that Meegan wouldn't let her kids go anywhere near a screen but she was basically plastering them across screens daily to promote products and land herself a book deal. Her online fans didn't seem to agree, because they erupted in praise and gratitude emojis as soon as she posted her news.

I spent three completely sleepless nights reading and rereading all her blog entries, going back to her very first one ("Mom Meets World") and to her most-read one ("When It Comes to Family, Bigger Is Better"). I even searched for other blogs on which she was either mentioned or on which she had commented. When I found myself shaking and short of breath, I shut my computer and forced myself to stop.

If my nights were bad, my days were no better. I was tired, jittery, and agitated, and I snapped at everything in my orbit—which meant that people in my orbit became increasingly rare. I still got up in the morning to make breakfast for the kids before school, but if they uttered a syllable of complaint, I was likely to take it all too personally and lash out at them.

Sam ran into the kitchen one morning waving his phone in my face. "I got an AWESOME room assignment for Albany," he said, skipping over to the fridge and getting some orange juice.

"That's nice," I said. "Want a corn muffin?" I'd made a batch two nights ago at 4:00 a.m., and most of them were still uneaten.

"No, thanks. I'll pass."

"What's wrong with my corn muffins?"

"Nothing," he said. "They're just a little dry." Sam looked down at his enormous feet, and I saw Harry, who'd just appeared, shake his head slightly out of the corner of my eye. He was right. My baking was off. Cooking food for other people is difficult when the only thing you're hungry for is attention from online readers who have no idea who you really are.

"A little dry? Maybe I should just stop baking altogether," I said, slamming the fridge door shut. "While I'm at it, I'll stop cooking, too. You people can feed yourselves."

"That's not what I—" Sam began.

"Bells . . . ," Harry said.

"Remember, I'm sleeping at Abigail's tonight," Alice announced as she walked into the room. "Her mom wants us to try on the rest of our play costumes."

"I thought I was helping you with that." I took an aggressive gulp of coffee.

"I just thought . . . You seem super busy, and Abigail's mom—"

"I actually don't want to hear anything else about Abigail and this wonder mother of hers. If you'll excuse me, I have a baby to feed or change." I banged my mug down, scooped Steven out of his bouncy seat, and left the kitchen. Harry made the mistake of following me out through the yard. The grass was covered in ice.

"Bells . . ."

"What, Harry? What is it that you want to say to me? Just spit it out."

"You need to calm—"

"You know what? I take it back. I don't want to know what you have to say to me, especially if you're about to tell me to calm down. If you want to help me, bring me the car seat."

"Where are you going?"

"The baby needs fresh air," I said.

"Why don't you take him for a walk? Do you need to take the car?"

"I need to see people, and there are more people in town."

"Bells?"

"Yes?"

"*You* need to see people?"

I don't need to see people, Harry. I need to write about them, and I can't write about them if I'm trapped in the kitchen with you and your ungrateful children.

"I know what you're getting at," I snapped. "But you can't complain that I never leave the house, then challenge me when I finally do. The baby is two weeks old, and I want to go out."

"Do you want company?"

I waited a few seconds too long before trying to respond.

"Fine," he said, throwing up his hands and walking away.

I'd apologize later. In the meantime, I quickly fed, burped, and changed the baby, then zipped him into his snowsuit. Harry silently brought in the car seat, and I strapped Steven in rather than attempt it outside while my fingers froze in the driveway. (On days like this, I would have gladly traded the garage kitchen for an actual garage.) I hauled the baby outside, latched him into a frozen Fulbright, and drove into town. I parked in front of the diner, in front of a row of now-barren trees, but I didn't see Joey, so I sent her a quick text (Any news?) and turned off the car.

Within moments, Steven began to fuss, and within fewer moments, the fussing turned into a shriek.

"Oh no," I said, turning around to face him. "Not now."

But the shrieking continued.

"OK, fine. I'm flexible," I said to a face that understood nothing I was saying. I unbuckled my seat belt and reached back, trying to calm Steven by singing lightly in his ear. When he began to root around, looking for more food, I had no choice but to climb into the back of Fulbright.

"OK, buddy," I said. "I'm here." I opened my coat and yanked up my T-shirt and sweatshirt, released him from his shackles and snowsuit, and nursed him in the back seat, sweating in my layers. He immediately soothed and looked up at me with grateful, woozy eyes. I prayed that nobody would see me and at the same time kept watching the street in case anything caught my eye. The only problem is that in December in the Hudson Valley, with the sky a perpetual milky gray and temperatures near freezing, few people are lingering on the sidewalk. I saw nothing, and when Steven's diaper failed and poop oozed out, I knew I had no choice but to admit defeat and go home.

The Dutchess was officially on the back burner, and there was nothing I could do about it.

-25-

The good thing about being in a constant state of anxiety is that at some point you stop noticing it and accept it as the new normal. I spent a particularly grueling night sitting on the bathroom floor, worrying about getting Steven to sleep through a performance of Alice's play and about whether or not Sam had what he needed for his trip to Albany. At no point did it occur to me that spending four hours worrying about both of these things could possibly be unhealthy.

The next morning, I was sitting on the tufted couch, wearing clothes I'd worn the day before, staring at my laptop and drinking tea. I'd spent all morning reading through old comments, hoping something would inspire me. I even wandered, yet again, over to Meegan's corner of the blogosphere, where in addition to updating all of us on the progress she was making living tech-free, she was also promoting another blog, *Henry and Me*, by a mom in Woodstock who made her own clothes and recently contracted with a big label to do her own line of rompers. I assumed that Meegan got at least one free romper in exchange for the plug. Whatever. These women still had a lot more going on than I did.

Enter Harry, who ran out after breakfast to hit the Pigkill farmers market and came back with a large brown paper bag, which he set down on the couch. "Are you going to ask me what's in the bag?" he asked, rubbing his cold hands together, looking very pleased with himself.

I looked up from my computer. "Is it Nutella babka?" Nutella babka was the only food I could get down and was therefore the only thing standing between me and a complete mental breakdown.

"About that . . ."

"YOU FORGOT THE BABKA?" I stood up to yell this and almost knocked my tea over.

Harry picked up the brown bag and held it close to him.

"You can tell me what's in there. I won't bite you," I promised.

"You sure about that?" he asked, still looking terrified.

"Harry," I said in the nicest voice I could muster. Damn, I could almost taste that babka.

"You've been saying that you want your baking mojo back," he said, gingerly placing the bag down again. "And I thought this might help." He reached in and pulled out a bundle of beige fabric.

"What is that?"

"It's a hemp apron," he said proudly.

"A what?"

"An apron made out of hemp," he said, taking a quick step back.

"I sent you for babka, and you come back with a feed sack for me to wear?"

"It has pockets," he said, smiling weakly.

"Harry, would you wear hemp?" I heard Steven moaning on the monitor.

"Actually, I bought a messenger bag . . ."

"What else did you buy?"

"I got you this glass teakettle and some leaves." He pulled out the kettle and a bag of dried flowers.

"Did you buy this for you or for me, and how much did it all cost?" Steven's moan was now a full cry. I must have been really yelling at this point because Harry had backed farther away and was wincing as I spoke.

"I'll go get the baby," he said, talking over Steven's wail. But before he walked out of the room, Harry turned to me and said, "You're not eating, you're not sleeping, and you basically roam the house all day yelling at people. You don't even want Suki to visit. Nothing any of us do is right."

"That's easy for you to say," I spat. "You get to leave, feel accomplished, and come back with overpriced, impractical gifts and act like a conquering hero."

"You're just really stressed out right now, and you're kind of stressing us all out."

"I'm stressing you all out? I spend my days and nights thinking of ways to help make your lives easier, and I'm stressing *you* out?"

"This is nuts, Bells," he said. "I think you need to get some help." He headed for the stairs, leaving me alone in the room.

Harry thought I needed help, but he'd just gone and helped me in a way he could never imagine.

~

The High Cost of a Low-Tech Husband

I know that unplugged living is all the rage, especially up here in Dutchess. I see all of you tech-free people and your oatmeal-colored lives. I see your typewriters, your moleskin notebooks, your art projects, and your smugness. That's right, I see *you*.

I also see how easy it is to tell the rest of us to ditch our screens without fessing up to the price tag of screen-free living—the household help that allows you to avoid using the screen as a babysitter, and the time you must have on your hands in order to take a year off and travel the world or homeschool your kids in a farmhouse you just built with help we'll never see. Even though we all know what screens have done to all our lives, I just wish everyone would be more honest about how much it really costs to unplug without shaming the rest of us.

It isn't just the unplugging, though. This whole low-tech lifestyle is far from cost-free. How do I know this? I live with the Duke, who just may be the biggest offender of all. That's right, the Duke is a *high-cost, low-tech husband.*

The problem is the Duke has caught the Hudson Valley fever for all things old-fashioned and now believes that anything we can make ourselves, and preferably with a glass device, is better. I have a shelf crammed with glass coffeepots in all shapes and sizes, and as of last week, I also have a glass kettle. What do I plan on doing with that, you ask? Oh, I plan on making tea with flower petals that cost eighteen dollars an ounce. If you think that's bad, don't ask me about the overpriced hemp clothing and the footwear made entirely of recycled tires.

The Duke recently asked me to assist him in some innocuous home pickling. Pickling your own veggies may be fun and may give you a reason to run out and buy mason jars by the dozen—and isn't that what we are all after—but it is not cheap. I did the math, people, and the cost of one jar of home-pickled cukes: TWELVE dollars and a few rounds of cleanup performed by yours truly.

I love my husband. Really, I do. But if he doesn't give up this habit, we're not going to have any money left for anything, including store-bought pickles and regular old tea bags.

(And I'm not just cranky because my local farmers market was sold out of Nutella babka.)

Xoxoxo

The Dutchess

~

Feeling pretty pleased with myself and finally productive, I sent the piece to Andy, stretched out on the couch, and closed my eyes.

I woke up ninety minutes later and instinctively checked my phone. I had a text from Andy.

So glad you're back and even happier to see you finally posted a clue!

Clue? I went to the blog and saw that not only had he posted, but the comments had already started coming in.

Me thinks the Dutchess has slipped. There are some real clues in here about her actual whereabouts . . .

Thanks, Dutchess! You've dropped a tasty hint ;-)

My face felt instantly flush, and I prickled with panic. Then I got a text from Suki:

> Dutchess Eaters post landed in my inbox. They know you're from Pigkill—something about babka at the farmers market? (And who only takes a two-week maternity leave!?!?!)

I raced over to the *Dutchess Eaters* page and read the latest entry, which had been posted ten minutes before. Those ladies were fast.

~

Peppermint Bark and Clues

Before we tell you all about our experiments with white chocolate brownies topped with peppermint bark, we must report that one of our local favorites, the County Dutchess, dropped a hint in her latest blog post. The Dutchess, an anonymous blogger who has been the subject of our own online speculation, may have just told us more about herself than she intended to. Did she mean to divulge personal info when she wrote that her local farmers market sold out of Nutella babka? Because any market regular in the Hudson Valley knows that the only local market that sells the Nutella babka is the Pigkill market.

Intentional or not, her slip means those of us desperate to unmask the Dutchess now have a little more info . . .

~

My hands shook and my head sweat as I read through the rest of the post and the early comments. I kept going until I was interrupted by the pings of incoming texts from Jess.

THE DUTCHESS LIVES IN PIGKILL!!!!!!! OMG YOU REALLY COULD KNOW HER. HER HUSBAND MAY EVEN WORK WITH HARRY!!!!!!

I probably would have felt calmer without the all caps. I texted her back.

So I hear.

Steven, who'd been napping in a bouncy seat, started to grumble and pull his tiny little arms out of his swaddle. I scooped him up, holding him close to me, as if he could ward off whatever was coming next.

"Your mother is a moron," I said to his little head, breathing him in. "I dropped a bread crumb, and now I'm doomed." I bounced lightly as he settled against me. "Maybe I should pack a bag, and you and I can escape before it's too late." I craned my neck and made eye contact with him. "What do you think?"

Steven didn't think anything. He just gave me a gassy smile, which I knew better than to read into, but I also knew that he was the only person who wasn't judging me. He knew nothing about the Dutchess, and if he had, he probably wouldn't care. I felt safer as I held him, braced by his unconditional love.

What Steven also didn't know was that even though I was planning our escape (including the mother of all apology letters to Harry), I'd just rekindled the Dutchess's fire, and I wasn't about to let it go out again. She was back, and people were reading. I spent thirty minutes pacing the ground floor with the baby in my arms. I was watching my stats climb and racking my brain for ideas for a follow-up post when Joey texted me a picture of a newborn baby in a pink hat.

Come meet my baby!

I zoomed in on the baby's tiny face and texted back.

What? That's awesome! Congrats!

Yeah! And I'm home. Tomorrow? Baby playdate?

I liked Joey. I really did. But I was way too old for a playdate, and even though I knew better, I also knew that time with Joey would be time spent away from the Dutchess. I may have declined her offer had I not gone back and checked my newest comments.

> Pigkill, eh? Watch out Dutchess—we're coming for you.

Maybe I needed a break after all.

-26-

Joey's parents' home was a small white house with black shutters and a trim, perfectly square, well-tended front yard. I heaved the car seat out of Fulbright and made my way up the path to their black front door, grateful that most of the snow on the ground had been shoveled.

Joey swung open the door before I'd even finished climbing the three stairs up.

"Bells!" she said with outstretched arms. She was beaming. Was I supposed to look like that?

I smiled back, and she gave me a huge hug, which might have been the first noninfant human contact I'd had in weeks. I held on to her for a moment, surprised at how happy I was to see her.

"I can't wait to meet Steven," Joey said, pulling away and peering into the giant swaddle of infant and snowsuit in the car seat. "And you have to meet Nicole."

"That's a lovely name," I said, following her inside. "I was sure you'd go with Jayden or Hayden."

She turned and looked at me blankly. "Her middle name is Kayden."

"Are your parents home?" I asked, changing the subject. "I'd love to meet them." I would have loved nothing less than to meet Joey's mother only to discover that she was basically my age.

"Nah, they're both at work," she said. I pretended to look disappointed and followed her into a small living room with a lit fireplace, some floral couches, and a glass coffee table with a vase of fake flowers in the middle—a coffee table that was going to need some serious babyproofing if Joey was still here when Nicole got mobile.

Joey bent down over a cradle in the corner of the room and scooped up her baby, swaddled in a pink blanket.

"This is Nicole," she said, not taking her eyes off the infant. Nicole had even more hair than Steven. In fact, she had more hair than any of my kids did until they were at least one. Her eyes were big and dark, like Joey's. I wondered briefly what her dad looked like and if he even knew she'd been born.

Joey just kept looking at her as if she couldn't believe her luck. I remembered looking at Sam that way. Staring at Nicole and Joey's beatific gaze, I could only think about Joey starting out on this journey and having no idea how hard it was going to be—not the early years of sleeplessness or the physical exhaustion of keeping up with a toddler, but the later years, when she'd lie awake at night and worry about Nicole's future. In a little more than a year, Sam would be eighteen and an official adult. Had I done enough? Was I running out of time?

"Bells, are you OK?"

I'd sat down in a large armchair (same floral pattern as the couch) and had Steven in my arms, my eyes closed. I opened them and looked at Joey and Nicole.

"Yeah. I'm fine," I said, forcing a smile and a less anxious posture. "How much time are you taking off work?" I asked, ready to move the subject from me and my not-so-subtle panic attack.

"The diner cut my hours, and it's just not worth it for me now that I have to think about childcare."

"Cut your hours? Why?"

"That place is really taking a hit. I guess kombucha and kimchi burgers weren't enough to compete with all the farm-to-table places or the vegan comfort-food place that just opened in town."

"Vegan comfort food? That's a thing?"

"Everything is a thing." She shrugged and then reached under her sweatshirt and unlatched her nursing bra.

"I'm really sorry to hear it." I took this moment to slide Steven back into his car seat. The last thing I needed was to see a twentysomething breast.

"Well, maybe people don't want burnt coffee and cakes made with five pounds of butter." She stroked Nicole's head as she latched on.

"Funny," I said. "That's exactly what I want."

"I promise to come over and burn your coffee for you," she laughed. "Anyway, I'm considering another gig that pays really well, and I don't need to be on my feet all day."

"Really? What is it?" Steven was stirring, and I was beginning to suspect I couldn't wait to feed him until I was back home, or even in the car, which was my backup plan.

Joey raised an eyebrow and bit her lower lip. "You promise you won't tell anyone?"

For a moment I was overcome with jealousy. Was Joey cashing in on Chore Donkey? Had her body recovered that quickly? (Even worse was the nagging realization that even when I recovered, I'd be recovering to a fortysomething body, which was nobody's idea of bouncing back.)

"I got asked to be part of the college scam," she whispered, even though it was just us and the babies in the house.

"Huh?"

"I thought all the moms knew about it."

"Joey, I'm sorry, but I'm really not following," I said, rocking Steven's car seat with my foot.

Joey hesitated and lifted Nicole over her shoulder to burp her. "All of those judgy moms you don't like?"

I nodded.

"They're terrified they're not gonna get their kids into college, so they pay people to take tests and write essays for their kids."

"That's not so new," I said. "It seems to be happening everywhere."

"I guess so, but there are a ton of overeducated, underemployed people with a ton of student debt up here. And they are all cashing in."

"Really?"

"Yeah. You know the smoothie guy with the huge goatee?"

I nodded, thinking about my post-yoga dirt smoothie.

"He has an MFA and has published short stories. He writes a mean college essay."

"Wow."

"Yup, and there's a yoga instructor with a PhD in applied math who can take the SAT, the ACT, and even some subject tests." She brought a now-sleeping Nicole down to her chest and cradled her.

I just sat there and blinked. SAT subject tests? Were those even a thing anymore, and why wasn't Sam taking any?

"And all this works?" I asked, shaking myself out of my very own college panic.

She shrugged. "I think so. There's a guy who runs the whole thing, and he's bribing test proctors and forging the applications."

"How much are people willing to pay?"

"I don't know about the essays, but I heard up to five thousand bucks for a full SAT or ACT, and they offered me fifteen hundred for a subject test. And in case you were wondering what my superpower is . . . *scientia ipsa potentia est.*"

"Huh?"

"Before I dropped out, I was a classical languages major. I could ace that Latin subject test."

"Joey, I don't know how to say it in Latin, but this is really risky."

"Don't *you* be judgy now," she said. "I probably won't end up doing it. But a lot of people up here really need the money. The city people have driven up prices, and many of us have lost our jobs or had our hours cut."

"If I'm judging anyone, it definitely isn't you," I said, feeling the stirring of curiosity and focus beginning to form.

~

I might have done nothing with Joey's information had I not experienced the mother of all blowups with everyone in my house that evening. After I'd watched them all ooh and aah over the latest meal-train delivery (*Get a grip, people, any idiot can make a tray of blondies*), I put Steven in his bouncy seat next to the couch and dove headfirst into my phone, which was rapidly becoming the safest, most comfortable place I could be. I was hate-reading Meegan's latest offering (Home Crafts to Beat the Winter Blues) when I got an email from Sam's guidance counselor:

> Dear Mrs. Walker,
>
> I wanted to let you know that Sam skipped the past two ACT practice tests you signed him up for. He's also missed a meeting with me. Please encourage him to come and see me and to email the test coordinator to sign up for the makeup tests.
>
> Thank you,
>
> Andrea Gambino

I scooped up the baby with one hand, and with a half-eaten yogurt in the other, I ran up two flights of stairs to Sam's attic bedroom. "What the hell is this?" I panted, shoving my phone in his face. Standing in between piles of clothes, shoes, and sheet music, I looked over at a small mountain of gray hoodies next to an empty overnight bag. Sam was leaving for Albany the next morning and told me he'd packed already.

"I had band practice," he said, recoiling and sitting on the edge of his unmade bed.

"Why would the school schedule band practice during a practice ACT test?"

Sam didn't say anything; he just looked down at his feet.

"Answer me!" I shrieked.

"It wasn't school band practice," he murmured, still looking down. "It was with Luke and Saskia . . . for a gig we have."

"Why would you be so dumb to skip a test so you and your two bandmates could practice to play in a shady restaurant? What were you thinking?"

"You don't get to ask me that anymore," he said, finally looking up. "Especially when you just had that accident." His eyes moved to Steven, stirring in my arms.

"What does Steven have to do with the fact that you're not taking your future seriously enough?" I saw spit fly from my mouth. "What's the matter with you? Don't you care?"

"Maybe you're not the right person to tell me I'm wasting my life," he said, his own voice rising. "You went to a fancy college and look at you. How much of your Ivy League education do you use to change his diapers?"

"I get enough of this from Grandma Hanna," I said, rocking Steven with one arm. "I don't need any more from you."

"Yeah, well, maybe Grandma isn't wrong."

"You don't get to talk to me like that," I said, wishing I had put the yogurt down before running up to Sam's room. "Not after everything." I rocked Steven, hoping to soothe him. "All of the work," I continued. "All of the hours I put in."

"What hours? All the other moms do so much more than you."

"Is that what you want? Do you want me to be one of those annoying moms?"

"They may be annoying, but they get results. You know that kid Jake Schiller?"

I nodded. Jake Schiller was a semiarticulate band kid a year ahead of Sam.

"Well, his mom quit her job when he started high school, just to focus on getting him into a good college. She basically took all of his classes with him and he got in early to Cornell."

"Really?"

"Yeah, and everyone knows that Adam Parker's dad writes all his essays." According to Luke, Adam Parker couldn't string a sentence together, but his dad was a history professor. "And Luke has a cousin in our class whose dad is the pharmacist in town and does all her problem sets."

"I did my best," I said. "You know I did my best."

"Well, congrats," he said, finally standing up and squaring off with me. "At your best, you quit your job to be a failed housewife who won't even be able to get her kids into college." He paused and looked at Steven. "Better luck next time."

I felt anger surge through me. I held Steven close to me with one hand and hurled the yogurt with the other. Sam ducked, and the yogurt slammed into a picture of the zeppelin in his framed Led Zeppelin poster, exploding all over the wall.

Harry came running in.

"What's wrong with you?" Sam asked, crying. "You're crazy!"

"Bells," I heard Harry say behind me. "Bells, you need to calm down."

I whirled around and looked at him. "DID YOU REALLY JUST SAY THAT?"

"Bells . . ."

"BECAUSE YOU KNOW HOW THAT WORKS, RIGHT? THAT BY TELLING ME TO CALM DOWN YOU ARE ONLY INCREASING THE ODDS THAT I'LL KILL YOU IN YOUR SLEEP?"

"Bells . . ."

"For god's sake! Stop saying my name over and over again." The baby was now full-on screaming. Alice, whom I didn't know had walked into the room, also started to cry.

I looked down at Steven, who had no idea I was rapidly falling apart, and handed him to Harry. Then I ran out of the room and down a flight of stairs. I kept running until I got to the front door. I grabbed my coat, keys, and laptop where it lay sitting on the coffee table and left the house. Sitting in a freezing Fulbright, I opened up my laptop and stared at the outline of my reflection in the dark screen. I had spent almost seventeen years doing one thing at the expense of just about all other things. I'd tried to be the kind of mother I thought I'd needed, even if my own mother thought I'd been wasting my time. But it turned out that my best wasn't good enough. Well, I wasn't going to waste any more time, and I certainly wasn't going to waste the opportunity to tell a really good story.

I took in a gulp of air and told myself I was actually helping Joey by saving her from making an even bigger mistake.

~

Millennials, College-Crazy Parents, and OH MY GOD, YOU GUYS, THESE PEOPLE ARE WILLING TO DO ANYTHING

Here I was, feeling guilty about being so hard on the badly behaving Dutchess moms. I mean, who among us doesn't want to use a task app to hook up with a millennial while your husband thinks you're having the gutters cleaned? But then, while minding my own business, I found that the connection between anxious moms and local millennials runs even deeper.

As a group, these millennials are not only overeducated, they're also underemployed, which means that many of them are swimming in a sea of student debt, paying for degrees they'll never use. What better way to pay off those extra degrees than by helping someone else get better educated?

Enter the college-hysterical parents of Dutchess County.

Some parents can do it themselves. They quit their jobs and basically take all their kids' classes with them, reading all their assigned books and doing the work they can't, then negotiating with teachers when their kids don't get the results they wanted. Some of these parents even succeed. Hell, one local parent did just this and got her kid into Cornell early. These parents take time out from teaching college-level history or filling prescriptions at the local pharmacy to write all their high schoolers' essays or do all their problem sets. But what happens when that's not enough? What happens when you need even more help to get your kid across that ivy-covered finish line?

Then you cheat even more.

Dear readers, task-app hookups were just the beginning. I have it on good authority that Dutchess moms and dads have also been paying local twenty- and thirtysomethings to write college essays and take standardized tests for their cherished, underperforming offspring. The entire enterprise is being masterminded by someone who is, to quote a perpetrator, "bribing proctors and forging applications."

Everywhere you look up here, someone's in on it: the goateed smoothie guy who's a published author and will pen your kid's college essay, the popular yoga instructor with the math PhD who will sit for his ACT, the heavily tattooed barista with two master's degrees who'll take his SAT subject tests. (You can't throw a stone up here without hitting someone who's in on it, which makes me wonder about that lovely young woman who introduced me to the bisnut—I wonder what her superpower is?)

What must it feel like for these parents, who've poured themselves into their children's success only to find out that their kids just can't pull it off without cheating? What must it feel like to spend hundreds of hours and thousands of dollars on courses and tutors and rigged evaluations only to find out that your little darlings are, at best . . . mediocre?

Maybe you shouldn't have lorded your children over the rest of us, who were just trying to stay afloat. Maybe you shouldn't have forked out all that cash only to have to cheat when your beloved, underperforming sons and daughters just couldn't cut it. Maybe it's time to admit that no matter how many PTA committees you chair, how many flyers you print out, how many hours of tutoring you pay for or essays you forge, average kids are always gonna be . . . average.

I know some of you are watching me.

But guess what?

The Dutchess is watching back.

-27-

What happened after that is still fuzzy. Sometimes I'm sure of the order of events, and other times, they blend, and I don't know who fell first.

I sent the piece to Andy, then shoved my phone in the top drawer of my nightstand and kept it there. I'd corroborated nothing in the story—not that I needed to as a blogger, and not that I'd bothered to do it before. But this accusation was bigger than sleeping with your much younger yoga instructor, and I hadn't asked Joey many follow-up questions or done anything to substantiate her story. I may have only covered fallen branches in the city, but I knew the basics of journalism. This story could derail people's lives—children's lives, Joey's life. What I'd done scared me. It just didn't scare me enough to stop it from happening.

~

An hour later, Andy called me.

"Hey, Andy," I said, taking a muslin from a shelf and wiping Steven's milky mouth. He opened his large eyes and watched me.

"Bells, this is a little nuts."

"I thought so, too, when I heard it. But it's true."

"How do you know?"

"Someone who is involved told me."

"A parent?"

"No, someone doing the actual test taking." *What makes a lie a white lie?*

"Did this person give you any proof that this is actually happening?"

"No," I said, burping the baby over my shoulder, hoping nobody walked into the bedroom while I was having this conversation.

"Does this person know you're planning on writing about it?" *No, and when she finds out, she may never talk to me again.*

"Are you running it, Andy?" I got up and walked around the room until Steven dozed off.

"I don't know if I can," he said. "It's uncorroborated, and frankly, really risky."

"Then tack on a disclaimer," I said, abandoning the mirror. "I'm a blogger, not a journalist." With the other hand, I googled "Can a blogger be sued for defamation?"

"Are you OK with me softening it up a bit?" he asked.

"Yes."

"And if you need to dig some more and write a follow-up—can you do that?"

"Yes."

"You know the knives are out, right? They know where you live."

"I know. I'll take the chance," I said, walking back toward the bathroom. "This is a big deal. Regular, non-superrich parents are paying cash-strapped millennials to take tests and write essays for their kids, and they're doing it on a pretty big scale. Andy, this is exactly the kind of thing we should be writing about." I felt myself growing taller and thinner as I spoke, and self-importance surged through me. I was a whole new version of myself by the time the call ended. Six feet, wiry, and on a mission.

~

I dragged myself out of bed at five the next morning and dropped a very silent Sam off at the high school so he could get on the bus to Albany. I came back, checked on Steven, and went downstairs, hoping to avoid Harry for as long as he needed to forget the scene I'd made.

Andy sent me a text at 6:00 a.m.:

Post is live now.

I set out breakfast for Harry and Alice and hid upstairs while they ate and then left. Nobody came looking for me. Nobody wanted to see me. I can't say I blamed them. Once they'd gone, Steven and I sat in the garage kitchen as the comments rolled in.

"Your mother is sort of famous," I said to him as he gazed blankly at me. "Try to contain your enthusiasm," I said, leaning down and kissing his forehead.

Dutchess! This is an awesome story! Thank you!!

Parents really need to know what lengths other parents will go to.

OMG DUTCHESS these parents are NO JOKE!

The yogi with the PhD! Love that!

Pat yourself on the back, Dutchess. This is a seriously screwed-up story you're telling.

I was doing just that when Suki called.

"Bells, you've got to be kidding me," she said, launching right into her reprimand.

"I know."

"You know and you still wrote it?"

"Yes, I still wrote it, and you would have done the same—it's a crazy good story." As I spoke, I saw a text from Andy.

NY1 is running the story. It's about to go live on the local NBC page. Stay tuned!!

"I'm worried," she said.

"About what?" I opened the NY1 page.

~

Dutchess Blogger Alleges College Scam

Just when you thought you'd heard it all, an anonymous blogger in Dutchess County is alleging that local parents are paying local millennials to take standardized tests and write college essays for their kids. The County Dutchess, whom some have deduced lives in Pigkill, claims that a Dutchess local is masterminding the whole operation.

~

"You can't make allegations like this without some fallout. Bells, you better have some proof that any of this is happening. Also, what if the college is involved? Have you thought about that?"

"You told me to be less gossipy, so I went and reported a real story—an actual story—and people are reading it. I'll deal with whatever fallout there is." I swallowed. "This is my time, Suki. Let people notice me."

"I don't know what you mean by that," she said.

"I mean that this is something I've wanted for a long time, and you should know that more than anyone else."

"I do know that. I just can't help but think that there may be better ways for you to get attention than this."

"Well, when you think of what they are, why don't you let me know," I said. "In the meantime, this is working for me."

"Until it isn't," she said.

"I have to go. Steven's crying."

"Nice try. We both know that's not true," she said. "Just say 'I don't want to talk anymore,' and I won't be mad."

"Fine. I don't want to talk anymore."

After the call, I scrolled through more comments.

> This is huge! (Also, what is a bisnut?)
>
> Mediocre darlings! LOL!
>
> Dutchess, YOU ARE THE BEST.

The comments, which were almost too numerous for me to read, were mostly positive. All were incredulous, as though it wasn't just a matter of time before more parents figured out how to exploit the college debt crisis just to get their kids into school. If you thought about it, something like this was just waiting to happen—I was just glad I was the one who caught it. Andy kept sending me random exclamation marks and links to other sites carrying the story. There was talk of a mention in the *New York Times* Style section.

I began to wonder if it wasn't time for me to come out of the shadows. Maybe with a story like this, I could pull back the curtain and reveal myself as the Dutchess. But when I tried to take a picture of Steven to send to Vivian and accidentally saw my own face in my phone, I got the fright of my life. I downloaded a makeup app I'd seen Alice use, promptly gave myself highlights and false eyelashes, and found a filter that erased ten years and two kids. If only I could walk through life looking the way I did in the gauzy, dreamy phone filter. I'd need some serious help for a book tour, especially if there was television involved.

Quick Richard came later in the day and punctuated the silence. He fixed the toilet seat and began working on the dishwasher, which had been leaking intermittently.

"Aren't you the chipper one," he said from underneath the dishwasher, as I hummed while stirring risotto, Harry's absolute favorite dinner. Alice was out late at play practice (a new development), and Sam was away. I figured I'd apologize for my outburst and feed Harry at the same time, a tactic I'd never seen fail.

I just smiled innocently at Richard and filed a mental note to google book agents when I was done with dinner.

I had just covered the risotto pot, rinsed the wooden spoon, and was waiting for Harry when my phone rang, Sam's freckled seven-year-old face lighting up the screen. Sam never called; at best he texted when he needed something. I grabbed the phone.

"Sam?"

"Mom?" He was crying. "Mom, don't be mad."

"What happened? What did you do?" Like so much of what I said to Sam, I regretted those words instantly.

"I didn't do anything, but they're sending me home."

"What do you mean? Why? What happened?" I heard some muffled voices in the background. "Sam?"

"Mrs. Walker? This is Bob Cutler, one of the chaperones on the trip."

I sank into a chair and put my head into my hands. "Yes?" I whispered.

"Sam was caught vaping marijuana in the bathroom of a rest stop earlier today," he said. "I'll be driving him home this evening, and Principal Nguyen will be calling you."

"Vaping?" I asked, my head bolting up. "Marijuana? Sam?"

"He's obviously denying everything. But a parent caught him, and he leaves us no choice."

"Of course," I said. "I'll be home all night."

~

Harry texted that he was running late while Steven and I sat waiting on the tufted couch. Even though the potbelly was roaring, the house felt huge, cold, and dark. I picked up my phone, hoping to cheer myself up, but Alice came running in before I could unlock it.

"Mom," she cried, her face blotchy and red, "I want to go back to the city!"

"What happened? Why aren't you at play practice?"

"They all hate me!" she said, and ran up to her room.

I sat outside her door and begged her to come out, even threatening to remove the lock if she didn't. But Alice wouldn't budge, and we both knew I wouldn't know the first thing about lock removal, and neither would her father. Alice just lay on her bed facedown and wept, which I knew because I sat and listened to her muffled sobs.

There was a knock on the front door. I ran down and opened it, hoping it would be Harry, but it was a miserable-looking Sam and a man with a smattering of red hair on either side of his head and small steel-rimmed glasses.

"Mrs. Walker," he said, "I'm Mr. Cutler. Sam can tell you everything, but he shouldn't come to school in the morning. A three-day suspension is in effect."

Maybe I should have fought there and then, demanding proof or more of an explanation, but I could tell from the look on Sam's dejected face that he wanted this man, with whom he'd just spent the longest car ride of his life, to be gone.

I nodded, let Sam in, and closed the door behind him. He dumped his bag in the hall and made for the stairs.

"Don't you think we should talk about this?"

"There's nothing to talk about," he said, not looking back. "I didn't do it. It wasn't me."

"Then why do they think it was you?"

"Because I was in the bathroom when it happened."

I wasn't above missing signs of drug use, but nothing about this felt right. I didn't have more than that to go on, but I believed him. "Well, then, let's fight it," I said, walking toward him. "If you didn't do it, then just tell them who did."

"You don't get it," he said, finally looking at me. "That's not how it works. Besides, Ms. Plank said it was me, and everyone believes her."

"Cynthia?"

"Yeah."

"She was on the trip?"

"Yeah, she's also a chaperone. Hayley plays trumpet."

Of course she does.

"I can help you," I said. "You just need to tell me as much as you can."

"No, thanks," he said. "You just make everything worse." And with that, he climbed up to the attic and left me on the staircase holding the banister, which I noticed had come loose again.

I was about to check on Alice when my phone rang.

"Bells, it's me," Andy said. "Who is Hudson Mom of Six?"

"Why?"

"Because she just outed you," he said. "It's everywhere."

The next thing I did was pull out my phone and text Suki:

THE BREAD DID NOT RISE.

~

The County Dutchess: A Royal Scumbag

She never mentioned she was a writer. She was just a new, unassuming, maybe even slightly dumpy mom (Wait, what???) who moved to town. She came from the city, which meant she thought she was better than the rest of us simple Hudson Valley folk, but we never bothered to check much. If we had checked, we'd have seen that Bells Walker used to write for a paper you've never heard of—and she used to write about things that nobody cared about outside the big city, like street parking and leaky hydrants. Maybe then we would have noticed that just when Elsbeth Cohn stopped writing about her boring city life and moved to town, the Dutchess started trashing life up here. OK, I'll get to the point—she started trashing the people who live here.

But we didn't notice because Bells Walker wasn't worth investigating. She really didn't seem to be the type—no zippy lines or clever observations. She just blended in with the minivans and the comfy clothes. Maybe those people are the worst—the ones you'd never expect. Also, the Dutchess claimed to be a longtime resident, and what kind of person would make up something like that, let alone anonymously trash the parents of her children's classmates? What kind of woman would make baseless accusations about people affiliated with Dutchess College when *her own husband works there*?

A scumbag? A psychopath?

Y'all know that I don't usually throw around words like that on this blog, but when you've been invaded and betrayed, you get mad. And readers, I'm really mad.

Bells Walker is a fraud. She moved up here and started lying and trashing the people in her own town. She claimed to be someone she isn't, and even worse, she's making up all kinds of stories and wasn't even brave enough to put her name on any of them.

We see *you*, Bells. And we are not happy.

Hudson Mom of Six

PS: I will now return to my regularly scheduling programming of cute crafts you can do with your kids and on a budget. Blessings!

~

Harry was not answering his calls. At first the phone rang, but then it started going directly to voice mail. I left Alice soaking in her woes and didn't even bother following Sam upstairs. I just ran downstairs to the tufted couch and threw myself down next to Steven's bouncy seat.

"It's over," I said to him as he opened one eye and then the other. "It's all over."

-28-

I knew immediately that Harry had heard when he walked through the front door and threw his bags down next to Sam's.

"Harry . . ."

"Were you ever planning on telling me?"

I nodded. He'd left the door open, and a blast of cold air rushed in.

"When?"

"At first I didn't tell you because Andy only let me write on a trial basis, and I had a total of three followers. I wanted to wait until I could make you proud."

"Proud of bashing everyone in this town?"

"This town was bashing me, Harry." I took a few steps toward him.

"What?" He held up his hands, motioning for me to stay back.

"Nobody saw me here. I was an old pregnant freak until I became the Dutchess." I motioned to the open door with my head, but he ignored me.

"Only you thought that. It was all in your own head."

"You don't know that," I said. "You didn't hear them talking. You have to believe me when I say that I didn't plan on it going this far, and I really didn't want to get you involved."

"Well, you screwed that piece up because I just got pulled into the dean's office."

"What?" My god, why wouldn't he close the door?

"Did you think it wouldn't affect me? Did you think you could write about these people, people in our community?"

"What happened?"

"My tenure decision isn't happening this month. Best case, it's delayed to April."

"Harry . . ." I wanted to rush to him and put my arms around him, partly to warm myself up but mostly to beg him to forgive me, but I was afraid to go much closer. There was a very good chance that if I touched him, he'd bolt.

"You knew how badly I wanted this," he said, his voice breaking. "You knew how much we needed this as a family, and you risked all of it. And I don't even know what for."

"I'm so sorry, Harry. You have to believe me." I was desperate to touch him.

"Are you sorry you did it, or just sorry you got caught?"

I looked at him mutely.

"That's what I thought," he said. "I'm going to bed." He walked upstairs and left the front door wide open.

~

I don't know exactly when Meegan pieced it all together, but once she did, she immediately called Cynthia, who quickly got Sam sent home. She then called her neighbor, who just happened to be the mother of the Abigail half of Abigail-Courtney, and told her that Alice Walker's mother was a lying, conniving blogger, and her daughter better keep her distance. Abigail's mom promptly made some calls of her own, and shortly thereafter, Alice was removed from various chats and pages and all the places where thirteen-year-old girls live online. Cynthia also told her husband, who called Dean Stone at the college. Harry was involved within the hour.

All of this was happening while I stirred risotto, imagining myself on morning television shows and at book signings with long lines of fans, all of whom looked like I did before the highlights, lashes, and phone filters. It happened while I googled “Best agents for new authors,” “Best agents for bloggers,” and “Best agents for middle-aged moms who wrote a book when nobody thought they could.”

Suki tried me a few times, but I was too ashamed to hear her voice. Jess called, and I sent her a text:

I know. It’s bad—so bad, I can’t really talk about it. Please don’t tell Vivian.

I ignored all of Andy’s texts as well as a string of calls from the *Gazette* asking me to comment.

Alice and Sam came out of their rooms and found me lying on the tufted couch staring at a crack in the ceiling.

“Mom?” Alice asked, holding up her phone. “Who is the County Dutchess?”

I sat up on the couch and faced them.

“I owe you guys an apology,” I said, looking at both kids. “I started a blog a few months ago. I used it to write nasty things about people in this town, and now I’ve been outed, and those people are really mad. Some of them are affiliated with the college. They’re also the parents of kids you go to school with, which is how you probably heard about it.”

Sam spoke first. “So it’s true?”

“Yes,” I said. “It’s true.”

“You wrote a blog about people in Pigkill?” Alice asked, looking baffled by all parts of that sentence.

“Yes,” I said. “I blogged under the name the County Dutchess.” I’d be lying if I said I didn’t feel just a little bit clever every time I said those words—Meegan and her low expectations could go straight to hell.

"You always lecture us about technology and safety!" Sam yelled. "You tell us over and over that anything we post will stay somewhere forever, and that the watchers are watching!" He used his fingers to make quotation marks for that last part, which was a direct quote from me. "And then you go and trash people online and barely cover your tracks? Are you that dumb?"

"So that's why my friends dropped me," Alice whispered.

"Yes," I said, looking at her with all the atonement I could offer. "And it's probably also why Sam got into trouble on his trip. It looks like I upset some of the wrong people."

"You're such a hypocrite," Alice said, shaking her head and tearing up. "You lecture me about caring what people online think, but you're one of those online people who make other people feel bad." She paused. "You're a bully, an online bully."

"Even worse," Sam said, "you didn't even have the guts to put your name on it."

I nodded.

"I don't even know what else to say," he said.

"I think," said Harry, appearing suddenly in the room, "that it would sum things up nicely to say that this is really fucked up."

Even Sam looked shocked at Harry's language. "What now?" he asked. "How do we even go back to school?"

"Who says we want to go back to school?" Alice said, playing with the zipper on her white hoodie. "I say we move."

"What if not all of us want to go back to the city?" Sam asked her. "Then what?"

"Nobody is moving anywhere," I said. "I made this mess, and I'll clean it up."

"You think you can just go on an apology tour and fix this?" Harry asked, finally addressing me directly.

"I don't know," I said. "But I have to start somewhere."

~

I started with Andy.

"I need to apologize," I said. "I need to come clean."

"I'm sorry, Bells, but I spoke to the publisher, and we're killing the Dutchess."

"What?"

"We got a letter from a group of Dutchess County parents, and the publisher wants you off the payroll. People are threatening lawsuits, Bells."

"But they're meritless—you know that."

"It doesn't matter. It will still cost us to defend them, and the publicity will be bad for us," he said.

"But this could be a really big story, Andy. Doesn't that matter?"

"It's a big story for someone else. We don't have the capacity to investigate or cover it—we're leaving it to the big guys."

"So that's it? I can't even apologize?"

"I'm afraid not," he said. "The blog is off the site, and all your old posts have been removed. As of now, the Dutchess is officially dead."

-29-

Statement from Kelly Wallace, CEO of the College Test Corporation

The College Test Corporation knows nothing of the alleged testing scandal in Dutchess County, New York, and will commence an internal investigation immediately. As of now, all SAT and ACT tests administered in Dutchess County are under such investigation.

~

Hudson Valley Gazette

Scandal Comes to Pigkill

As for the recent alleged college scam in Pigkill, the district attorney has launched a full investigation, and while nobody has yet been named, rumor has it that Pigkill's high school will not be boasting the same number of Ivy placements as in years

> past. An anonymous source inside the PTA told the *Gazette*, "Some schools are now afraid to touch us with a ten-foot pole, which is unfortunate because nobody works harder than the kids at Pigkill." When asked about the revelation of the identity of the County Dutchess, the anonymous blogger who first uncovered the rumors of the scam, the source said, "No comment."

~

Harry did not come to bed that night. He came in when Steven cried and helped after feedings, but then left the room. I found him in the kitchen, fully dressed and pouring coffee into a thermos. It was barely 5:00 a.m.

"Are you leaving?"

"It would appear so."

"Harry, look at me, please."

"I can't do that," he said, grabbing a yogurt from the fridge and putting it into his lunch bag. "In fact, I can't really be around you right now."

"When will you be ready to talk to me?"

"I don't know. It's *my* turn to marinate." He closed his lunch bag, grabbed the coffee, and left the kitchen.

Alice refused to leave her room, and Sam wouldn't talk to me. Later that morning, after I left a blueberry muffin in front of Alice's door only to find it uneaten an hour later, I discovered a reporter from the *Gazette* standing on my porch. Funny how now they couldn't get enough of me when only months ago they had been so dismissive. *Is this what you thought I should do, Gary Wallace? Was this what you had in mind when you said, "Go home, write a blog, and see what happens"?*

"No comment, and I'll thank you not to trespass," I said to the reporter, channeling all the Hanna Cohn I could muster. But once inside the house, I breathed heavily for about thirty minutes until the panic had subsided.

The doorbell rang again five minutes later, and after I'd jumped out of my skin, I peeked and saw Quick Richard standing on the porch. I opened the door, and he handed me a Bundt cake.

"I thought you might need this," he said. "It's maple."

"Richard, what did Emerson and Thoreau say about trashing people in your town?"

"I don't know what either of those fellows would have said, but I thought you were darn hysterical." He left before I could thank him for the cake.

~

If the house was big before, it was even bigger when I was left alone in it. Sam was the first to leave for school, texting me at lunch.

Staying at Luke's tonight.

Please don't. I really need to talk to you.

About what? How you used all the info I gave you about kids I know? I read your stupid blog and you rly screwed me over.

Please, let me apologize.

When he didn't respond, I sent another text, and then another. When he responded to none of them, I called, knowing that it had been about two years since Sam had answered one of my calls. I put my phone facedown on the kitchen counter and left it there.

I took a piece of cake up to Alice. At the very least, her social isolation would force her to have to talk to me.

"Alice, honey," I said, standing in front of her door, "I have some cake for you."

No answer.

"Alice, please. You have to eat something. You have practice."

"I don't. I quit."

"What?"

"I emailed Ms. Shrub. I just can't get up on a stage in front of all those people."

"You can't quit, Alice," I said into the closed door. "Not because of my mistake. You're good, so good."

"Oh, so now you care about me," she said, suddenly opening the door. I expected to find her tear-stained and blotchy, but she looked remarkably refreshed—her eyes bright and shiny, her hair straightened.

"Of course I care about you. I always care about you." *And what have you done to your hair?*

"Abigail said that no mom who cared about her kids would do something like this." She showed me a string of texts as proof. Apparently her social fortunes had been reversed.

"I thought none of your friends were talking to you?"

"They texted me this morning," she said. "Also, Courtney's mom is coming now to pick me up. She said I could stay there for as long as I needed to."

"You're going to stay at Courtney's?"

Alice nodded.

"For how long?"

She shrugged, and her phone buzzed.

"That's her," she said, grabbing the bag and her backpack and brushing past me.

"Alice," I said, following her down the stairs, "you can't run out like this."

But she did run out, grabbing her raincoat on her way, and I could do nothing but watch. I threw myself on the tufted couch, listening to rain hit the windows and wondering if this is what it would feel like when the kids grew up and left and I was all alone. The house was no more than a collection of rooms with no people in them and furniture that would go untouched, unused. I'd been so stupid to want more space, because pretty soon, space would be the last thing I wanted.

~

With Harry as my last hope for company, I spent two hours making pad thai for dinner. For good measure, I made a curried tomato soup to go with it. When he didn't show up by six, I called him.

"I made pad thai," I said. "What's your ETA?"

"I don't know. I'm working late. I'll grab something here."

"Harry, I'm all alone. The kids won't come home."

"Can you blame them?" he asked. "Have you thought about how much damage you've done? Alice was so desperate to fit in, and you went and blew up her social life. And Sam? Do you even know how a suspension for drug use is going to look on his record? Have you thought about that?"

"I know I screwed up, but how am I going to make it right if none of you will hear me out?"

"You need to let us be angry for now." He paused. "You need to let *me* be angry."

"Until when?"

"Until I'm not angry anymore. I'll see you in the morning, and I'll take Steven off your hands then."

He hung up, leaving me alone in the house with an infant who probably would have walked away, too, if he knew how to.

I called the one person I knew would always take my calls.

"I'm in real trouble here."

"I know you are," Suki replied.

"You warned me, or at least you tried to, but I just wouldn't hear you."

"It was more like you *couldn't* hear me," she said.

"That doesn't make me feel any better."

"Believe it or not, I get it. The Dutchess was feeding you, and there was nothing I could say to make you stop."

"I feel like such an idiot," I sobbed.

"People have done worse things," she said. "Remember Missy Bender?" Missy Bender went to college with Suki's husband. She was now Melissa Bender-Block, and when she wrote a tell-all about the rash of open marriages in Park Slope, her entire Brooklyn set turned on her. Melissa Bender-Block had to move to Los Angeles. Her husband and the mini Bender-Blocks moved with her.

"Except that Harry and the kids won't come home," I said, blinking and releasing a fresh set of tears. "I'm all alone here, except for the baby."

"They will all be back. I mean, eventually they're going to miss all those desserts." Suki laughed softly at her own joke. "You're a good mom, Bells, and a good wife. Just keep apologizing, and eventually they'll hear you."

I had one person left to try and apologize to, but she was the person I was most scared to see.

~

"I'm sorry," I said as soon as Joey opened the door. "I didn't do this to hurt you."

"You cost me a lot of money," she said, stepping outside and wrapping a gray cardigan around herself. "Plus, they know we're friends, which means they also know I'm the one who ratted out the scheme. I can't really show my face in this crappy town anymore."

"I know how that feels," I said, smiling in solidarity.

"Do you? Do you know how it feels to grow up somewhere and have people you've known your whole life avoid you? Do you know how it feels to realize you were dumb enough to befriend someone who probably laughed at you behind your back and then ratted you out?"

"I never laughed at you."

"You never looked down on me for being naive? Uneducated?"

"Of course not."

"Not even in your head? Go home, Bells."

"Can I come in? Can I at least explain to you why I did it?"

"I get it. We all want to be famous and have a billion followers."

"That's not why. I did it because I felt empty and inadequate. I did it because I wanted to be seen."

"I have no idea what you're even talking about."

"You don't now, but one day you might."

"Stop harping on your age—it's getting old. I thought you were actually interested in me. I thought you were a friend. But you were using me for info the whole time, and you made me look like an idiot."

"I'm so sorry, Joey."

"Don't come back," she said, walking into the house and closing the door.

-30-

Joey's rejection was the final straw. I was officially persona non grata. I tried my sisters-in-law, but even they were passing regular judgment. Molly heard me out and then said, "I just don't get why you had to do it. I just don't understand." Jess was no better. "I'm not mad at you," she said. "I'm just confused. How did you think you'd never get caught? Everyone always gets caught."

Sam and Alice came home after two nights away, but they were still barely talking to me. I'd tried just about everything I could think of, and my desperation led me out of the house to Green's, Pigkill's swanky grocery store. Maybe if I bought everyone's favorite foods, they'd forgive me. After breakfast, I drove into town with the baby, holding my breath until we were in the store, praying I wouldn't see anyone I knew. Once inside, I attached the car seat to a shopping cart and started walking, but minutes later, Steven started to bray. I did the math, figured he was probably more than a little hungry, and looked around for somewhere to nurse. I saw an empty table in the café at the front of the store. I pushed the cart over and pulled him out of the seat.

Once Steven latched on, I exhaled, leaning back into my chair and looking over at a small group of moms and babies huddled around a cluster of tables. I heard them talking about sleep—always sleep—and pumping and feedings and vaccinations, but I couldn't tell much more because I was flummoxed by their youth. It wasn't the plump, full faces that got me, the absence of hollowed-out undereye circles, or the hair that seemed less angry and more shiny (it occurred to me for the first time in that moment that hair may actually age, which is something I might have known had I read women's magazines or the occasional beauty blog). No, it wasn't the damage of the years that separated us. It was the hope.

Because hope was for mothers who were still at the beginning, who hadn't made mistakes they could never undo, who had time to reverse course or even up their games and become the mothers they wanted to be—the moms they thought they'd be, even if their own mothers disapproved and told them to make sure to build lives for themselves. In short, hope was not for mothers of daughters old enough to leave the house for a few nights when they were mad at you or of sons with an oversize foot out the door, sons who regularly played the "This time next year, I'll be getting ready to leave" game.

In short, hope was not for me.

I didn't belong anywhere near these moms. Why was I even here? And why was it so hard to breathe?

I looked down at Steven, who had fallen fast asleep during the feeding, and held him close to me, a talisman against all my worst thoughts.

I burped him gently, slid him back into his car seat, and started to walk the aisles. Minutes later, I stood, still breathless, staring at a wall of vegetables, squinting in search of snap peas, Alice's favorite. Eventually, my eyes landed on a bag, which I threw into my cart. I'd come in search of more food but still couldn't really breathe and was starting to sweat. I leaned on the cart. Steven was moaning again. When my vision began to blur, I realized it had been a mistake to think I could do this. I needed to leave.

I had to walk up through the condiment aisle to get to the cashier so I could pay for the one bag of snap peas I had in my cart, never once thinking it might be best to abandon ship entirely and go home. As

I neared the top of the aisle, the strap of my purse caught on a cardboard cutout of a giant bottle of some micro-batch olive oil. When I tried to tug the strap free, I knocked the giant cardboard bottle over and watched as it took down an entire display of olive oil bottles with it. I tried to grab the bottles as they rolled past me, but I was not fast enough, and instead I spilled out the contents of my purse when I bent over and got my foot tangled up in my purse strap. Splayed out on the floor, I looked up at Steven, who was now crying. "I have so much to do," I told myself as I fell down to the floor. "I have so much to do, and Sam's about to leave, and then Alice will, and I'm not sure I got any of it right." I slid to the corner of the aisle and put my head in my knees. "My baby," I heard myself say. "He's my baby, and it was all so fast. Nobody told me it would all be so fast."

Steven screamed even louder. "It's OK, Sam," I said, realizing my mistake instantly. I reached for Steven but saw Sam's baby face instead. I looked at him and said, "Please give me one more chance. Please let me have a do-over."

"Bells? Is that you?" I heard someone say.

I don't remember anything else. I don't remember Cynthia Plank throwing her coat over me and calling Harry while she knelt next to me in the store holding my hand. I don't remember Anna scrambling to pick up the contents of my purse and soothing Steven until Harry arrived.

-31-

The kids opened the door. Alice swept Steven into her arms, and Sam guided me to the couch. Harry took off my coat, laid me down, and covered me with a blanket.

"I'm sorry," I kept saying. "I'm so sorry."

Harry said nothing. He just took off my shoes and sat there until I fell asleep.

I woke when they handed Steven to me. After I'd fed him, rolling over onto my side, sliding him alongside me, and lifting up my sweatshirt, I handed him off to Harry or one of the kids and then fell back to sleep, or whatever nonwaking, catatonic state I was in.

Whenever I opened my eyes, I saw Harry. Harry sitting at the end of the couch, Harry's head in his hands, Harry's hands on my feet, my legs. I'd occasionally sense him getting up off the couch to put wood in the stove or tend to the baby, but he'd return quickly and resume his position.

He was walking around with Steven over his shoulder, patting his tiny back in an effort to soothe him, when my milk rushed in and woke me. I reached out, and he placed the baby in my arms. I sat up, and when Steven latched on immediately, I lay back against the couch.

Harry spoke first.

"Two things can be true at the same time," he said, staring straight past me. "I can be incredibly angry with you, and I can also understand why you did what you did."

"If you understand what I did, why can't you even look at me?"

"Really, Bells? You don't know why?"

I knew why. Harry told me everything, every small detail, even the ones I didn't need or want to know, and I'd told him nothing about what I'd been doing.

"I understand why you wanted to be the Dutchess," he continued. "I'll just never understand why you spent months sneaking around behind my back."

"You make it sound like I cheated on you."

"You did."

I felt myself gasp sharply. Having spent all of our marriage worrying that Harry would let me down, or even worse, betray me, I'd anticipated and even rehearsed this conversation; I was just playing a different role.

"At first I was embarrassed," I said when my breath finally returned. "I thought you'd think I was doing something so dumb and insignificant, especially after you'd called blogging silly. I didn't want to do something you weren't proud of."

"That's not fair. This isn't my—"

"Please, I'm not done," I said, cutting him off. "If I'm being really honest, I was also ashamed, even at the beginning, before things really heated up. I didn't want you to think you'd married someone capable of doing something so awful." Steven pulled away, and I put him over my shoulder to burp him.

"I don't think that," Harry said.

"But you don't forgive me yet."

Harry opened his mouth to speak but was interrupted this time by a knock on the door. Harry got up to open it, and Cynthia walked in.

She looked like a 1980s news anchor in her boots, jeans, and a silky black blouse with full makeup and blown-out hair. I both regretted my sweats and made a mental note to blog about how it wasn't just millennials coveting decades-old fashion. I shuddered when I realized what I was doing. *What is wrong with me?*

"Hello, Harry, and hello, Baby Steven," she said, reaching down and letting Steven hold her index finger while he did his postfeed grunting.

"Cynthia," Harry said, "what brings you here?"

"Bells and I have some unfinished business," she replied. Harry, taking the cue, picked up the baby, who was now officially ready for a diaper change, and flew upstairs at record pace, the house shaking with him.

Cynthia sat on a chair opposite the couch as my stomach sank between my knees. "How are you, Bells?"

"Better than I was the last time you saw me," I said.

"That's good." She smiled.

"About that," I began. "Thank you. You didn't have to help me, and you did."

"You would have done the same for me. You just might have written about it afterward."

"I deserved that," I said, feeling myself begin to sweat from the head down.

"When I saw you lying on the supermarket floor, I realized that I had no idea you were going through whatever it was that you were going through. You always seemed so cool, removed, and pretty together. I guess what I'm saying is that I realized that everything is not what it seems."

"I guess not," I said, having no idea where she was going.

"And what I mean by *that* is that I didn't see Sam vaping."

"What?"

"I saw his friends vaping," she said, looking uneasy in the chair.

"Was Sam even there?"

"Yes, but I didn't see him doing it. I just assumed he was because some of the others were."

"Did you tell the school?"

"Of course I did," she said, alarmed that I'd even asked.

I sat, speechless.

"Bells, I came here to tell you that I've cleaned up *my* mess, and now you have to clean up yours. You slung a lot of mud in that blog. It's time to clean some of it up."

Before I could respond, she stood up and headed for the door. She began to let herself out and then stopped.

"Oh," she said, turning around to face me and raising a tote bag, "I made you dinner."

"Thank you," I said, walking over. I took the bag, saying the silent prayer of gratitude of mothers who realize they don't have to think about what to cook for dinner. "Not just for the meal, but for helping me when you didn't have to."

"That's what we do here, Bells," she said. "When someone is in trouble, we pick her up off the floor and we get her home. Then we check on her, and sometimes we even bring dinner." She smiled again. "We aren't all bad."

"I know that," I said, placing the bag on the chair. Once Cynthia left, I lay down and closed my eyes, taking in what she'd said but not sure exactly what to do about it.

I knew that whatever I was going to do, I wasn't going to do it from this couch.

-32-

I was stepping out of the shower when the doorbell rang again. I threw on another, albeit clean, pair of sweats and called for someone to answer it, but nobody ever does, so I ran down and found Ernst standing on my porch.

"Hello, Elsbeth," he said in his clipped accent.

"Is everything OK? Is Vivian OK?"

He turned and gestured to the limo parked in front of the house. The limo door swung open and revealed Vivian and Hanna, both in the car, both in black. Having spent most of my married life making sure that my mother and mother-in-law were never in the same place at the same time, I can say with certainty that there are few sights more terrifying than the sight of Hanna and Vivian together in a car.

"Is this a joke? What's going on?"

"Get in the car, Elsbeth," my mother called. "We'll explain everything."

I looked down at my sweatpants, hoodie, and shearling slipper boots and turned back to get my coat.

"You don't need a coat, I brought one," Vivian called, lifting up a coat made of what I assumed were a thousand dead minks.

"But my outfit . . . ," I said.

"Really, Bells, now's not the time to wake up and realize you are too old to be wearing clothes you've had since college."

"And Harry?"

"He's the one who called me," Vivian said, looking at my mother. "And I called for backup."

"Get in the car, Elsbeth."

I followed Ernst down the steps and climbed into the limo, sitting opposite both women.

"Did you color coordinate?" I asked.

"You'd be surprised how flattering black can be," Vivian said, sitting next to a woman who'd made that discovery about forty years ago. She handed me the mink, which I put on my lap.

"I'm pretty sure you and Vivian didn't come to stage a makeover intervention," I said, stroking the coat. "Why are you here?"

"Drive to the water, Ernst," Vivian commanded.

"Are you planning on killing me and dumping my body in the Hudson?" I asked, half joking.

"First things first," Vivian said, reaching into a large black overnight bag with leather handles. She pulled out a stack of photo albums tabbed with Post-it Notes. She took the top album and handed it to me.

"Look at the pictures," she said. "What do you see?"

I paged through pictures of a very young Harry, Alex, and Mark fishing, biking, skiing, lying on their stomachs reading, or playing rounds of chess, some of which were familiar to me from the walls of Vivian's home. Harry's father was in many of the pictures, often wearing a suit or sport coat, and had a full head of dark hair, which he'd started to lose by the time I came into the family. I flipped through the album, focusing on the pages Vivian had tabbed. I smiled when I saw Harry wearing Star Wars pajamas, playing a piano duet with his father while his brothers looked on.

"Where are you?" I asked.

Vivian said nothing and just handed me the next album, and then the next. The pictures went up through Harry's college graduation, where I saw my first appearances in the Walker albums. My hair was enormous and my face was round. I was so young and full that it was hard to see.

Like the pictures on her walls, there were no pictures of Vivian alone. She only appeared alongside Steven and the boys or in family portraits where someone else was behind the camera, and even then, she looked beautiful and well dressed but never comfortable, and none of the pictures captured her vibrancy or energy. I could almost hear her counting the moments until the portrait sessions were over.

Before I could say anything, she handed me scrapbooks stuffed with write-ups from various medical events and pictures from the gardening club, golf tournaments, and dinners with doctors and their wives sitting at round tables.

"My whole story," she said, "was his story."

"I know that."

"But now that he's not here, I don't have anything that's mine. All I have are the things that were his—the gardening, the golf, his friends, his boys."

"I thought that was what you wanted."

"It was. And now it isn't."

"But you love your boys . . . you are a different person when they're all around you." I pictured her at the head of her dining room table, puffed up and full of them.

"I let myself get squeezed out of the picture," she said. "It was a slow thing. I didn't even realize I wasn't in the frame until I went back and looked."

"Why are you telling me this?" I asked her. "Do you want me to go out and find some hobbies of my own?" I looked at my mother. "Or are you here to tell me to go back to work?"

"We want you to tell your story, Elsbeth," my mother said.

"What does that even mean?"

"We want you to write." She paused. "*I* want you to write."

"I tried that."

"You tried writing about other people. You told their stories. What about yours?"

"You always said writing is only a hobby, not a career."

"I also said that coloring your hair undermined women and upheld the patriarchy, and I was clearly wrong about that." She ran her hand through her own cropped, recently dyed hair.

"Nobody wants to read my story. Nobody wants to read about being the invisible support staff of a demanding family, about the middle-of-the-night anxiety when you realize it's all happening so fast and there's nothing you can do to slow it down. Nobody cares."

"Elsbeth," my mother said, "that's exactly what people want to read about."

"Would you read about that kind of invisibility?" I asked.

"I was a single mom when you were ten. Nobody has seen me for over thirty years."

"More like forty, if we're being honest," Vivian chimed in. My mother shot her a healthy dose of side-eye.

"The point is this," Vivian continued. "Feeling invisible *is* a story—and it's not just your story. If you want to write, and we both think you should, then turn the camera on yourself."

"Why not just come over and tell me this? Why hold me hostage in a car with Ernst?" I looked out the window. We were parked along the river.

"Because you can't walk out of the room, or ask us to leave, or even change the topic," my mother said.

"Also, I love a little drama," Vivian said, smiling.

"I've had enough drama," I said. "Have you ever had a meltdown in the condiment aisle of the supermarket?"

"No, but don't ask the boys about the incident in the tennis club with Bitsy Parker."

"Really? That's a name?"

"You have no idea," Vivian replied.

"I have something, too," my mother whispered. She reached into her own enormous purse and pulled out a stuffed manila folder. "I put a dollar in there every time I said something to you I wish I hadn't. I was going to give it to you when you graduated college, then law school, then when you got married, but I kept needing the folder." She opened it up and revealed an enormous stash of dollar bills.

"How much is in there?" I asked.

"Who knows," she said. "More than I want to count. Ask me when I last put money in here."

"When?"

"Last month," she said, handing me the envelope.

"What was it you said?"

"I'd like to say 'Who remembers,' but I remember." She paused. "I told you that you could kiss the next five years of your life goodbye. I think I may also have made an offhand comment about baby weight."

"Nice," Vivian said. We both shot her some side-eye.

I looked back at my mother. "I know this isn't what you wanted for me at all. I know you wanted me to have a big career and a big life. I'm so sorry I've been such a big disappointment."

"You listen to me, Elsbeth," she said, leaning forward and taking my hands in hers. "I was the one who let you down. I was the one who made you feel like you were never good enough." She was crying now, which was not something I had seen often, even in the years right after my father left and when her own parents died. "I'm the one who should be sorry. I'm sorry I made you feel so inadequate and so alone."

I squeezed her hand. "Tell me what to do, Mom. You always know what to do."

"I don't."

"You picked yourself up after Dad left. You put your life back together."

"Actually, I ate everything in the apartment. Twice. Then I had a giant meltdown at the playground on Seventy-Second Street, when you were about three."

"What?"

"Yup. And then your grandma Pearl told me to get my act together and go back to school. She told me I needed to set a better example for you. But I ended up doing the opposite. I had my mother to lean on, and I was so busy with my own life that I wouldn't let you lean on me. Even worse, I made you feel like crap every time you needed me. I left you all alone."

"Mom, I've made such a mess of things."

"You just lost your way. We've all done that." She looked at Vivian. "Let us help you find it."

I took the envelope, put it on top of all the minks, and held on to my mother's hand. With my other hand I wiped my eyes and looked at Vivian.

"I think I've got this," I said. "Ernst, take me home, please."

-33-

I begged Alice to return to the play, and she relented, probably because I looked like I'd been through a spin cycle in the washing machine and because she never really wanted to quit in the first place. I'd baked coffee cake muffins for Sam and left them in the kitchen with a note when I knew he'd be home. "I'm so sorry I screwed up so badly. I'll fix this, and I love you." When I returned to the kitchen a few hours later, the muffins and the note were gone. Baby steps.

Andy proved to be harder to convince than I'd anticipated.

"Please," I said. "Just this one time. From then on, I can start writing on my own site. I just need people to read it."

"I don't know, Bells. I think we ought to wait until everything has died down." The man who was running the scheme, the assistant principal at the high school, had struck a deal with investigators and handed over a list of everyone involved. Several families I'd never heard of had been officially named. I flinched when I read Joey's name in the paper.

"Please, Andy. This will have nothing to do with anyone other than me. No gossip, no scandals, I promise."

Eventually he relented, and for the sake of a public apology, we resuscitated the County Dutchess.

~

Who Is the County Dutchess?

Despite pretending otherwise, the County Dutchess is neither royal nor a longtime resident of Dutchess County. She's a middle-aged wife and mother who moved up to the Hudson Valley when her husband took a job at Dutchess College. She has two adolescent children and a brand-new baby. She spent years convinced that neither her mother nor her mother-in-law liked her. Her best friend is a food writer in Brooklyn, a borough that she refuses to enter, let alone live in, because she's certain that to live there you need a book deal or a byline. Also, she likes to bake in the middle of the night, and she really hates her hair.

She would have told you all of this, and maybe more, if she'd had the confidence and courage to write about herself, to tell her own story.

Sadly, she had neither.

I am the County Dutchess. My real name is Bells Walker—or Elsbeth, if you're my mother, who doesn't like nicknames. There are lots of things my mother doesn't like, and until a week or so ago, I thought I was one of those things. In addition to my mother and mother-in-law, I also thought my husband's colleagues didn't like me much, either—not that I ever gave them a chance to like or know me. Ditto for the mothers of my children's classmates. You see where I'm going here.

When you aren't such a big fan of yourself, you assume nobody else is, either, and even though you've wanted to write for as long as you can remember, when your self-worth is in the toilet, you don't seem like such a good subject. Also, when you're fortysomething and feeling like not much more than the family chef, wiper of spills, loader and unloader of the dishwasher, maker of appointments, and driver—and you're about to go through it all again because OOPS, YOUR IUD JUST FAILED—rather than write about yourself, why not gossip about your new neighbors?

Enter the County Dutchess. As it turns out, it's so much easier to take down someone you don't really know than it is to write about being up at 2:00 a.m. because you're worried that you haven't pushed your high schooler enough just to prove a point to all the moms who push their high schoolers too much, or that you've decided to have a baby at an age when all the other moms you know are finally making time for themselves.

As for all those rumors, I don't really know for sure that everyone up here is sleeping with millennials, but at least a few people seem to be, and you know what—it's none of my business. Also, drink whatever the hell you want, people. Kombucha may taste like a blend of Listerine and pickle juice, but have at it. Same for chia pudding. That stuff is nasty, and everyone who says otherwise is pretending. Regarding the whole college-scam brouhaha,

I have no comment other than to say: WHAT THE HELL, PEOPLE.

I've learned that there are some good people up here. People who help you when you don't deserve it. People who cook meals for you when you've had a baby, even though you don't ask. People who help you off the floor of a grocery store when you're having either a panic attack or something of a breakdown. People who call your husband to check up on you the next day. To those people, I'm sorry for what I did. I'm sorry for judging all of you secretly and trashing you publicly. If you can ever forgive me, I make a mean pie and very good coffee. I will also continue apologizing to the people closest to me, even though I know that it will take time for them to forgive me for what I've done.

The County Dutchess has retired. And along with her, I'm retiring the gossip and the backbiting. I have wanted to write for as long as I can remember, and from now on, if I'm going to write, it's going to be about me. I may not be anywhere near as riveting as fortysomething moms using job apps to hook up with younger men or paying millennials to take the SAT for their kids, but it will be my story. It will be mine.

If you want me, I'll be at BellsWalker.com—where I'll be telling it like it is, or at least like it's happening to me. Find me, if you're interested.

~

A few months later . . .

Silver Bells and Cockle Shells (www.BellsWalker.com)

Everything that made me a pretty decent baker also made me a pretty awful gardener. Give me a set of instructions and I'll follow them. Then tell me to walk away, and I'll do it—happily. (One of my favorite things about baking is knowing that not only do I not *need* to open the oven to check on the cake inside, but that I am expressly prohibited from doing so.)

Gardening, on the other hand, is different. There is no oven to close and no walking away, and although there are rules, there is mostly instinct. And, big shocker here, but my instincts are often . . . a little off.

H. came home with a sack (hemp, naturally) of all sorts of seeds he'd procured from local gardening stores (I glazed over while he explained them to me, but I'm pretty sure he said the word *heirloom* about eighteen times). After almost costing him his job, the least I could do was plant his seeds (and yes, I am well aware of the double meaning of that sentence, and no, I still have not lost all the baby weight). So, I dutifully planted, following the rules—even germinating some seeds indoors in whatever container I could find and labeling them with Popsicle sticks (those ladies on Instagram really do have many ways for making some of us feel inept, but you've never really felt it until you've gone down the home gardening rabbit hole)—but not much grew, and what little did grow shriveled up and died when I transferred it to the garden beds outside. I stood over the beds, like the grim reaper of all things green, and wondered where I'd gone wrong, what step I'd missed, what ingredient I'd forgotten.

You know who was good at it? My teenage son. Every time I looked outside the kitchen window, he was moving pots around to better spots in the sun, watching the plants, and occasionally getting up and sticking his hands in the dirt. He was eventually joined by a reluctant, recently minted teenager (and recent star of the Pigkill stage) who had decided that the light outside was good enough for her selfies. Turns out that teenagers have some pretty good instincts about what it takes to put down roots and flourish. (You see where I'm going here, right?)

They knew what I didn't. They knew that some things take time, trust, and patience. They knew that if you don't like where you've been planted, you can always readjust and shift, and that just because one part of the garden box isn't working for you, that doesn't mean the whole box is bad. You just have to find your place in the sun. And that's about as much belaboring as I can do of that metaphor. (I'll be honest: I could never get as excited about Italian kale as I could about French pound cake. Go figure.)

As for H., just when the garden was starting to look alive, his number came up and he got tenure, which means we aren't going anywhere now. We celebrated by throwing a party in the yard, right alongside the vegetable boxes—a party I let the kids plan. We invited some old friends but mostly new friends, friends who helped me when I was at my lowest and probably didn't deserve much help.

And in a move that will come as a surprise to those of you who knew me before I was the Dutchess—when, as I am now, I was just myself—we even invited both of the grandmothers.

At the same time.

ACKNOWLEDGMENTS

I am forever grateful to Danielle Marshall for taking an early chance on me, and to my editor, Alicia Clancy, and the entire crew at Lake Union for continuing to support me, being a pleasure to work with, and believing in the Dutchess early on.

I was honored to receive the Kathryn Gurfein Writing Fellowship at Sarah Lawrence College and equally as lucky to be mentored by Mary La Chapelle, who was tremendously generous with her time and her wisdom. A special thanks to Patricia Dunn and the entire Sarah Lawrence writing program.

I'd also like to thank:

Jill Marsal, my agent, for her sound advice and general unflappability. Kathleen Carter of Kathleen Carter Communications for helping get the word out about the Dutchess.

Eileen Palma for being my sounding board, writing partner, and overall inspiration. You move through the world with grace and resilience, and one day I'll write about someone half as cool as you. Also, I'm so glad you grew out your bangs.

David Naggar, early reader and giver of the best notes, who took me to lunch one hundred years ago and told me to write a book—thank you.

I continue to shout from the rooftops that everyone should have a friend and first reader like Johanna Shargel. A huge thanks to my other early readers: Hilary Buff (peddler of all the best plot advice and essential oils), Baroness Eleanor Menzin (also a fake title, but so royal to me), Shoshana Radinsky (my middle school colleague and reader of every cozy mystery ever written), Shami Shenoy (to whom I gave one of the earliest drafts and whose advice is *always* spot-on), and the brilliant Dahvi Waller (whose vegan baking skills put even Bells Walker to shame). Thank you to Rebecca Amaru for her help with the geography of Dutchess County and the ob-gyn consults. A big shout-out to all my pals in the SAR middle school teachers' room, and to the real Beeks for bringing me on board.

The internet and writing communities are full of people who show up and support writers, and I'd be remiss if I didn't thank Amy Poeppel, Annabel Monaghan, Suzy Krause, Camille Di Maio, Camille Pagán, Andrea Peskind Katz, Jamie Rosenblit, Athena Kaye and the Great Thoughts' Great Readers community, Marilyn Rothstein, Rochelle Weinstein, Suzanne Weinstein Leopold and Thelma Adams of Suzy Approved Book Tours, and Linda Levack Zagon of *Linda's Book Obsession*. A special thanks to the entire Lake Union community—both writers and readers—who continue to support and lift each other in ways I'd never imagined.

I was (and am) a blogger like Bells, and it was my kids who gave me the very best material and just may be responsible for helping me find my voice. One day, I hope you guys all have kids who do stuff so crazy that you have to write it down and hit "Publish." I'm also indebted to all my blog readers who lift me up and cheer me on, chief among them Sharon Sturm and Laura Shaw Frank.

My cat, Lois, is my mostly companion when I write, but it is my husband, Michal, who continues to make everything possible for me and pushes me to do more and try harder when sometimes all I really want to do is buy a dress and take a nap. I love you.

BOOK CLUB QUESTIONS: *THE TRUTH AND OTHER HIDDEN THINGS*

1. Bells's life changes when Harry takes a job at Dutchess College and the family moves from Manhattan to the Hudson Valley. Have you ever had to move or make a big change to your life because of your spouse or partner's career? How do you think Bells handled Harry's career crisis and his decision to take the job at Dutchess?
2. Harry and Bells would probably say they are equal partners in their marriage—do you feel this is accurate? Is there such a thing as an equal partner, especially in parenting?
3. Bells initially keeps her pregnancy a secret from some of the people closest to her—and as the book rolls on, she keeps more and more to herself, ultimately keeping the Dutchess from almost everyone. Did you sympathize with her reasoning? When does it make sense to keep a secret?

4. Consider Bells as a mother. She tries so hard to be a better mother than she thought her mother was. Do you think she succeeded?
5. Bells likes to distinguish herself from the pushier moms she knows. Later in the book, she admits to worrying that she didn't push her children enough. Do you think she strikes the right balance? Could she be more demanding with Sam and Alice?
6. Suki is Bells's oldest and closest friend, but Bells never really succeeded in making "mom friends." Do you think Bells's life would have been any different if she'd had a group of women to support her? Do you think she will make more of an effort to make mom friends this time around with Steven?
7. Bells decides pretty quickly that Pigkill is not for her. Have you ever moved or lived somewhere and known immediately that it wasn't the right fit for you? Did that opinion ever change? Were you able to make the place work for you? Do you think Bells was too quick to judge?
8. Before she starts writing as the Dutchess, Bells considers Suki's advice to write about herself. Do you think she would have been as successful had she written about her own life? Are there times when you think you couldn't possibly be interesting enough, when you're sure your stories might not be worth telling? How do you know if you're right?
9. Bells considers telling Harry about the Dutchess but keeps it from him when he downplays blogs after reading *Hudson Mom of Six*. Do you think Bells would have told him otherwise? Or do you think she knew that she was doing something wrong from the beginning? Have you ever undertaken something you knew was misguided or

wrong and told yourself that you kept it a secret to protect the people around you?

10. Bells had several opportunities to come clean to Harry and to pull back from the Dutchess. Was there a time when you thought she should have told him or should have pulled the plug on the blog?
11. Vivian ends up being an ally—keeping Bells's secret and even letting her wear her tiara while she writes. Why do you think Vivian supported Bells, knowing the risk to Harry, and do you think that if she'd had the opportunity, Vivian would have done something similar? Could Vivian have been a Dutchess?
12. Hanna, on the other hand, does not know about the Dutchess because Bells cannot imagine her mother approving of any of her life choices. Hanna's biggest criticism of Bells is that she doesn't put herself first. Is Hanna right?
13. Bells loves Harry, but she is just not that interested in all the details of Harry's work. Can you still be a good spouse if you're not interested in all the details of your spouse's day?
14. Bells discovers Cynthia's infidelity and writes about it but ultimately comes to an understanding with Cynthia when all is said and done. Can the two women ever really be friends when Bells knows about Cynthia's history, and when Cynthia knows that Bells has the capability to write about the people she knows?
15. Do you think Bells will ever hear from Joey again? Should she?
16. While in the limo with Vivian and Hanna, Vivian shows Bells the albums and scrapbooks that she's kept herself

out of. Many women take family pictures without themselves in them. Why do you think that is?

17. Until she learns about her mother's envelope, Bells had no idea Hanna ever realized how bad she made her feel. Why do you think Hanna waited so long to tell her? Do you understand why Hanna's own experiences made her act the way she did?
18. At the end of the book, although Harry understands why Bells did what she did, he still hasn't fully forgiven her. What do you think Harry and Bells's relationship will look like going forward? How will it be different? How will it be better or worse?
19. Who was your favorite character? Why?
20. Movie time: Who would you like to see play each part?

ABOUT THE AUTHOR

Photo © 2017 Jason Roth

Lea Geller is the author of *Trophy Life*. A recipient of the 2019 Kathryn Gurfein Writing Fellowship at Sarah Lawrence College, she began her writing career by blogging about her adventures in the trenches of parenting. Lea lives in New York with her husband and children, for whom she frequently wakes up and makes several separate breakfasts. When Lea's not writing and eavesdropping on her children, she can be found running, gardening, drinking diner coffee, and occasionally teaching middle school English. She is a graduate of Columbia University and Stanford Law School. You can find Lea at www.leageller.com.